Madness and Murder

By

Jen Hilborne

Echelon Press
Publishing

MADNESS AND MURDER
An Echelon Book

First Echelon Printing / December 2010

Cover © Karen L. Syed
With Nathalie Moore of Graphics Muse

Echelon Press, LLC
9055 G Thamesmeade Road
Laurel, MD 20723
www.echelonpress.com

ISBN: 978-1-59080-592-3
eBook: 978-1-59080-556-5

PRINTED IN THE UNITED STATES OF AMERICA

10 9 8 7 6 5 4 3 2 1

This novel is dedicated to my beloved Dad, Robert John Hilborne, and Nanny King.

Love you forever.

The author wishes to express grateful thanks to the following: senior editor, Kat Thompson; Karen Syed; Deputy Marek Janecka; Carol Givner; Alison Hilborne; Pam Lowes; Brad and Genna Olson; Hilda Flores; Tim Geary, and all others who shared their valuable time reading, listening and encouraging.

Chapter One

Sacramento 1982-1983

"You have committed the most heinous of crimes, and you have shown no remorse. The court imposes the maximum sentence the circumstances will allow...life without parole."

A woman's penetrating scream drew every eye in the courtroom. From his seat in the back, Detective Mac Jackson looked over at the family of the convicted and at the boy glaring back at him with dark, hate-filled eyes. Even when his mother's cries grew louder, and the uniformed officers dragged away his father–a brutal murderer with a shaved head and a spider tattoo curling all the way around his thick neck–to begin the life sentence Judge Marshall had just handed out, the child's rigid stare didn't waiver. Jackson read a warning in those eyes: this isn't finished.

Detective Shaun Hodges leaned in closer to his partner. Together, they'd brought Bodie Allure to justice for killing a child younger than Jackson's own son. "We did it." The jubilant punch struck him in the side of his leg.

Jackson glanced at the family of the victim, a few rows in front of him, eyes cast down in despair, exuding anguish so raw, he had to close his eyes for a second. A life for a life, that's what they'd wanted. Taking the advice of his lawyer, Bodie had pleaded guilty and escaped the death penalty.

Unlike Hodges, Jackson didn't feel like celebrating. Murder left him weary. The murder of a child left him drained, used-up, like somebody had sucked all the good air out of the world and extracted the energy from his body. Although he'd spent many years on the force, seen some terrible things, he never got used to the death of a child. Perhaps it was the one remaining sense that reminded him he was still human; that this damn job hadn't turned him into a machine.

He nodded. "Yep, we did it." Finally, he got up to leave, passing the victim's family; a broken mother and father, clinging to all they had left: their seven-year-old twins. Tears ran down their cheeks, droplets falling from the end of their noses and onto the children's heads. The twins looked bewildered.

Jackson doubted they understood the significance of today. As he made his way from the courtroom, he thought about Bodie's long criminal history. The man had grown from a violent teen into a brute with no conscience. A true psychopath. Thanks to the guile of his lawyer, a technicality had resulted in his previous crime, a rape and robbery, being thrown out. Jackson couldn't help wondering if the law had failed the Croft's; if Cameron might still be alive had the judicial system done its job.

He drove back to the station in a pensive mood. Cameron Croft had been the eldest of the Croft's three kids. Tall and skinny, he'd made it to eleven. Then he'd crossed paths with Bodie Allure, who'd snatched him from the driveway of his Sacramento home. His neck had been snapped like a twig, only a week after the rape and robbery charge had been dropped. Jackson switched lanes, trying simultaneously to change his train of thought. No such luck. Events soon after the murder filtered back. He remembered the family's reaction; how they'd crumbled in front of him when he'd given them the news that Cameron had been raped, sodomized, choked, and broken. He thought about his own son, Bryce, unable to imagine anything worse than losing a child. Raymond, Cameron's father, had told him he wished he were dead.

An experienced officer in his mid-thirties, Jackson found telling the families a loved one had died the most distressing part of his job. When a youngster had died the stress doubled. In solving the Croft case, he had excelled. Good instincts and an uncanny accuracy with a hunch had enabled him to track down Bodie quickly. From time to time, that sixth sense he seemed to possess even got Hodges spooked, or so he'd said. Jackson reached the station and pulled into his usual spot, chewing on a hunch that Bodie would not fair well in prison for raping and murdering a child. Even hardened criminals detested child molesters and Jackson knew it. He imagined if Bodie didn't, he was about to find out the hard way.

"Seems like the Croft's got their wish."

"What d'you mean?" Jackson frowned when the *Sacramento Bee* landed on his desk six weeks later, almost knocking over his coffee. Ready to berate Hodges for his carelessness, the words caught in his throat when he saw the article Hodges'd circled. He read it quickly. "Well, well, well. Can't say I'm surprised." He grinned up at his partner. "He should have pleaded not guilty. He'd have lasted longer on death row."

"Nah, saved the state a lot of trouble," said Hodges, perching on the corner of Jackson's desk. "Saved the taxpayer's money." Ironically, Bodie had been sodomized and beaten to death by other inmates housed in the general population at San Quentin State Prison. He'd died the same way he'd killed Cameron, thanks to his lawyer's advice.

"Ironic, huh?" Hodges took back his paper.

"Certainly is. Good to know there's still some justice out there."

"Think the Croft's know about it yet?"

"I don't know." Even if they did, Jackson doubted it would bring them any comfort. Nothing would bring back their beloved son.

"He's dead. He'll never hurt anyone else." Her father's blunt words echoed in her head, but Jessica Croft didn't feel safe. What did he know? He didn't know about the bad man who came to her at night, terrorized her in the dark, an arm like a tree branch around her dead brother's neck. The vicious, snarling brute that made her wake up in the dead of night in sopping wet sheets.

She couldn't tell him. After Cameron died, no one spoke about the murder. No one spoke about anything to do with the murder, or the trial. Instead, the fractured family withdrew into themselves, withdrew from life, the parents dragging their scared, confused children into a bizarre existence that rarely strayed past the walls of their small, two-story home.

One chilly evening in late November, twelve months after Cameron's death, Jackson got another call that horrified him. "You're kidding me?" he said to the dispatcher when she gave him the address.

"I'm afraid not. The neighbor reported hearing a gunshot. You better get over there."

Did Bodie have someone on the outside who'd gone back to the Croft's to settle a score? Had someone murdered the rest of the family? Hurt the other children? "Jeez, I hope not," he muttered, gunning the engine of his black and white.

The twins had been in bed for hours. Sometime earlier, Jessica had woken, hair stuck flat against her sweaty forehead, nightdress stuck fast to her clammy legs. Only babies wet their beds. At eight-years-old, she felt like a baby. The moon's illumination cut a sliver of light through the blackness of her room, and she used it to chase shadows while her eyes focused. Out of her sodden bed, she pulled the wet nightdress over her head and felt around in her dresser for another. Once she'd put it on, she closed the creaky drawer slowly, and did what she did almost every night.

With Bear, her beloved, scruffy, brown teddy, under her arm, she made her way out of her own cream-colored room, that never seemed so terrifying in the daylight, and inched along the hall toward her brother's room, and his dry bed. His bed would be safe. The bad man never ventured into Judd's room. The evil in her nightmares had no face, yet she knew it well. Always at the core, she saw her dead brother, a massive, tattooed arm tight around his neck, his chest muscles open, mouth drawn back, teeth exposed. He made no noise as the scream originating in his diaphragm lost its tone in his throat, and died on his lips. Trapped forever in the inky darkness of her dead brother's eyes and the horror that filled her nights, she wondered how, if Bodie was dead, he could still get to her in the night?

Judd barely moved when she slipped into the bed beside him, so familiar had the ritual become. Gradually, Jessica slipped into a fretful sleep.

The ominous boom jolted them awake. A deep, loud crack bounced off the walls, creating a rumbling, evil echo. Terrified, Jessica clung to Judd. "What was that?" she whispered.

Before he could answer, a chilling scream filled the night air, and then a strange sound came, a kind of wailing; the sound of insanity.

"Come on," Judd urged, sliding out from under the sheets.

Against all her eight-year-old instincts, Jessica climbed out of the warm bed behind him, shivering in the cold night air, and clinging to his old, blue-flannel pajamas. At the door, he craned his neck and peered into the hall. When he stepped out, she followed. Together they crept toward the stairs.

"Who's down there?"

"I don't know," Judd whispered, "but something's happening. Something bad." From the top of the stairs they heard another low wail. "Mom." As soon as Judd said it, Jessica began to sob. "We've got to go down there," he said.

"No, I'm too scared."

Judd sounded miserable. "Me, too. But we can't stay here." Jessica buried her face into Bear's neck. If Judd went downstairs, she would go, too. She didn't want to go; she wanted to run far away, wanted to hide. She knew she'd do whatever Judd said, for she trusted no one more than her brother.

"Come on, Jessie." He stood up with a bravery she didn't understand, took hold of her hand, and pulled her slowly down the stairs.

Chapter Two

Raymond had been to the grave earlier in the day. No one had spoken about the murder, or about Cameron, for so long, but, today, he had something he wanted to say. He blamed himself, and they needed to know. "I wish I'd never bought him that hoop," he'd told Marianne that morning.

"He loved that hoop, and besides, that's not what killed him."

"But he wouldn't have been outside right then; and he wouldn't have died."

"Yes, he would," Marianne had replied. "He would have been out playing somewhere. You couldn't have prevented what happened."

"He was my son. I was supposed to protect him, and I didn't."

"Stop it, Ray. He was my son, too. We did the best we could. Think about the twins. They need you, and so do I. Please, you have to see that it's not your fault."

Her words failed to reach him. Mentally remote, he left, and eventually found himself at the graveside, where he could be alone with Cam. The earth smelled damp from the morning rain, and an unpleasant coldness filled the air. Raymond shivered, wondering if the rain could soak through six feet of earth and rot a coffin. He thought about what his son's body might look like now, after laying in the dark, damp earth for a year. Ashamed of his morbid thoughts, he tried to push them away, but they kept coming. He switched thoughts to the counselor and how she'd tried to help him through the process of grieving. *What do you know? Have you ever lost someone you love?* The woman looked barely out of her twenties.

"Move through the phases," she'd explained. He could barely remember what they were.

Something about sadness, anger, acceptance. He'd hardly heard her. There was no new phase; nothing beyond the endless, empty abyss; the cavern of despair created by the loss of his son. After a while at the grave, he stood up, brushed his hand across his cheeks to wipe off the tears, and made his son a promise. "I'll see you soon, Cam."

Later that night, when the moment arrived, it was late. The twins had been upstairs for hours. Marianne, sweet Marianne, sat in her favorite armchair, eyes closed, head titled back, her forehead slightly less wrinkled in sleep than in the waking hours that kept it rutted. Raymond watched her sleep, watched the gentle rhythm of her breathing. *You're wrong, my darling, this is all my fault.*

He reached into his waistband for the pistol he'd concealed earlier…and faltered. He closed his eyes, and tried to think of a reason not to. Images of Cameron alone in the dark flashed behind his eyelids. "I'm sorry," he whispered. "I love you, but I can't leave him alone another night." His eyes flickered open, and with one final look at Marianne's sweet face, he raised his hand, placed the pistol at his temple, and squeezed the trigger.

Jessica and Judd stood in the doorway, frozen by what they saw. Gruesome chaos. Blood everywhere. "Momma?" Tears stopped Jessica from saying anything else; and Judd blocked her path. His small hand on her arm warned her not to move forward, not to step into the room. "We have to call the police."

Numb and scared, she followed him to the phone in the hall, listened while he spoke to the grown-up who answered, heard him tell the lady that someone had shot Daddy. She waited in shocked silence, next to his stiff little body, in the chilly, black night for help to arrive. *Everything bad happens at night.* She clutched her teddy, and waited for the bad men to appear.

As soon as the call came through, Jackson remembered the family. "I'm on my way," he told the dispatcher. The tragedy of Cameron's murder, one year earlier, which had made Jackson more protective of his own son, had been the lowest point of his career; until he got to the house, and confirmed the suicide.

"Can you tell me what happened?" he asked Marianne.

Marianne Croft couldn't tell him anything. She just sat on the floor next to Raymond, hugging herself, rocking back and forth; a woman on the brink of insanity. The twins only stared with silent eyes, frightened, locked inside a terror he couldn't imagine.

Forensics arrived and did their job, the body was carried away, and a female officer took the children into another room to get them away from the appalling sight in the living room. Jackson wondered what would become of them. After Cameron's death, he'd learned from their mother that she had two brothers, another set of twins, but no other family. Her brothers had moved to New Zealand more than twelve years ago. They had lost touch with Marianne, and they had never met her children. Scarred and terrorized, and practically orphans, their futures didn't look good.

Chapter Three

San Francisco, December 1995

Although more than a decade had passed since he'd seen them, occasionally Jackson still thought about the twins. Foster care could be hard, and he hoped they'd been kept together, even if he knew it unlikely with the overburdened families to whom foster kids usually were sent.

With one week to go before Christmas, late on a Monday night, he turned his thoughts to a more pressing matter. Puzzled, frustrated, and cold, he warmed his hands on his sixth cup of coffee and stared at his notes. The San Francisco Homicide Unit, where he'd transferred from Sacramento six years ago, in order for his wife to be closer to her ailing father, had presented a set of circumstances that bothered him.

Within the past month, two bodies had been pulled from the San Francisco Bay. The female, thought to be between forty to forty-five, had been found in November, right before Thanksgiving. The male, believed to be about fifty, had been discovered late last week. Two murders, both near the holidays. He pushed away old, unpleasant memories of another death close to the holidays–a suicide, more than a decade ago–and continued to work through the evidence.

"Making any progress?" Red Dennis, his partner of three years, called out.

"Nah, not much, except I believe we're looking for one guy; and he's good."

He took a slurp of coffee and re-read the coroner's

report. Both bodies had been found within twelve hours of death. Both badly mutilated, multiple stab wounds, and no ID.

"Brutal, more like."

An autopsy on the female revealed massive blows to the back of the head resulting in multiple fractures, and stab wounds to the face and chest. Empty lungs revealed her body had been tossed into the bay postmortem.

"She had no defense wounds," Jackson said, tapping his fingers against his mug, "which indicates she didn't see it coming."

"Or she knew him."

"He must have hit her from behind, killed her instantly, then stabbed her from the front."

"That's the bit I don't get," Red said, "why carve her up if she's already dead?"

Jackson shook his head. "I don't know."

"That's what tells me he knew her. Hated her. That's not anger, that's rage."

The male had been less fortunate. A soporific drug had been detected in his bloodstream, and where his genitals had once been gaped a hole. However, he'd drowned. Water-filled lungs had told the coroner that. *Poor bastard.* Jackson went back over the report once more. "I don't think he knew her," he said to Red, "I don't think he knew either of the victims."

"Oh? Then why the rage? Why so sadistic? So violent?"

"There's definitely hatred, no doubt about it. But I think these are the bodies of two dropouts. Maybe that's got something to do with the anger."

"Homeless?"

"Yeah. Both had missing teeth, the male had a corroding liver, and the female had needle marks in her arms. No ID, no wallets, and no valuables."

"An alcoholic and a drug addict. That doesn't mean they were homeless."

"No, but no one's come forward to claim them. No one's reported anyone missing that matches either of their descriptions."

"Yeah, well the female would be hard to recognize," Red said, his usually laid back voice somewhat agitated.

Jackson ran his eyes over the victims' wounds noted on the report. The killer had done a number on the woman's face. He'd stabbed her cheeks clear through to the inside of her mouth, smashed her nose so that it hung at an angle, and left empty black sockets in place of her eyes.

"I still think they're homeless."

"Is that another hunch?"

Jackson shot him a look that dared him to challenge his statement. "What if it is?"

"Well, then I'd be more inclined to believe you."

The killer hadn't left much evidence for the detectives to go on, which had stalled Jackson's usually prompt progress. He had only a vague idea about the killer. The weapon used on both victims, determined to have been an eight-inch blade, like one a chef might use, only gave him clues to a possible profession, and the suggestion of a double homicide.

"You really think it's a serial killer?"

"Going by the blade marks, I'd say yes. Rape wasn't a factor in either case." Jackson drained his coffee mug. "So it's not sexual."

"So, we've got an angry male who hates the homeless. Terrific."

"I know. It's not much to work with." Jackson sighed with frustration.

"We'll get him. Sooner or later, he'll make a mistake."

"They usually do." That's what Jackson was counting on.

He sat at his beaten-up mahogany desk, elbows planted one on each side of his notes, and pushed his fingers deep into his brow. He checked the time–eight-thirty–and groaned. "Got time for a drink, Red?"

"Go home, Jackson." Red shook his head. "You can't keep 'em waiting all night."

At home, Jackson had a wife and a fifteen-year-old son waiting for his return, waiting to go Christmas shopping. He lacked both the energy and the inclination. He pushed a hand through his hair, scratched his scalp, and, sensing Red's disapproving stare, buried himself once more in his notes.

A few minutes later, he tossed down his pen, rubbed his forehead, and cussed. "Shit, I don't even know where the crimes took place." He huffed with tiredness and frustration. "Not even a damn blood trail."

"Pick it up in the morning. Go home," Red repeated.

"There's gotta be something." Sighing, he flipped the page in his notebook and made a list, which he titled *What am I dealing with?* and began jotting down questions: Is this a serial killer? What's the motive? Is he local? What's the level of brutality? What's the true crime scene? and, finally: What time of the year were the murders committed?

He thought harder about the last question, stuck his pen between his teeth, and chewed on the end. *Both killings took place near the holidays. A loner?* "Hey, Red, what d'ya think about this? Both killings happened near the holidays. Maybe we're looking for a loner, someone with no family."

"Maybe." Red didn't look up.

Jackson's mind churned. "Or maybe he finds the holidays traumatic. Possibly something happened to him."

"Possibly."

"An abused child, maybe. An abandoned husband. Perhaps he's a deserted lover."

"Perhaps. And perhaps you should call it a night, stop fucking stalling, and take that poor wife and kid of yours Christmas shopping, like you promised."

Jackson looked up, and saw Red's big brown eyes, spaced wide apart in a freckle-face that was framed by a mass of copper-colored hair, glaring back at him. He thought about the two unfortunate souls lying in the county morgue. Even those poor bastards deserved respect, deserved justice. But they could wait one more day. They wouldn't give him the hassle his wife would for keeping them waiting.

"You're right." He snapped his notebook shut.

"That you should call it a night?"

"No, that I'm fucking stalling." He flashed a grin at Red. "Sure you won't have that drink?"

"Get outta here."

"You should get married," he said, reaching for his coat and looking at Red, whose legal name was Jon, and whose red hair and freckles reminded him of a young Ron Howard.

"Why? So I can be as miserable as you?"

Jackson chuckled. "I'm not miserable. I'm only miserable at Christmas."

"I've given up trying to find someone special." Red turned back to his work.

"You mean, you're a closet homosexual."

"Yeah, well at least I wear the pants in my own house."

"Ya got me there."

The detectives worked together well. While Jackson loved that Red gave him room to do most of the thinking on the cases they worked, Red enjoyed Jackson's expertise and broader experience; and sometimes even his sarcasm.

Jackson bid Red goodnight when he couldn't talk him into a quick drink at The Flag, a favorite watering hole for the cops, and left the station, turning up his collar to shield his neck against the December chill. As he drove home to collect Suzette and Bryce, he sensed a sickening in his stomach at the Christmas lights hanging in the street and in the windows of people's homes. The reds, yellows, blues, greens...they reminded him of a chocolate box painting or a Thomas Kinkade, but he'd been sidestepped by the festive mood. He found the seasonal festivities falsely cheerful in comparison to the real brutality of life, and the two dead, unclaimed bodies lying in the morgue, waiting for justice.

"I hate Christmas shopping," he griped, trying to think of any possible, last minute way to get out of it and envying Red for one brief second, "I hate any kind of shopping."

Chapter Four

Christchurch, New Zealand, December 1995

At the end of her walk with Lucky, her parents black Labrador, Alex Sullivan looked around her quiet, tree-lined street, still dappled with morning dew, relishing the peace and quiet. Today carried an aura of mystery; something she sensed in her gut, which bubbled with a knot of anticipation. A glance skyward showed her long fingers of fiery red stretching across the dawn Christchurch sky, unfurling a promise of another beautiful day ahead.

"Come on, Lucky," she called, tugging his lead and turning right from Newport Street onto Avonside Drive. Today, her day off, she planned to do something special; not go to the mall, which is what all the other young girls did on a Saturday. Alex hated the mall, having worked there for the past two years, in a small music store, alongside a hippie, a punk, and two ecstasy-loving, rave fanatics, all of them weird. Today, she sensed something different, something about to happen.

"Come on, boy." Lucky hadn't budged, busy sniffing the ground. Impatiently, she tugged harder on the lead, until his big brown eyes searched hers, and he obeyed. They turned into the large concrete driveway of her parent's three-bedroom, Avondale home. Alex knew they wouldn't be up. They rarely got up before noon on the weekends. Quietly, she let herself in, tiptoed past their bedroom, down the hall, and into the kitchen, where she pulled back the sliding glass door and let Lucky out into the yard.

"Can't read to you today," she called gently, watching him plop down in his favorite spot, under the old wooden bench where she read aloud most of her crime fiction novels. "You'll have to wait for another day to find out what the mysterious, antique key means." Lucky cocked his head, and she could have sworn he understood.

After a quick breakfast, she grabbed her bag, wrote her parents a note, and backed out of the garage in her old, yellow, Volkswagen bug. Whatever mystery she sensed about today, that bubble in her belly, she hoped she would find it at Sumner Beach.

John Donnelly had decided to capitalize on New Zealand's superb summer months. A handsome, unscrupulous, native Californian, he had come by the money through dubious means. Today, a few days after he'd shaken off killer jetlag, picked up his rental, and hit the road, he found himself eyeing a quaint looking place in the beachside village of Sumner.

"Looks as good a place as any," he announced to no one in particular, parked the van, and sauntered across the parking lot and inside the Yarbelle Restaurant and Café. "Wow."

"Know what you want?" a pretty, buxom waitress asked after a few seconds, smiling like pretty girls did when trying to catch his eye.

"I certainly do," he replied, returning the smile and dragging his eyes away from her ample bosom, straining to find its way out of her snug uniform. "I know exactly what I want, uh...Marika." He stole another glance.

"It's Maori," she explained.

"Huh?" He gazed back up at her face, confused.

"The name, it's Maori."

"Oh. Pretty."

She took his order. He wandered out through the French doors to a patio area dotted with cute little tables and shady umbrellas. The warm sun kissed his face and he turned it toward the ocean. Right there, in that single moment, all his plans flew out of his head, and he stood transfixed, gaping at the beauty a few feet away.

"My, my, my, this must be my lucky day," he said, barely moving his lips, and shielding his eyes against the streak of sunlight reflecting off the water, sizing her up with fascination. Not since Leslie-Anne Powell had he seen anyone so lovely as the beauty at the next table.

Lacking a little upstairs. He preferred bigger breasts. *Petite. Long legs.* Figure came first, most importantly the legs. They must be flawless, and certainly no cellulite dappled thighs.

His eyes skimmed over her body and rested on her long, brunette hair, sliding over her shoulder and hanging like an expensive silk curtain, partially concealing her face, not that it mattered.

She was a knock out even with half a face.

"Or maybe it's *your* lucky day." He wondered how she'd compare to Leslie-Anne, his first lover and the mother of his old college buddy, Brett. He bit back a snigger, remembering how Brett had come home from class early one day, and found them together, writhing about on his parents sweat-soaked sheets. *Shit, she taught me a thing or two.* The incident had cost him Brett's friendship, but it had been worth it. *Brett was a dweeb.*

Alex's skin prickled. She paused, brought her head up out of her novel, and glanced around, gaze darting quickly from side to side. She caught him on the double-take, and immediately realized he'd been staring. *I knew it.* She'd always been able to tell when someone was watching. For an instant, she mistook him for her ex, Ian Charles, the only boyfriend she'd ever had. They had the same hair. A second glance set her straight. This man was gorgeous, tanned, alone...and smiling. She grinned back, and felt her innards wilt at the strong jaw, defiant chin, straight, narrow-bridged nose, and dark tousled hair. *Whose bed did you just climb out of?* She blushed at the thought.

Oh, yeah, you love me already. John noticed the flush creeping up her neck and staining her cheeks. Like a lion on the prowl, closing in on its mate, he moved to her table and extended a hand. "I'm John." *And that's all you need to know.*

"Alex." *Self-assured, but that's hardly surprising.*

She sipped her coffee and John spotted the absence of any rings, or one in particular. Not that it mattered, but it made for less drama. "Let me guess, you're taking a day off from modeling?"

Alex giggled. "No."

"Then you're a wealthy princess?" *Shit, wouldn't that be nice. I wouldn't have to work.*

She shook her head, giggling again.

"Mind if I sit?" Encouraged, he assembled the few manners he had.

"Please." Her body language, tilt of the head and shuffle of her bare shoulders, told him she'd like nothing better.

"Thanks." He pulled up a chair. "Well, all I can say is...a girl as beautiful as you puts these stunning views to shame." *Corny, but true.* He let it settle for effect. "What brings you here?"

"I live here." He watched the shy smile curve the corners of her mouth. "You?"

"Just visiting for a few days." *She's too young.* Younger than he'd realized.

"I thought so. I knew I hadn't seen you before. Where are you from?"

"Oakland."

"Where's that?"

"America." He laughed. Who hadn't heard of Oakland? Apparently, she hadn't.

"I thought so. I could tell by the accent."

He watched her shy smile. "Have you ever been to America, Alex?"

"I haven't been anywhere. I've been told I have a distant aunt and a couple of cousins somewhere in California, but I've never met them."

"Well, Oakland is in California." What did it matter? Who cared about Oakland when the most beautiful girl in the world was sitting at his table. He'd forgotten he'd joined her.

"I've never left New Zealand," she said, a pout in her voice.

"I can see why you wouldn't." John stretched out his arms, and looked around. "Look at all this. It's such a beautiful country, although not as beautiful as you."

The red flush deepened in her cheeks. *Perhaps she's doubting my sincerity.* He smiled. *Who cares? She's too beautiful to be smart.*

"Traveling alone?" she asked.

Ahh, and now we're doing a little fishing. He didn't mind it at all. "Yes." He saw his advantage. "Would you like to show me around?"

"Now?"

"No, not now," he said, laughing at her surprise. "Have dinner with me tonight." He hadn't meant to say it, it just slipped out. At first, he thought she'd refuse. Her blue eyes opened wide with astonishment. Expertly dialed in to the female species, he knew some moved faster than others, but eventually he got them all. He breathed in the pungent scent of sea air and squinted into the sunlight. Normally, he'd be wearing shades, but, well aware of the effects his penetrating eyes had on women, he'd slipped them off and stuffed them into his pocket the minute he'd spotted Alex. She still hadn't said anything. She hadn't said no. As he opened his mouth again to win her over, his mobile phone rang in his pocket. *Damn*. He didn't even have to look. He knew who it would be and knew he'd have to answer. If he didn't, she'd keep calling. He pulled it out and flipped open the lid.

"Yes, yes, I'm fine. No, nothing's wrong, I'm with someone. I'll call you back later." He snapped it shut and turned his attention back to Alex. "My mother. She worries if I don't call. I'm her only child. Plus it's almost Christmas." He laughed, embarrassed.

"That's sweet. And yes, I'd love to have dinner."

"Great." *Who knew mothers could be so useful?*

"How long are you here, in New Zealand?"

"I haven't decided. A few months, maybe." John winked. "Until it's safe to go back." She didn't need to know that was the truth. The new boss would soon be placing fresh, more dangerous demands on him. As a new recruit, he had yet to prove himself, prove his loyalty. Streetwise but inexperienced, he needed to create some distance while he decided if he could handle the risks. Drug-trafficking could be dangerous.

Suddenly, Marika arrived with John's coffee and pancakes. He had forgotten all about his hunger and brunch. "Can I get you another coffee?" he asked Alex, hoping she'd hang around for a little while longer.

"Sure."

As Marika disappeared, John worked the conversation around mouthfuls of food. "Tell me about you, about this wonderful place."

Long after he'd finished eating, they stayed sitting on the patio, ignoring daggers from Marika, discussing Alex's ambition to get out of retail and John's incredible itinerary for touring the north and south islands. Listening to John, Alex found herself with a renewed appreciation for the splendor of her own country.

"I'm going to explore the South Island first, visit all these beautiful lakes and mountains," he said, pulling a brochure out of his pocket for Alex to see. "Then I'm going to hike and bike in some of those valleys, swim with the dolphins, right here…look," he pointed to a picture on the flier, "and I might even go penguin spotting or whale watching."

"Wow." Alex blew out a breath when John stopped to take one.

"Oh, and I want to taste a possum burger. Maybe we could do that tonight?"

She laughed; a tiny, tinkling sound he liked. "Maybe *you* could."

"And I want to see a glacier…you know…close up."

"I can't believe I've lived here all my life and done none of this."

"Well, maybe you will." He studied her face, suddenly serious. She seemed so naïve, he almost felt cruel. *Probably got a stern old man with a shot gun warning her away from guys like me.* "So, where are we going tonight?" he said, before she could change her mind.

"I've got somewhere pretty special in mind."

"Somewhere that serves local food would be nice, I'd like to give that a try."

"I believe I know just the place."

As John walked her out of the café, returning Marika's smile over the top of her head, he couldn't help thinking that, whatever tonight brought, he'd already hit the home stretch.

Chapter Five

Tiffany's, a one-hundred-year-old Tudor House Restaurant in Central City, fronting the Avon River, and boasting an enviable reputation for its excellent local cuisine, service, and atmosphere, would be the ideal place for a romantic dinner, Alex had decided. As she drove down Oxford Terrace to meet John at the restaurant, her eagerness threatened to ruin her desire to appear casual. She checked her makeup in the mirror for the tenth time. Dressed in snug-fitting blue jeans, a black silk shirt, and strappy black sandals, her hair held up in an elegant twist, even she had to admit she looked good. At seven-thirty, the time they'd agreed to meet, she pulled off the road and into a parking bay behind Tiffany's. "Beautiful place," John said, appearing at the door of her bug before she'd even stepped out.

"Yes, it is," Alex said, pleased with herself. With two days to go before Christmas, the restaurant looked especially beautiful with the festive trimmings. "Did you know this is an award-winning restaurant, right across from the Bridge of Remembrance?"

"I noticed." John draped an arm over her shoulder, and steered her toward the entrance. "Honoring the sacrifice of your soldiers from the First World War." After she'd told him of the place she'd picked, he'd researched it that afternoon.

"Wow, John. I'm impressed."

"Don't be." He smiled, like a sly cat preying on a mouse. "I'm fascinated with history."

Conversation over dinner flowed easily. They feasted on freshly baked herb bread with sun-blushed tomato paste; Akaroa salmon; vegetable tortellini with asparagus; and beef fillet with creamed beetroot, spinach, potato gallette, and Kikorangi blue.

"It's a triple-cream blue cheese," she explained to John, "made right here."

"Delicious," John said, gracious and charming, his eyes shining with purpose. He insisted on dessert, even though the button on his pants seemed to have shifted. One delectable chocolate and Cointreau mousse with crème Chantilly arrived at their table, accompanied by two forks. Far more romantic to share; and cheaper.

As the last mouthful disappeared from his fork, John sat back and sighed. "I can't move. What a superb meal."

"I'm glad you approve."

As they left Tiffany's, after John had picked up the check, and strolled back to Alex's car, he pondered his dilemma. Alex seemed considerably younger and far less experienced than the women he usually took to dinner. *They* usually repaid him with a hot, steamy night of passion, the way he preferred to end an evening with the woman for whom he'd opened his wallet. The meal tonight hadn't been cheap.

His budget rental wouldn't impress her and would hardly entice her out of her clothes.

She'd already mentioned she lived with her parents. That would work for him, but perhaps not for her. *Damn.* Alex acted like a virgin. *And what the hell do you do with one of those?*

"Well," she said as they reached her bug, "I guess this is goodnight. Thanks again for dinner."

"My pleasure." Like the tide he'd watched ebb that same afternoon, he saw his chances of a night of hot sex fade equally as fast. Discontentment swirled in his gut.

"I had a wonderful time," she went on.

"What? Oh...me, too." He forced a smile. "Seems a shame to end the night so soon." A frustrated sigh sneaked out, and he quickly coughed to cover it up. It seemed hopeless.

"Did you enjoy your first taste of New Zealand?"

Now you want to chat? You want to prolong the agony?

"Yes, Alex, I did. You picked a fine place." He had an idea. *Maybe a little sexual innuendo will move things along.* "I hope I'll get to see a lot more of the local flavor." *What the hell, nothing ventured...*

He grinned at the sharp pain of Alex's elbow digging his rib. *Aha.* His spirits rose. *Perhaps she isn't so naïve.* "Ouch." He laughed. "I mean it. I'd like to see more of you."

She faltered slightly. "You...would?"

Damn, girl, have you looked in the mirror? He smiled. "Of course. But only if you'd like to." He could be polite when he had something to gain.

"Yes." She smiled, revealing perfectly straight teeth. "I think I would."

"Good." The effort was killing him. He'd never had to work so hard to get laid.

"But how?"

"What?"

"How would we do it? You're traveling all over the islands. I have to work."

"Oh, that's easy. Take some time off. It's Christmas. You could join me for a bit."

You make it sound so simple. Maybe you don't need to

work, but I do. And retail means I have to work the holidays. She couldn't push off the little voice that told her otherwise. She hated her job. She'd get another. Someone else said yes, even as she recognized the voice as her own.

He watched her drive away, unsure where it could all possibly lead. *Perhaps I was wrong about her*. He turned back to his camper van and climbed inside. Not used to dating respectable women, he wondered if he shouldn't be toying with such a trusting, young girl.

Chapter Six

After leaving Christchurch, John stopped fifty miles away in Akaroa, where he took a cruise around the harbor, watched a small pod of Hector's dolphins swim alongside the boat, and thought about Alex. He'd had time to think. *Maybe she shouldn't come*. He'd embarked on this trip to avoid complications, and virgins counted as complications.

Christmas Day, a scorching hot day, he lazed around on the beach, surrounded by a bevy of beauties in bikinis, a couple of whom he took home. They didn't care about the camper van. He called his mother, like the good, dutiful son, filling her in on his ventures around the island.

"The country's awesome," he told her, "there's hardly any traffic."

"When are you coming home, son?" she whined.

"Sorry, Mom, bad connection." More than once he used that line, and hung up.

Moving on to the West Coast town of Haast, he spied a ravishing redhead exiting a sports car. She flashed him a smile, and later that night, after she left his camper van, he scratched up another notch on the underside of the table. He smoked a cigarette, snorted a little cocaine the redhead had left, and cracked open a beer. *This is the life.*

Away from the boss, he could relax. The first drug trade had been successful, but left him nervous. He'd never done anything of that magnitude, and, for a while, he needed to lie low, figure things out, decide if he could do it again. He'd made a lot of money and now he wanted to enjoy it. Alex would only mess things up. Three weeks later, when she met him in Alexandra, John had almost forgotten about Alex's fabulous ass, pert little tits, and heavenly legs. Now, standing in front of him outside The Nook, the restaurant where he'd told her he'd be, he had to adjust his jeans to give himself a little more room, glad he'd finally called and agreed to meet her.

"I wasn't sure you'd come," he said, staring into her beautiful blue eyes and folding her into his arms. She went willingly, they shared a tight embrace, and he let out a low groan of frustration at the way her soft body molded into his, hoping she would be less uptight than she'd been before.

"Of course I'd come. You made quite an impression, in case you hadn't noticed," she said shyly, while he watched that same old flush creeping its way up her neck.

He lowered his head and pressed his lips against her full, red mouth, marveling at the softness of her lips, surprised at his control not to devour her right where she stood. When she didn't resist, he twirled a lock of her hair around his finger, curled his other hand around the base of her neck, and pressed down harder, sliding his tongue between her lips, into the warmth of her willing mouth. He pulled her closer, and felt the pulse of her heart race against his chest, the tightening of her fingers pressed into the small of his back. *Damn the comfort.* With one hand still around the back of her neck, and the desire of an animal, he half carried her across the parking lot to where he'd parked his van, flung open the door, and lifted her inside. With absolutely no resistance from her whatsoever, he laid her down on the collapsible table that also served as a bed, practically tore off her clothes, and owned her, over and again, until they both lay there exhausted.

Later, that evening, over a Cajun dinner at the Blue Lounge, Alex ruined everything.

"I'd like you to meet my family."

He almost choked on his mouthful of beer. "Already? Isn't that what you do when you go steady?" he tried to joke. *Fuck, I barely know you.* Unless he had marriage in mind–and he didn't–he didn't want to meet her family. He couldn't see the point. "What's the occasion?"

"My uncle lives here."

"Oh." *Terrific.* He took another swig, the afterglow of the afternoon fast disappearing.

"They're laid-back people, John. It'll be fun."

"It will?" He doubted it. Meeting family didn't sound like fun.

"Of course. What could be better than your own tour guide, someone to give you the inside scoop on all the best things to see, the best places to eat? And, you'll like my Uncle Edward. He's smart, knows a lot, and he's well-traveled."

"Uh-huh?" The warm beer was beginning to taste better.

"And he's been to America. He knows about Oakland. I told you I had cousins there."

"You did?"

Just when her pleading had brought about the start of a headache, she stopped, and stared down at the table, and he watched her begin picking awkwardly at the table cloth. He shifted uncomfortably in his seat, wishing the waitress would bring the check, anything that would deflect the unease that had suddenly settled like a storm cloud. *Way to kill a moment.* "Uh, well…I," he started, unsure what to say.

"It's okay." She shook her head before he could continue, before the indignity of rejection. "It doesn't matter. Sometimes, I get too pushy, I'm sorry. Forget I asked."

"Well…wait a minute." Maybe he could still salvage a hopeless situation. With a forced grin, and an inward grimace, he nodded. "Sure, why not?" *If it means I get another afternoon like today.* And just like that…within a few hours he found himself face to face with Uncle Edward, a compact, wiry man he guessed to be in his mid-fifties.

"Pleased to meet you," Edward offered, extending a hand. He had an Aussie twang even stronger than Alex. John grasped his hand, pumped it up and down vigorously, perhaps a little too hard. He peered down into the man's upturned face and beady, brown eyes. At over six feet tall, he towered above him. Something in the way Edward's eyes darted about, from John to Alex and back to John, hinted he hadn't been honest; that he was far less than pleased.

"Likewise," John lied.

"Come, come." With surprising strength, Edward tugged on the hand still in his grip, half dragging him into the living room. Alex trailed behind.

"Alex tells me you're a Yank--"

"Uncle--"

Edward flapped a hand at his niece, brushing aside her embarrassment. "Whad'ya doing all the way out here?"

Straight shooter. No doubt with a deadly aim. John had already decided he liked Edward no more than Edward appeared to like him.

"Traveling." The less he said, the less ammunition he provided for Edward to use.

"By yourself?"

"Yes."

"For how long?"

"I haven't decided."

Edward rubbed his chin. "I see."

The two men stood awkwardly, each weighing the other like two boxers in a ring, unevenly matched in size, but intellectually perfectly paired.

"Uncle, I want your advice on something."

Whether she'd done it to save him, or truly did want his advice, John only knew he was grateful for the escape, and threw Alex his silent thanks. While she engineered her way around John, grabbed her uncle's arm, and dove into conversation about her career concerns, or mostly how to break out of retail and into real estate, he became aware of another set of eyes in the room.

Curled up in an armchair in the far corner, he noticed a brown-haired, unattractive woman of about thirty, blending so well with the dowdy piece of furniture in which she sat that he almost missed her.

"Hello." He shot her a cautious smile.

"G'day."

He clasped his hands in front of him, let out a sigh, shifted from one foot to the other. No one had even invited him to sit. *Fun, Alex said. I'd rather have surgery.*

"So, you're John."

"That's right." *I should have refused.*

"Amanda. Alex's cousin." She didn't get up. "Alex told us all about you. Well…not all, perhaps." A loaded pause. "What do you do, John?"

And there it is. A flash of anger tightened the muscle in his cheek. *Barely out of the gate, hardly know each other, and now they all want to know what I do. I deal drugs, cocaine. Happy?* A smile forced its way onto his lips. "I'm in marketing."

"Marketing, huh?"

Edward appeared behind him, Alex was nowhere in

sight. "Tell me more about that."

"Not much to tell. I promote large companies, travel a bit, nothing glamorous."

"Are you working now, while you're here?"

"No. I'm on vacation."

"What's the name of your firm? Maybe I've heard of them. I'm in advertising myself."

Fuck. Wouldn't ya know it. "Ah. Doubt it. It's a small, American firm. Anyway, who wants to talk about work when they're on vacation?" He laughed, shuffled his position, and glanced over Edward's head, desperate to find Alex so she could save him again. His eyes flickered back to Amanda, took in her short, wavy hair, bony face, and pencil thin body. She looked just like her father, Edward; two sharp-eyed little birds waiting to peck him to pieces.

I was right. I shouldn't have come.

Chapter Seven

Time passed quickly, and four days later, when Alex bid John goodbye and headed home to Christchurch, she drove with a head filled with doubts.

Uncle Edward hadn't liked John. "I've seen his type before," he'd told her, "charming and handsome, a womanizer."

Amanda was only slightly better. "He's shady, not on the level…but he is gorgeous. I can see why you like him."

"Forget him." Edward scowled at Amanda. "You'll get hurt." As Christchurch loomed in the distance, Alex knew she wouldn't forget. Couldn't forget. It was far too late to worry about getting hurt. John had already wormed his way into her heart. "It's not a fling," she cried indignantly, when she got home and her father sided with her uncle, "and I'm not some stupid, love-sick teen pining over a holiday romance."

As the days dragged by, and slowly turned into weeks, she had to admit she'd been wrong. They'd all been right. John didn't call. She stumbled through her days, hurt, angry, feeling foolish, struggling to pick up the routine in her colorless, boring life. The monotony of her dead-end job with the bunch of cacophonous weirdo's didn't help. Six weeks after she'd left Edward's place, she looked at her calendar, and realized John would soon be leaving the south island to head north, and then in another few weeks he'd be gone, headed back to the States. She huffed out a sigh.

Wonder what that's like. The States. Oakland. Another

world in which she didn't belong.

Bored and moody, she stared out from the counter at the record store, punk sounds pounding through her head. For the first time she heard the lyrics. They sounded eerily applicable to her own life. John had been a 'brief encounter'; she had 'no assurance of his love'; her world felt like 'life had nothing else to offer'.

I'm nineteen. Hell, maybe I'll just slit my own wrists. She even eyed the box cutter under the counter.

"How much for the box-set?" someone asked.

"What?" She looked up from the counter into a pair of impatient, grey eyes.

"The box-set. It doesn't have a price. How much?"

She pointed to a poster on the wall. "It's a new release. The price is up there." The customer turned away without another word, dropped the empty case back into the rack, and left the store. The manager shot her an angry glare. If bluntness had cost her the sale, if it even cost her the job, Alex didn't care. Life had never seemed more dull, or more empty. *Damn you, John.*

Hours later, as she neared the end of her shift, her mobile phone rang in her pocket. Just for a second she let herself dream, hope, and then snapped herself out of her stupor. She dug her hand in her jacket to get it. Too many disappointments had her no longer bothering to check the number.

"What?" Whichever friend wanted to know why she no longer called, why she never wanted to hang out, she'd tell them the same thing she'd told the others. I don't want to.

"Hi." That rich, smoky voice, the American accent. "It's John."

She could barely breathe when she heard what he said.

Chapter Eight

"I'm going," she told her parents. "I'm nineteen. I can do what I want."

"You don't know anything about this man," her father argued, "what if he's a mass murderer? You'll be thousands of miles away. Too far for us to help you."

"That's ridiculous." Alex scoffed. "John's not a killer, Dad."

"Try seeing it from our side," her mother tried more gentle tactics. "You're still a kid, our only kid. Even though you're a pain in the ass, we're rather fond of you. We don't want to lose you."

"You won't." Alex turned back to her father, the one whose permission she needed. If he caved, she knew she could get to her mother. "Dad, I'm young, but I'm not stupid. Maybe it's time I ventured out a little bit. You can't deny it will be good for me to travel and explore the world. This way I'll have someone to show me. Safer than doing it on my own."

"Is it?"

"If you have to go, why not go with a friend?"

"If she has any left," her father retorted, sarcastically.

"My mind's made up. I'm going. Look," she pleaded, not really wanting to go without their blessing, but fully prepared to if they wouldn't give it, "it's only for a couple of months and I'll come back sooner if I'm unhappy."

"What about your job?"

"What about it, Mum? I'm a retail clerk."

"Don't be flippant, young lady." Her father spoke harshly. "That's a valid question."

Immediately, Alex realized her mistake. Immaturity about her job wouldn't help win their approval for a solo trip half way round the world. She sighed. "You're right, I'm sorry. But it's a retail job, not a career. I can't listen to pop tunes for the rest of my life, Dad. You even said so yourself."

Gotcha. She watched his mouth twist into a wry scowl and knew she'd made progress. "I'll get another job when I come back." She hung on to her small advantage. "Something serious. Plus, if I travel now, I won't have to leave a good career behind, will I?"

"Damn, I should never have taught you how to argue."

She grabbed at his arm with the excitement of a child. "Does that mean I can go?"

He paused, glanced at her mother, who looked away, covering a tiny smirk with her hand, and looked back at Alex. "If you promise to check in at least once a week, I...suppose I can't really stop you."

"Thanks, Daddy," she squealed, hugged him, and grinned at her mother.

"When do you tell John?" he asked, grumpy and begrudging.

"I already did."

"I thought as much. Well, I'm telling you this," he glowered, "if I get a whiff of anything funny, I'll be over there myself to collect you. And I don't care how much I embarrass you."

In early March, after John concluded his tour of the north island, Alex boarded a flight with him in Auckland, and flew out to begin what she hoped would be the start of a wonderful relationship. A lot could happen in two months.

"What time is it?" she asked, groggy and disheveled after the long, grueling flight to Oakland, made longer by several connections.

"I don't know." John hurried them through the airport and out to the parking bay where he'd left his car.

"I feel weird, like my body's all out of whack."

"That's called jetlag, Alex. Don't worry, it wears off in a couple of days."

He rolled down the window, slid his ticket into the pay meter, and waited for the barrier to lift.

"What's your apartment like?" She looked out the car window as John left Airport Road and veered onto Interstate 880, following a sign directing them to downtown Oakland.

"Small."

"Everything's so huge," she said, gazing out at the late afternoon traffic, across multiple lanes of highway, and massive billboards way up on the embankment, "I've never seen so many cars."

"The curse of Oakland," John said sourly, stepping on the gas and weaving in and out of lanes.

"I never imagined it would be like this. It's so weird, being on this side of the car and not being the driver."

"Or this side of the road."

"Yes. I'm glad you're driving." She laughed. "I don't think I could handle that as well as all this traffic."

"You'll get used to it."

Alex smiled, stole a glance at his handsome profile, and settled back into her seat, closed her eyes. Something about the way John had said that stirred a warmth in her belly, a sense of satisfaction, like she'd just eaten warm apple pie.

John wanted her to stay, to get used to it. John hadn't kidded her about his apartment. Compared to her three-bedroom home in Christchurch, his tiny, one-bedroom place seemed barely big enough for one person, never mind two.

"Sleep first, sightseeing later," he ordered, dropping down onto a king-sized bed that seemed to fill the room.

"I'm too excited," she squealed, bouncing up and down on the bed beside him with the vigor of a teen, all keyed up and full of a second wind. "There's too much I want to do."

"All in good time." John gave her a tired smiled. "We've been up for over thirty hours. Get some rest."

The two months whipped past with the same speed she'd come to expect in America. Everything in America moved fast; the cars, the community, the way people spoke, the decrease in her cash. America was expensive.

Sometimes, John disappeared for days at a time. "Working," he explained, "out of state marketing campaign."

On those occasions, she occupied herself with walks around the unfamiliar streets of his neighborhood. Other days she rested. She checked in with her parents, and John checked in with her. Everything seemed good. Alex liked America.

John made up for the time he left her alone by showering her with attention on his days off. He showed her around his town, his city, took her into Los Angeles, and down to San Diego. The flame he'd brought into her life lit her up until she glowed. Even her parents noticed.

"You sound happy," they remarked, on her calls back home.

"I am happy. Everything's perfect."

Chapter Nine

San Francisco, 2002

The twins stood side by side at the top of the small hill, in front of the old Victorian building. Jessica stole a glance at her brother, drained of energy, hoping he wouldn't get them thrown out of this apartment, too. Every day he got older and angrier, and a few months later, when the inevitable happened and he lost his cool, they'd have to move on. The pattern had grown predictable.

She'd lost track of all the places they'd lived. After an often abusive ten years in foster care, finally leaving at eighteen, they'd spent the next eleven years drifting in and out of a variety of dubious places, surviving in dodgy neighborhoods, hunting out cheap digs and merciful landlords, who would pardon late rents and Judd's explosive outbursts. When he'd spent time in Juvenile Hall for drug and theft offenses, Jessica had learned how to navigate the dangers of local gangs and break-ins alone. Judd's mouth was set in a hard, grim line. Jessica wondered if he could read her thoughts.

"It looks nice," she offered, with a stab of guilt. No matter how hard he'd made things, he'd always managed to take care of her.

"I thought you'd like it. But we're further away from Mom. We won't be able to visit as much."

"It's not like she'll know."

Murder, suicide, and lunacy. Ninety miles away, secure in a mental home, and locked away in 1982, Marianne Croft no longer knew her own children.

"Well, are we gonna stand out here all day, or d'ya wanna check it out inside?"

"It doesn't matter what it looks like inside," she said, "I know I'll love it. We're in San Francisco. I love San Francisco."

"I know. That's why I chose it."

Jessica squeezed his hand, and then reached into the back of her old Ford Taurus for a jacket to shield her against the early October breeze.

A few steps ahead of her, Judd's voice, sounding happier now, floated over his shoulder. "We've got two of the three floors, and we even get the garage. It parks two, tandem," he explained, checking behind him to make sure she'd followed. "Both the bedrooms are big, so we don't have to fight over that, not that I'd get much of a say." She heard him chuckling, a deep, rich sound she loved yet barely ever heard.

"Oh, wood floors," she cooed, stepping over the threshold, "I love wood floors."

"I know that, too."

She followed him into the living room, grinning at the wood-burning fireplace in the corner, imagining cozy, winter evenings, just the two of them, reading or watching television in a room they'd furnish with the few things they'd collected over the years.

"Kitchen's a bit small," Judd said, moving on through the apartment, "but it comes fully equipped."

"I love it." Jessica smiled.

"The bedrooms are on the second floor."

She trailed behind him, up the stairs, a sense of longing in her gut; longing to make this spacious, bright apartment on Baker Street, in San Francisco's Western Addition, into a home. The brochure had called it a unit. Jessica didn't like that. Such a cold and clinical classification, like an irrelevant entity or component that represented only a part of something not yet whole. *This isn't a unit, this is a home. My home.*

"So, you approve?"

She turned to look at Judd, leaning against the doorway of what would be her bedroom, grinning with pride. From the glow on his face, she could tell he knew he'd chosen well. This place was nothing like the hovels they'd stayed in before. "I do...but," she didn't want to ask.

She didn't have to. "Yes, we can afford it." He laughed and turned on his heel to head back down the stairs. "I got us a good deal."

Catching up with him at her car, Jessica hugged him from behind. "Thank you, Judd, for being my brother. I love you."

"What, even though I'm a screw up?" He shrugged off her hug, and seemed almost embarrassed. Perhaps he thought he didn't deserve her affection, or her love. He had caused her more than her fair share of worry, and they both knew it.

"Yes, even though you're a screw-up. And besides, I have to love you, you're all I've got."

As she yanked the bulging, red monstrosity she called her suitcase from the trunk of her beaten-up Taurus, and Judd took it from her to haul inside, she angled a glance down the street, and sighed. Maybe someday, she might have a few luxuries in her life, like a nice, new vehicle to drive; maybe even something sporty, like the silver Mercedes parked just down the street.

"Our furniture won't arrive until tomorrow," Judd apologized, grabbing her other bag. "But at least we've got the fridge."

"And the TV. How about a quiet night in? Me, you, movies, and Milky Ways?"

"Sure. There's a store close-by. I'll pick some up."

Judd noticed the look that crossed her face; a rare look of peace, like she'd gone back in time, to their old lives in Sacramento, before any of the tragedies. A long time ago, it had been her favorite treat; to sit in front of the TV in her pajamas, with her mother, father, and two older brothers, eating frozen Milky Ways after dinner.

"I don't feel like doing anything else," Jessica continued, "I'm starting my new job the day after tomorrow."

Chapter Ten

"Shit."

The coffee cup burned his fingers; Jackson set it down so fast it splashed onto his desk. He'd been up all night, had already downed two cups in the past hour, and needed another to get him through the long morning. "Damn." He looked around for something to mop up the rapidly spreading, brown mess.

"You look like shit," Red said, tossing him a roll of paper towels.

"Yeah, well you're no sleeping beauty. Thanks." Jackson caught the towels and tore off a few pieces, blotted the liquid seeping closer to a stack of files on his desk.

"You still think it was murder?"

Last night, Thursday, October third, a man's body had been pulled from the harbor. That made four suspicious, unsolved deaths Jackson had been dealt; another had been found torched in a car near Telegraph Hill a month ago, and he hadn't been able to close the two cases in the Bay from seven years ago. They'd been turned over to the cold-case division, where Jackson feared they would stay.

"Yeah, he couldn't swim. Why would he walk by the harbor, alone at night, when he couldn't swim?"

"He was Paul Lowe." Red Dennis had bagged the wallet, containing the man's ID.

"This one's different, not like the others."

"You mean 'cause of the ID? Because this one's not

homeless?"

"Yeah, but not just that." Jackson tossed the sodden towels into the trash can and sat down at his desk. "Both these two recent ones are different. Paul Lowe's wife said he couldn't swim, and even she doesn't believe he'd have walked along the harbor at night, by himself."

"Well, his body didn't have a mark on it, so maybe he fell in and drowned. He had been at the bar...maybe he was drunk."

Jackson chewed the end of his pen. "He wasn't robbed, his wallet was full of cash."

"So what's the motive for murder? It was probably an accident, like the coroner said."

"I don't think so."

"Is this another hunch?"

"No." Jackson pulled the pen out of his mouth and tapped it against the desk. "The barman said he was alone, he only had one drink."

"Maybe the barman forgot...or didn't remember. He said it was busy last night."

"True, but Paul sat at the bar. And the barman did remember him–he remembered the black mole on his cheek, it's the size of a quarter. Said he only served him one drink."

"Okay, so he wasn't drunk. But why push someone in the harbor for no reason, Jackson? The killer, supposing there is one, would at least have taken his wallet."

"There was a reason," Jackson said, taking a slug of what was left of his coffee, "I just have to figure out what."

When they'd interviewed the barman last night, he'd remembered Paul, remembered him sitting alone, talking to no one. "He came in late, had one quick drink, and left," he'd explained.

By the time Paul's body had been spotted floating in the harbor, and dragged out at ten-thirty the night before, he'd only been dead for about thirty minutes. The barman said he'd closed the bar at ten and stayed to clean up, verified by the manager. "Did you see him leave?" Jackson had asked.

"Nah, sorry, just saw he'd gone." They'd eliminated the barman from their inquiries.

"Why didn't he yell, scream for help?" Jackson thought out loud. "Someone would have heard him."

"Could be any reason. Scared, voice froze, water too cold and couldn't get a breath. That frigid Bay water'd take anyone's breath away."

"You'd find it if your life depended on it."

"Maybe the alcohol numbed his senses and he didn't realize the danger until it was too late."

"A successful businessman who can't swim isn't likely to walk by the water at night and alone," Jackson repeated. "Someone knew he couldn't swim."

"The one last month doesn't fit the mold," Red said, "I see what you mean by different."

"I've been thinking about that," Jackson agreed, staring at Red. "That one doesn't involve the water, but it does involve a knife, among other things."

The male body, found in the car near Telegraph Hill, had been torched beyond all recognition. A month later, no one had claimed the remains. Forensics determined the use of an accelerant on the torn cloth shrouding the head. No traces of drug had been found in his system. Under the cloth, duct tape had been found over the victim's mouth, and rope tied tightly around his neck. The autopsy revealed puncture wounds to the heart. The poor bastard had been gagged, stabbed, strangled, and burned.

"Neither of these last two are homeless." The wallet left intact on the drowning, the expensive watch seared to the wrist of the burn victim told him that. The homeless didn't have those luxuries.

"Yeah, his pattern has changed."

"You think it's a he?" Red raised an eyebrow.

"Well, it's one helluva strong, angry bitch if it isn't."

"Anything come back from the accelerant?"

"Nothing solid."

The last place he'd checked that had sold accelerant around the time of the murder had turned out to be a divorcee and her daughter, planning a barbeque. Jackson had kept their details anyway, just in case. Maybe the divorcee was a cheat. Maybe an angry ex-husband had exacted revenge.

"The water and the knife–they're the connections," Red said, getting up from his desk and joining Jackson at his.

"You mean the two from ninety-five?"

"Yeah. I know you think I forgot about those. I didn't."

"I didn't think that," Jackson said, with a sigh, "I just wish we could nail this bastard before he does it again."

All the killings, except one, had involved brutal stabbings. All except the drowning had involved extreme injuries to the victims. A brutal rage.

"If we're looking for a serial killer," Red said, going along with Jackson's suspicion, "then why the long gap? They span more than seven years."

"That's puzzling me, too," Jackson said, reaching for his coffee cup again. "Most serial killers take a break, but not usually that long." He cussed at the empty cup.

"Still got your old notes?"

Jackson unlocked a drawer in his desk and pulled out a file.

"You know you should have turned those over to Cold Case," Red said, with a grin.

"Kept a copy. Had a hunch we might need 'em."

Red peered over his shoulder and scanned the questions Jackson had written out seven years earlier. "Yes for question one, serial killer. You convinced me."

"The evidence should do that."

"What evidence? He never leaves us much."

"Hmm." Jackson wrote YES against the question.

"Motive…that's a tough one."

Jackson rocked the pen back and forth between the first two fingers of his left hand, and let out a sigh. "Yeah, I still haven't figured that out." He wrote UNKNOWN.

"Let's say I'm with you on this," Red said, "about the drowning–and I'm still not sure–then I'd have to say the killer's local."

Jackson wrote YES against the question. "He is local, I'm certain of it."

"How can you be so sure?"

"There are never any witnesses. It's hard to murder someone in a busy city with no witnesses unless you know the city. You've gotta know where or when to strike."

"Or know who can swim and who can't."

"Exactly." Jackson snorted out a tired laugh. "I knew you'd come around."

"All the killings are brutal," Red said, reading the rest of Jackson's notes, "except the drowning."

"It's a brutal crime against a man who can't swim. To watch him flounder and drown." Jackson drummed his fingers on the desk.

"What do you think about the timing, then?" Red pointed to the next question. "These two weren't near the holidays like the others."

"Yeah, another break from the pattern. It blows out my theory of him being antagonized by the holidays."

"He's not after sex, he's not after money, and he's not after power…so, what is he after?"

Jackson shook his head. "Without any motive, I'd say he's a hedonist. A psychopath murdering purely for pleasure."

"Terrific," Red said, through gritted teeth, "the worst fucking kind."

"Think he owns a boat? I'm thinking that he likes the water…so maybe he owns a boat. And he's got money."

"How do you know that?" Red looked at him in astonishment.

"Well, he isn't robbing his victims."

Chapter Eleven

Yesterday, October third, had marked Alex's sixth wedding anniversary. Part of her wished she'd listened to the warnings about marrying a man she'd only known for a year, and hadn't known all that well, but her reckless side meant she could live with no regrets. She'd had to find out for herself, even if they had all been right. The discovery of the little packets of cocaine hidden in his closet had turned a disastrous marriage dangerous. John wasn't only using, he was dealing. Now she'd been to the police, she knew she had to get out. John ran with a bad crowd. She knew better than to confront him.

A week ago, before she'd gone to the police, she'd found herself the new apartment. Of course, by the time she'd spoken to Narcotics, the packages had disappeared from the closet.

"You did the right thing," the officer told her. "We've had him under surveillance for a while. You could have been implicated if you hadn't spoken up."

That horrified her more than the discovery of the cocaine. Even with the new apartment, she'd put herself at risk. Once the police picked him up, it wouldn't be long before he made the connection, and sent someone looking for her.

The one-bedroom unit, in San Francisco's upscale Pacific Heights, took up only the ground floor of a four-story building on Fillmore Street. It offered a Queen sized bedroom, one bathroom, a tiny kitchen and a combination living and dining area, and had been freshly painted. To Alex, it symbolized freedom and fear: freedom from John, from terror, from his life of drugs and dangerous friends; but fear of making it in a foreign country alone.

This morning, as she ran up the steps into the office of Home Hunters, Oakland, where she'd worked for the past eleven months, she thought about the fact that he still knew where she worked. He didn't care she'd left, hadn't even batted an eyelid when she'd moved out all of her things, but she'd only be safe until he figured out she'd been to the cops.

"How's the new apartment?" Sammy Cole smiled.

Alex shot Sammy a grin. A co-worker in the leasing department, and her only friend, Sammy had helped her find it.

"It's fantastic. I love it."

"Any word from John?"

"No, nothing."

"What about the police?"

Sammy knew all about John and the drugs. She'd been the one who'd encouraged Alex to go to the police. "I haven't heard from them, either."

"Then they still haven't picked him up."

"They said they'd call when they do. How long do these things take?"

Sammy shrugged. "I don't know, sweetie, its not my specialty. I'm sure they'll call soon."

"Do you think thirteen miles is far enough away?" Alex picked up the list of the day's showings. She'd deliberately stayed close. John would expect her to go further. When he discovered what she'd done, and sent his cronies looking, they'd hopefully search wider than a thirteen mile radius.

Plus, thirteen miles kept her close enough to watch her own back.

"I'm sure you'll be fine, but you should think about a new job." Sammy moved her chair closer to Alex, clearly in the mood for a chat. "Did you hear about the latest?" She lowered her voice.

"The latest what?" Alex didn't have a clue.

"Here…read."

Sammy handed her the morning's paper, tapping her finger on an article half way down the first page. Dutifully, Alex skimmed through the article. …another suspected murder…young male, pulled from the Bay…last night after…his wife said…police believe… The words went on but Alex stopped reading.

"That's why the cops haven't nailed your John," Sammy said, "they're too busy trying to catch up with this killer."

"That's a different division, Sammy," Alex said, handing back the paper, "and he's not my John."

"They still haven't figured out the one from last month. You remember…the one that got torched in his car?"

"Of course I remember."

"Well, I think it's a serial killer. He's killed two, and probably getting ready to do it again. Hey," she stared at Alex, "do you suppose…" she thought for a second, "nah…forget it."

Alex shot her a contemptuous look. "No, I don't. John's a drug dealer, not a murderer."

"Just a thought. Could be a deal gone bad." Sammy shrugged, and moved back to her own desk across from Alex, obviously thinking it a fair assumption.

"You watch too much TV, Sammy," she said, somewhat annoyed and wanting to change the subject. However, the thought had occurred to her, too, and hearing Sammy say it made it all too real. The burned man could have been an ordered hit. So could the drowning last night. Alex didn't want to think about it.

"Sorry. I didn't mean to upset you. I just thought..."

"I know what you thought. It could have been an accident."

"Oh, come on, Alex, how the hell could it have been an accident?" Sammy said.

Alex couldn't tell if her suggestion had Sammy amused or amazed. Anyone could fall into the harbor after they'd spent the night in a bar. Before she could say that, Sammy had launched off into a tirade.

"How could that poor bastard strangle, stab and then burn himself? He had a cloth wrapped round his head, a rope round his neck. That's one clever son-of-a-bitch who can do all that, and then set fire to himself."

Alex stared at her friend's wild eyes. "I meant the drowning. I didn't mean the one last month."

"Two suspicious deaths in two months?" Sammy snorted. "That's murder."

"Have you been tracking them?" Alex was amazed her friend could remember so much detail.

"I'm just vigilant," Sammy said, defensively. "And I'm scared. I live alone."

"I know. I'm sorry. I guess I'm trying not to think about it too much. Getting away from John is about all I can handle."

"Well, speaking of him again," Sammy said quickly, "what about a new job? You really should get away from here."

"And I will, but I've other concerns to take care of first."

Her thoughts switched to her new apartment. Apart from the small refrigerator and a washer and dryer that had come with the unit, she didn't have another lick of furniture; not even a bed. "How much does it cost to kit out an apartment?"

Sammy laughed. "A lot. But don't worry, I can lend you some stuff."

"My rent alone will gobble up half my pay check."

"Tell me about it," Sammy moaned, "but hey, what's the price of freedom?"

Chapter Twelve

The six o'clock alarm on Alex's mobile phone woke her the following morning. She rolled out of her sleeping bag on the floor and reached across to where her purse lay to shut it off. In her yellow jammies, with the phone still in her hand, she padded out of her bedroom into her tiny kitchen, and opened the refrigerator door. *Hmm, not much to choose from.* Settling for orange juice and a slice of bread, she grabbed a pen and notepad from the kitchen counter, and dragged the yellow pages out from one of the drawers. *If Sammy thinks I need a new job, I'll find a new job.*

What she had in mind this morning, however, was something to help her make ends meet. Seven nights sleeping on the floor had already tweaked her back and robbed her of sleep. She had to get a new bed, and soon. *What I need right now is a second job, something flexible, with plenty of tips.*

A loud buzzing from the kitchen counter interrupted her thoughts. *Damn.* When she hauled herself up from the floor to check it out, she saw John's digits had flashed up on her phone. At six-fifteen, he had to be just getting home. *Screw you, John.* She let it go to voicemail, wondering if he'd leave a message. The call made her anxious. Maybe he'd start calling around, try to locate her. Goose bumps rose on her arms. *I'll have to change my number.* That would make her feel better. If John didn't have her number, he couldn't call. Another layer of separation.

Under the shower a few minutes later, she turned the dial

to hot and closed her eyes, letting the strong jet of water cascade over her shoulders and back. The force pummeled at her tension, until she sensed it splinter into tiny pieces that swirled down the drain with the soapy water. *Another step away from you, John.* Eyes still closed, she turned around so the water splashed over her face, washing John's image further and further from her mind.

After several more minutes, she stepped out, dried herself briskly, and pulled on a pair of beige cotton pants and a pale pink sweater. With the tangles brushed out of her hair, and leaving it to dry naturally, she wandered back into the kitchen, recharged and ready to make progress. Only a few minutes later, she threw down the pen. *Shit, I can't concentrate.* John's call had rattled her cage. He hadn't called all week, so why now? Narcotics hadn't called…it couldn't be that. Could it?

She tried to shrug off the returning anxiety, and grabbed her leather jacket, threw on a pair of boots, and let herself out into the crisp, fall air, hoping a walk would sort out the jumble creeping back into her head.

"Nice morning," a bald man said, passing her a few seconds later, only a few yards outside her apartment, walking a beautiful, black dog that reminded her of Lucky.

"Yes, it is." She tucked her head into the warmth of her collar, and picked up her pace. Did John know him? *Don't be ridiculous, you'll turn yourself into a nut.*

Invigorated by the wind, despite the sting on her cheeks, Alex braced herself and strode down Fillmore Street. The sharp, early morning Bay Area breeze punched fiercely at her nose and ears and whipped at her wet hair. The bite brought tears to her eyes, masking the real ones behind them that began to fall. *How did I end up in such a fucking mess?*

When it felt safe, she risked a quick glance behind, to check if she'd been followed by the man with the dog. He was nowhere in sight. With her sleeve pulled down over her hand, she wiped her nose, wiped the tears from her face, and turned onto Pine, with no idea where she was heading.

Two hours passed before she returned to her apartment. She had zig-zagged so many side streets she couldn't even be sure how she'd found her way home; but she had...and safely. John hadn't sent out any henchmen. *Time to get busy.* With the directory flipped open to the businesses beginning with A, Alex began pouring over pages of restaurants. San Francisco had so many good places to eat. *Wow.*

She reeled off names, sounding them out, deciding which she liked best: "Chez Nous, Fifth Floor, Hyde, Quince, Rustic, Slow Club, Town Hall." *Wow, they all sound so fancy, too up-market for me. I don't have the experience.*

Her eyes fell upon a name that made her laugh out loud. "Phat Harry's. I like it." She picked up her phone and dialed the number.

"We do have a position," a friendly voice told her, introducing its owner as Sarah. "Can you come in today and meet with Harry? He likes to do the interviews himself."

Phat Harry's, on Fillmore Street, was only two blocks from her apartment. Alex found herself with her small hand being gripped in a hearty handshake by Harry ninety minutes after she'd hung up the phone.

"Bet you thought I'd be fat," Harry said, winking and chuckling at Alex.

"Well," she couldn't help but laugh herself, "I wouldn't have cared if you were."

"It's alright, I'm just testing...seeing if you've got a sense of humor. Gotta have one to work here. I don't employ boring stiffs."

"Where did you come up with the name?" she asked, genuinely interested.

"Ya like it?"

"I do."

"You're not an American. Where ya from?"

"New Zealand. Do foreigners count as boring stiffs?"

Harry roared, and his infectious laugh rubbed off on Alex. She hadn't had a good laugh in ages.

"Phat in American speak means cool or entertaining," Harry explained, "I like to think I'm both, that this place is both, but more than that…it's a testament to my former physique."

Alex listened with a twinge of sadness while he explained. "I used to be fat, huge actually. Then, when I was forty-seven, I had a heart attack. Doc said I was a casualty of my own making."

"What do you mean?"

"He eats here regularly. Knows my cooking. He said I have an extraordinary flair in the kitchen and that if I didn't curb my appetite I'd be lucky to see fifty."

"And did you?" Alex blushed, realizing what she'd said. "I mean…you're not fat anymore. I'm sorry, I didn't mean to…"

Harry chuckled again. "I did. Lost over eighty pounds just to keep doc happy. But humor's what saved me. If you can laugh at yourself, laugh at life…you'll lengthen your days."

"I've never believed that more than I do right now," Alex said, smiling at Harry. "So, will you interview me for the job? I'd like to work here."

"I just did."

Alex stared up into his cheerful face, framed by a shock of unruly, grey hair, blue eyes twinkling under bushy, grey eyebrows. She imagined him to be about sixty. "You did?"

He laughed. "I told you, humor is all you need. I go by a sense I get about a person. I don't care if you've got experience, where you've worked before, or whatever fabulous things you could get your friends to say about you. You need a job, I've got one to offer."

"I don't have experience," Alex said, thinking it best to be honest, "but I do work hard."

"A fool could learn this job," Harry said, and added with a wink, "'though I'd never hire a fool. Sarah says you've worked in retail."

"That's right, a music store."

"Well, it's all customer service, except it's food instead of CD's. I like you, Alex. I'm offering you a chance. Trial run for a month, if we like each other…you get to stay; if not, nothing lost. Sound fair?"

"More than fair."

Alex relived their brief conversation, buzzing with glee, on the short walk back to her apartment.

"You can start Wednesday," Harry had said, "Wednesday's are slower."

I'm on my way. She swiped the air with her fist.

Her first call, when she let herself back in, was to Sammy.

"Score," Sammy shrieked, when Alex told her the good news. "Can I be your first customer?"

"I was hoping you would. I start this coming Wednesday. Be there around seven."

"This calls for celebration," Sammy said. "My place, tonight. Bring a bottle."

Later that evening, Alex drove the thirteen miles from her apartment, over the Bay Bridge, to her friend's town-home in Oakland, a bottle of red wine nestled on the front seat of her four-year-old Honda accord. A twinge of unease nestled in her gut–the same unease she always felt driving back into Oakland. She realized she still hadn't filed for divorce, pushing it off so she didn't have to think about John, or give a divorce lawyer her new address. Was she afraid they might pass it to John? *I'll do it on Monday.* She scolded herself for being so paranoid. If she knew John at all, understood anything about his ceaseless energy, incessant demands for attention, and voracious appetite for sex, she knew he'd have already moved on. *He's not going to come looking for me.* Even if she couldn't be sure she believed it.

Chapter Thirteen

"You better get going," Sammy murmured across her desk to Alex, her head buried in a pile of rental applications.

"What time is it?" This Wednesday had been unusually busy with both of them spending almost the entire day driving all over Oakland, showing property to prospective tenants.

"It's already five-thirty."

"Oh, shit, I should have been out of here half an hour ago." Alex quickly tidied the mess in her in-basket and shut down her computer. "If traffic's bad on the bridge, I'm screwed."

"Traffic's always bad on the bridge. Get going. I'll finish up here."

Alex blew her friend a kiss and went for the door. "See you around seven."

At six-thirty, she raced inside her apartment, stripped out of her business suit, leaving it in a crumpled heap on the floor, and dived into black, fitted slacks, a maroon polo-shirt with Harry's logo embroidered above the right breast pocket, and shoved her bare feet into a pair of ugly, flat pumps. *You'll have to do.* She scraped her hair up into a pony tail–Harry had said she'd have to do that if she wanted to keep it long–grabbed her keys, and began the two-block march to Phat Harry's.

Slightly sweaty and winded when she arrived, she pushed open the door a few minutes after seven. Sammy grinned at her from a corner table. "Sorry," she mouthed, "I couldn't wait." She shrugged an apology, and dug her fork into the pile of mashed potatoes on the plate in front of her.

"Put this on." Sarah hurried over. "You're late."

Alex tied the bib around her waist. "Sorry." She brushed a lose tendril of hair from her cheek.

"You're lucky, it's busy tonight. Harry's out back, he won't notice."

"What do I do?" Alex asked, "I've never worked in a restaurant."

"Nothing. Just follow me. Watch what I do tonight, and help. It's busier than usual, we have been assigned the lower level."

Alex nodded, and followed Sarah to a booth, listened to her take an order, while angling a swift look around Phat Harry's, figuring it could seat about a hundred. Split between two levels, the restaurant had a deep yellow, Saltillo clay tile floor, and rustic seating, giving it an earthy feel. Customers already filled many of the booths, and she sensed a twinge of nerves. The door bell jangled, both waitresses turned, and Alex watched a small group of men in business suits enter the restaurant. Sarah nodded at one of them, with tousled, blond hair, and pointed to a corner section.

"Regular," she muttered to Alex, "always sits there. Big tipper."

The blond nodded, moved toward the section, and cast a glance back over his shoulder at Alex. She blushed, embarrassed to have been caught staring.

"Forget about it."

"Excuse me?"

"Him. The blond. Always a different chick. Buys discretion."

"What do you mean?"

"The big tips? He pays us to be discreet."

"Oh." Her stomach rolled a little. "Maybe I should have eaten." Alex chuckled, risking another quick peek. The man in question, wearing an expensive blue suit, white shirt, and yellow tie, had a boyish quality that Alex found appealing. He winked, sending a crimson flush up her cheeks.

"Your funeral," Sarah warned, and headed toward their table.

Alex followed. "I'm only looking." *Hell, I've got enough hassles already.*

"Gentlemen. So nice to see you, again."

Alex listened while Sarah took care of their order, kept her head slightly bowed, stealing shy, furtive glances at the blond when she thought she wouldn't get caught. Occasionally he rewarded her with a wink, or a smile; blue eyes following her around the room while she shadowed her mentor. Less than half an hour later, Alex noticed the section empty. The three men had conducted their business, eaten quickly, and gone. Not that it mattered. *I forgot how good that feels.* She smiled to herself, standing at another table, listening to Sarah take another order. After years of insults and being ignored by John, a man had made her feel attractive again, desirable even. He'd awakened senses she thought had died.

The rest of the evening passed in a busy, but uneventful, blur. At the end of the night, she plopped down onto a bar stool next to Harry, and sighed. "I'm wiped out."

"Did you have fun?"

"Yes. Actually, I did."

"I knew you would." Harry patted her back. "I'll see you Friday. And, this time, try not to be late." He winked, and left her with Sarah.

"I can't believe it's already eleven." Alex yawned, real tiredness starting to set in.

"Yep. It's tough working two jobs." Sarah handed her an envelope. "You did okay tonight."

"Thanks." Alex inspected the contents of the envelope. She pulled out a fistful of bills and a business card. "What's this?"

"Tips."

"No, I mean the card." Alex turned it over in her hand.

"The blond you were batting your lashes at. Seems he liked you, too." Sarah shrugged on her jacket. "Don't say I didn't warn you."

Alex fingered the raised lettering on the card. Anderson Collins. Collins Real Estate. A couple of numbers. A tiny smile lifted the corner of her mouth, and she pushed it deep into a corner of her pocket, where she imagined it would stay.

"Need a ride home?" Harry called out a few minutes later, from somewhere in the back.

"No," Sarah yelled.

"I'll walk," Alex called back.

"Is that wise?"

She looked at Sarah in surprise. "Why not?"

"With a madman on the loose?" Sarah jangled the keys in her hand. "I can give you a ride."

"It's two blocks." Alex laughed. "I'll be fine."

Around midnight, tossing and turning in her sleeping bag on the bedroom floor, she realized the futility of trying to find sleep among the myriad thoughts crowding her brain, and fixed her eyes on the ceiling. Outside, a breeze was rustling through the trees, making shadows in the moonlight that danced on her ceiling.

What a whirlwind five days. John would soon get the petition. *I wonder if he'll open it.* Most mail, he tossed in the trash, unopened. *Don't disappoint me now.* Ben Ryan, a young attorney with law firm, Whitley, Weston, and Young, where she'd filed the divorce petition on Monday, had warned her to expect things to get messy if John contested. She hadn't mentioned the drugs, or the police. *Maybe I should have.* Irreconcilable differences. That's what they wrote. *Insanity would have better.* She watched the pattern on the ceiling, bending, swaying, dancing, this way and that, not in control of itself but at the mercy of the wind, waiting for the next gust to tell it what to do. *Kind of like me.* In limbo when the flurry let up.

Anderson Collins. Anderson Collins. Who are you? She had no intention of beginning a new relationship. She smiled in the dark. *But thank you.* Telegraph Hill; the corpse in the burned-out car; a business man pulled from the Bay. *Such madness on the streets…the busy streets of America. Nothing like back home.* Lucky.

How are you, boy? Do you miss me? Big, brown eyes. Her own lids began to droop. *I miss you.* A white-washed house on a quiet corner, an old bench in a peaceful backyard. You can always come home. She closed her eyes. *Maybe I will.*

Chapter Fourteen

"He must still be under surveillance."

"Well, hell, how long does surveillance last?" Alex grumbled to Sammy in the office. "It's been almost two months."

"These things take time. I'm sure the police are doing all they can."

"Well, I'm not." She dropped down into her chair, tired and frustrated by the lack of progress, and fed up with the tedious daily trek into Oakland. "What do we have for today?"

Sammy passed her a list of prospects. "I'm glad you're already in a stinking mood so I don't have to spoil it. We're swamped again. You won't even have time for lunch."

"Terrific." Alex perused the list. The last few weeks, the story had been the same. Every day, back and forth into Oakland, driving all over town, in and out of homes, filling out forms, taking deposits, handing them back when the credit check failed, listening to complaints, tears, haggling over rents and terms of a lease. All the while, waiting to hear from the police; hoping to avoid John on the busy streets.

"You look exhausted," Sammy said kindly, "you can't keep working two jobs like this. You've gotta find something else."

"And when do I have the time?"

The phone rang, Sammy pounced, and Alex put her head in her hands. *When are you going to make a move?* She wished the cops would pick John up. *Then maybe I can relax.* Could she? Would she really be safe with John in prison? Would he be free during trial? What if he figured out what she'd done? The police had promised to keep her name out of it if they could. *What if you can't? What then? Who's going to protect me? I won't be safe here, I won't be safe anywhere. He'll know how to find me.*

The voice calling her name sounded far away. "Alex?" It gradually grew louder. "Alex? Are you all right?"

"What?"

Sammy had several sets of keys in her hand and seemed to be saying something. "You need to get going."

"Oh." Alex shook herself, tried to brush off the worrying thoughts.

"Do you need a few minutes? You look pale?"

"No." She stood up, faltered, and sat back down. "Maybe just a few."

"Look, you can't drive like that." Sammy frowned. "Let me make some calls. I'll try to reschedule–"

"I'm fine." Alex stood up again, grabbed her jacket, and stepped out from behind her desk. "I just need to eat and I'll be fine."

A small but fast moving line had formed at the bakery, a block from the office, where she stopped to get a muffin before heading out to her appointments. Alex dug her hands into her pockets, tightening her jacket against the crisp, morning breeze, and folded her fingers around a small piece of card. She pulled it out, stared at it, shuffled a few feet forward…and blinked with the formation of an idea.

"Next."

"Blueberry muffin." She gave her order. "Can I ask you a question? Have you heard of this firm?" She showed the salesman the card.

"Sure. Everyone's heard of Anderson Collins." He dropped one blueberry muffin into a bag and handed it to Alex. "Dollar-fifty. He owns a real estate firm in Pacific Heights." He handed her the change. "Ruthless, but very successful. Next."

Alex moved out of the line and slid the card back into her pocket. She'd forgotten she had it. *Real Estate, huh?* She recalled her first night at Harry's, let herself into her car, remembered how the blond had liked her, fired up her engine; thought about Uncle Edward's words–there's a first time for everything–and peeled out onto Broadway to head for her first showing of the day, a piece of muffin melting on her tongue. With one hand on the wheel and the other feeding herself pieces of muffin, Alex expertly maneuvered through Christmas traffic–already out in droves by December third–and felt her spirits pick up. *First time for everything. You're right, Uncle Edward. Time I made my move*.

A full twelve hours later, an exhausted Alex set off for one last journey, back over the Bay bridge, through the still traffic-clogged arteries of San Francisco, to her small apartment in Pacific Heights. Snarled traffic, horn-honking drivers, and obscene gestures brought her close to tears. Wistful memories of home didn't help. Too tired to bother with dinner when she finally stumbled through her front door, at eight-thirty, she scrambled out of her clothes, and lay naked on the floor with a bowl of cereal. Her head propped up on one elbow, she flipped through the channels, hoping to find something good on TV. *Maybe the news.* Perhaps there'd be something good. She spooned in another mouthful of cereal, winced at the cold milk on her teeth, and listened in horror:

"...Caucasian female...twenty-four-years of age...along the Embarcadero...motive not known...robbery unlikely...valuables intact. Throat slashed...tongue cut out..."

Alex stared at the TV, grabbed a blanket from the corner of the room, and covered herself with it. Another murder. The thought of a tongue hacked off made her shiver with disgust. *Why?* A mutilation. *Did he know the victim?* Without conscious effort, she'd assumed a he. A drug deal gone bad. *Damn, Sammy, why did you have to say that?* A chill ran through her. Do you think it could be?...nah. Sammy had said that, too. *But it could be John.*

Thirteen miles. That's all that stood between her and a serial killer. *Don't be ridiculous*, her right mind said, wanting to focus on more pleasant things. *Think about it*, the cranial twin on the left chimed in, *it's entirely possible*. Her right side thought about walks alone along the Embarcadero. *You've always been safe. It isn't John.* Again the left. *You take too many chances. Next time you won't be so lucky.* She flicked off the TV, clutched her head, squeezed her eyes shut, willed both halves of her brain to be silent. *A warm bath, that will help.*

Eucalyptus oil under the running water. The steamy aroma soon filled the room. Alex breathed it in. Maybe it would clear her head. Water continued to fill the tub around her. She closed her eyes and leaned her head against a rolled-up towel. A soft tinkle, ebbing thoughts, warm water folding like a blanket over her stomach. Someone must have turned the water off; Alex didn't remember doing it. Gentle waves lapped at her chin. Rest.

"A few more minutes," she whispered, her voice sounding drowsy, as though it came from far away, "a few more…"

Much later, with the wrinkled skin of a dried out prune, Alex crept quietly from the bathroom. She donned a pair of old pajamas and slipped into the comfort of her new bed. As her head sank into the plump, soft pillow, and her eyes closed for the final time, her mind became a kaleidoscope of bizarre but peaceful images: John imprisoned in New Zealand; walking Lucky around San Francisco; her parents having dinner with Phat Harry Hammond; and a stranger called Anderson Collins promising her a chance. The complex series of colorfully shifting events played out in her mind, as she sank deeper, and deeper, to some unknown place, muddled, yet restful.

Chapter Fifteen

Every morning, for the past two months, Jessica had arrived for work at exactly eight o'clock. Routine helped her stay sane. Routine provided an anchor in a bizarre world in which she might otherwise have floated away. The job, personal secretary to the proprietor, in a small suite of luxury offices on Letterman Drive, had been just enough to keep her mind off Judd and her troubles at home.

Anderson Collins hadn't proved to be an easy man to work for. The rumors had already reached her, despite keeping a low profile, and refusing to join in with the gossip. A ruthless, hard-driving businessman, he had powered a small real-estate firm, started ten years ago, into a successful enterprise, evidenced by not only a row of accolades and awards displayed in his office, but by the swanky location itself. Thick, blond hair, intense blue eyes, and a toned, muscular body belied his true age–somewhere in his early forties–and gave him the appearance of a man at least twenty years younger.

Handsome, boyish, witty, intelligent, charming when necessary, Anderson had all the advantages that enabled him to conduct his business with a shameless disregard for morals and ethics yet somehow emerge unscathed. He exploited his advantage to its full potential, especially when it came to women. Jessica had heard the stories, knew all about his life, how he'd married young when his girlfriend got pregnant, how he'd stayed a ferocious womanizer and played around, had shown no interest in either of his kids and hadn't cared when he'd lost them in the divorce eight years ago, how he'd scoffed at his wife's chances of making it alone, mocked the judge–a woman–and almost been held in contempt.

All he'd cared about was money; keeping his money and not losing half of his business. He'd already toughed out that two years before his divorce, when he suffered an acrimonious split from his previous business partner, Kelly Kirkland. Or so went the rumor. Jessica believed the rumor.

Jessica hated working for Anderson Collins. She hated his foul mouth, his roving eye, and despised his quick temper. She hated how the men looked up to him, wanted to be like him, used him as a yard stick to measure success.

"He's an animal," she wanted to scream, but no one would have listened. Jessica was partly to blame. Unpopular would have described it, but unsociable would be more accurate. Jessica had made no effort to fit in. She'd ignored invitations to join the women for nights out, declined friendly requests to have lunch. She'd shunned all her colleagues, and alienated herself. No one understood her, least of all Judd.

"Why don't you want to make friends?" he said, on the evenings they spent together. Even those had become more rare.

"Because they talk."

"People do. That's how you make friends."

How would you know? "Not that kind of talk. They gossip."

"So?"

"About each other. They dig for details. "

"You're afraid they'll find out about our crazy family?" Judd sneered. "About all the madness, the suicide, our lunatic mother. You're afraid they'll think you're crazy, too?"

The harsh words hurt. If he was trying to help, she'd rather he didn't. "No."

"Then what? I don't understand you. I thought you wanted friends, to feel normal."

What is that? To feel normal? I'm not sure I've ever known. "I don't want them to find out."

"Why not? They might understand. Maybe they could even help."

Every time it had come up, Jessica would just shake her head. This morning, she'd told him the truth. "I don't want their pity."

He'd given her one his looks; empty, hollow, devoid of compassion, and shrugged his shoulders. "Have it your own way."

This morning, sitting at her desk, with two more days to go before the weekend and the trek into Sacramento to visit her mother, she thought about the change that had come over Judd in the short time they'd been in San Francisco. He spent more and more time away from home. He spoke less often; seemed harder, meaner, and his voice, when he did speak, always had an edge. He'd snap, had less patience, and always appeared pre-occupied. It was the reason she hadn't told him the rest about her boss; how he'd summon girls to his office, how she'd hear the giggling, the scuffles behind the door before they'd come out looking flushed. Always the same girls.

He'd have told her to leave, but she couldn't. Her life had already been one constant upheaval. Depleted of vigor or ambition, she needed routine. So far, Anderson had not looked at her. If he did, she'd deal with it then. In the meantime, they needed money. And she couldn't rely on Judd.

A glass of water on her desk gave her an excuse to cover her face. She took a sip, wiped a tiny bead of wetness from the corner of her eye, set the glass down, and glanced across the office. No one had noticed. She sighed, thinking about Judd, and how he lacked psychological control and emotional stability. He seemed incapable of sustaining any kind of rhythm in his life. Subsequently, he hadn't been able to hold down a job. He'd drifted from one crummy thing to another, and now he had nothing at all. Jessica's was their only income. The only way to keep their apartment was for her to keep her job.

"Morning, Jessica."

"Morning." She nodded briefly at Anderson, passing by her desk, directly outside his own office, a few minutes after eight. On the bridge of her nose, she'd balanced a pair of black, square-framed glasses with plain lenses, parted her hair down the middle and tucked it behind her ears, and dressed in grey, loose-fitting slacks, brown sweater, and low-heeled black shoes. At first glance, she looked dowdy. Anderson didn't take a second look, strode into his office, and closed the door.

She waited the usual few minutes. Then it came. She lifted the receiver the minute her line buzzed. "Yes, Mr. Collins?"

"Please send in Nicky Drew."

"Right away." She dropped the receiver back into its cradle. When Anderson wanted something, he always managed a 'please'. Across the office, about twenty feet in front of her desk, Nicky Drew's cubicle faced her.

Nicky's head had already whipped up. Ready and willing, she'd already checked her watch. Jessica nodded, lowered her eyes, and swallowed the bile in her throat. If

Nicky wanted to indulge her boss, Jessica didn't care. Nicky, a young, waif-like blonde, no more than twenty-two, skipped across the open-plan floor, shot Jessica a smug look of amusement, and disappeared into the lion's den–the name Jessica had dubbed Anderson's office.

Jessica perused her calendar. *Slow day. Calls for improvisation.* Anything to divert unwanted attention. She dug into the box of old papers under her desk, fished out a week-old pile of documents Anderson had asked her to shred, and built them into a messy arrangement on her desk. Next, she stacked a new transcript he'd given her yesterday to type. A few old computer manuals finished the look, and, before long, she looked busy.

She pounced on the phone at first ring, glad for the distraction of what was happening behind closed doors, some of the shenanigan's she could hear. "Collins Real Estate, Jessica speaking." Enthusiasm had long since deserted her voice.

The accent made it a little harder to understand, but she realized the girl wanted Anderson. Didn't they all? The young voice continued, "I've had his card in my pocket for weeks. I've been meaning to call…met at the restaurant…I'm not entirely sure…"

For lack of anything else to do, and slightly charmed by the lilt in her voice, Jessica let the young woman twitter on for a while. "I'm sorry," she finally admitted, "he's in a meeting. Leave your number and he'll give you a call." She knew he would. He'd left her his card, the woman said. *Another poor sucker.* She sighed quietly, and scribbled down the name.

Alexandra Sullivan. She jotted down a number, hung up, and posted the note onto Anderson's board. She'd barely sat back down when his door swung open and Nicky bounced through, marginally flushed but barely disheveled. Jessica checked her watch. Eight-forty-five. For a man in his forties, Anderson could keep pace. With a sidelong glance as Nicky passed, she smothered a cynical chuckle.

"Good meeting?" she called out, squashing down another giggle at the falter in Nicky's otherwise steady stride.

The young woman ignored her, regained her composure and touched her lips, where her red, glossy lipstick had been some forty minutes earlier. *That'll teach you.* Jessica smirked.

All hands back on deck, the afternoon much quieter than the morning, Alex glared down at her phone. She picked at her nails, and checked her watch for the umpteenth time. *Ring, you stupid thing.*

Seven hours had passed since she'd left her information with Jessica, the secretary at Collins Real Estate. Anderson hadn't called back.

"No call?" Sammy said.

"Not yet. I wanted to talk to him before the end of my shift."

"Harry's tonight?"

"Yes. And I want to know before I have to hit the road. It'll help me keep my cool in all that traffic." She thumped her desk with the heel of her hand and let out a frustrated breath.

Sammy grinned. "He'll call. Give him a chance."

"I'm still not sure why he left me the card." Sammy glanced up in surprise. "I mean, it might *not* be a job," Alex explained, "Sarah didn't say that. I just assumed."

"And you left it two months to call?"

"We got busy. I forgot."

Sammy turned back to her work. "In that case, I can't say

I'm surprised he hasn't called back. I wouldn't either, if I offered you a job and you took two months to respond."

"He didn't offer me a job."

"Then what *did* he offer?"

"I don't know. A date?" Her eyes twinkled. "That might be fun. I remember he was cute."

"And you took two months to call?" Sammy screeched, louder this time, "What are you? An idiot?"

A date might be fun. Alex hoped the card would be about business. With two jobs, she'd have to rely on good fortune finding her.

As she snatched up her phone for the third time, it rang in her hand. A smooth, velvety rich voice that sounded like melted chocolate came from the other end.

"Alexandra?" Her heart leapt. She glanced across at Sammy, who bit down on her lip.

"Yes, this is Alex."

She liked the voice. She hadn't paid it much attention back at the restaurant, although she remembered their little flirtations. A date would be okay, she felt ready, but she'd prefer a job.

"Alex. Sorry." He corrected himself, and she heard the smile in his voice. "I've been meaning to call. I didn't catch you at a bad time, did I?"

Courteous, even better. "No, this is fine. Actually, there usually isn't a bad time to call." Sammy stuck two fingers in her mouth and made a gagging motion. Alex ignored her.

"Well, that's good." She heard his smile again. "Look, I'm not really sure how to begin so I'll just get right to the point. You may not remember me, it's been a while."

"I remember. I've been waiting for your call."

"You have?" Now the voice sounded puzzled. "It's Ben

Ryan, the attorney from the law firm where you filed your divorce." She winced. Her heart plummeted in her chest, like an elevator in a high-rise crashing to the ground floor.

"I hope you don't think me improper. I've wanted to call since you came to our office." Surprise and disappointment had suddenly rendered her speechless.

"I know you've had a lot on your plate, what with everything you've been through, and I don't want to complicate things any more for you, but," he hesitated, "it's just that I haven't been able to get you out of my mind."

While Alex struggled to find her tongue, Ben continued.

"I hoped we might go for a drink. Or perhaps I could buy dinner. I don't know, we, I mean, I thought…" he faltered, "actually, I don't know what I thought."

Alex still said nothing.

"Cat got your tongue?" Sammy mouthed across from her desk. She'd been so sure it would be Anderson. She closed her eyes, and couldn't help the sigh that slid out. Ben must have heard. Her eyes flicked open. "I'm sorry," she began.

"No, I'm the one who should apologize," she heard him say. The smile had slipped from his voice. It reminded her of a long time ago, back in New Zealand, behind a record store counter, when she'd been waiting to hear from John. She remembered what it had been like to have the stuffing knocked out of her each time someone else had been on the other end of the line.

"It's okay." She smiled into the phone.

Quick to cut in, perhaps to cover his hurt, he apologized again. "Alex. Look, I'm sorry, it seems I made a mistake. I just thought you might like to…you know what, it doesn't matter. I'm sorry if I bothered–"

"It's no bother. And I didn't mean to be rude. Jeez, you

must think I'm awful."

"Not at all. No need to explain. I've overstepped the mark."

An awkward pause hung between them.

"Good thing I'm not the one assigned to your case," he finally said, managing something of a chuckle. "That could have made things embarrassing."

Alex clearly remembered Ben and the way he'd stopped her in the hall on her way out of her divorce lawyer's office, even given her a few words of free advice. "Good thing, indeed, Ben," she heard herself say, "because it wouldn't be proper to fraternize with my lawyer."

Ben's chortle, deep and throaty, had her smile widening. He sounded as nice as she remembered. "Does that mean…?"

"I think I can manage a drink." Alex looked across at Sammy, grinning from ear to ear.

"Really? That's fantastic. Is tomorrow too soon?"

Alex chuckled. "Tomorrow's fine." After tonight, she wouldn't have to be at Harry's again until Friday.

They agreed to meet at seven, but when Ben suggested the Embarcadero, Alex suggested The Gold Dust Lounge at Union Square. She hadn't forgotten about the poor woman with her tongue hacked out, and the drowning, near the Embarcadero. Or the fact the police still hadn't picked up John.

"Sure, it's a date."

Chapter Sixteen

With the body count at five, and the blade marks left on the latest victim determined to be have been made by an eight-inch blade, Mac Jackson had little doubt in his mind that they had all died at the hands of the same killer. Another serial killer on the streets of San Francisco, but this one left no cryptic clues or taunting letters, made no demands to the police or the general public. He didn't appear to want attention or recognition. Jackson suspected he had a particular grudge, or some type of personal vendetta, only he hadn't been able to figure out what.

Exhausted from working through the night–even with a little extra civilian help to which he'd consented–he rubbed at his eyes, and took a slurp of coffee that had already turned cold. He'd been making notes and sifting through the scant evidence left behind since the young woman's body had been found by a lonesome jogger, during the early hours of Tuesday morning. *What the hell is your motive?* He set the mug down, sighed, and looked at the photo of the deceased. If he'd been called to the scene half an hour sooner, he might have been able to ask the killer that question. Her body had still been warm.

"She was just a kid," he said to Red. "Twenty-four. Only two years older than Bryce."

Red shook his head, no more enlightened than Jackson. "I know. There's no pattern. He butchers men, women, old, young, but never rapes them or robs them. What's the motive?

What the hell does this bastard want?"

"I wish I knew," Jackson said, grimacing at another mouthful of cold coffee, "but one thing's becoming clear; he's getting careless or cocky. Thirty minutes sooner and we'd have had him."

"Doubt it. That was deliberate, Jackson. The bastard knows what he's doing. He doesn't want to get caught until he's ready."

"Well, so far he doesn't have to worry about that. We've got extra cops patrolling the streets, and he still manages to leave us a warm, dead body and no witnesses. There's something we're missing." He pressed his hands and finger-tips together, hooked his thumbs under his weary chin, and closed his eyes, trying to get inside a killer's head.

"This is his arena, man, his stage," Red said. "He's killing right under our noses like there's not a damn thing we can do about it. And the warm body? ...he's performing. That's arrogance."

"Or anger." Jackson opened his eyes. "Or maybe he's bored."

"He's not bored," Red said, shaking his head. He strode around his desk to sit on the front edge of it, facing Jackson. "He thinks he's superior. He stays one step ahead, but barely, he leaves virtually no clues, and he seems to murder at random."

"And always in a busy location." Jackson drummed his long fingers impatiently on his desk. "Why do you think he makes no effort to conceal the bodies?"

"He wants them to be found. He wants us to know he's killed again, and we've failed again."

"Failed?"

"To protect the city. To do our jobs. He's not just

satisfying some sick thrill, you know, he's making fools of all of us, of law enforcement."

"So, maybe that's his message. There's a reason for the killings, I'm sure of that, but the real anger is against the law. And he wants us to figure out why."

"I'm going out on a limb here," Red said. "Call it one of your hunches, but I'd say he's never done time. He's not going to be in the database."

"What makes you say that?" Jackson looked at his partner with interest.

"Something tells me he hasn't reached his zenith. He's leading up to something, and until we figure out what it is, he's not going to get caught. He wants to get caught, but not just yet, not until he's ready. And another thing...I don't believe he kills at random. He picks his victims."

Jackson nodded, thinking, pinched the bridge of his nose while he contemplated. Finally he looked back at Red, still perched on the edge of his desk and looking as beat as Jackson felt.

"You know," he began, "I can't stop thinking about the tongue. He'd already slit her throat, so she'd have been dead already, bled out, so why cut it out? And why didn't we find it?"

A thorough search of the area where the body had been found had not turned up the missing muscle.

"I'd say she pissed him off," Red suggested. "Maybe she said something he didn't like."

"You think he knew her?"

Red shrugged. "Maybe, probably not. But I'd say he'd been in close proximity the night he killed her, maybe listening to her conversation."

Jackson picked up the report on his desk and reread the

notes about the young woman's last night. "She'd been out with friends," he read aloud, "celebrating a promotion, according to her friends." He searched Red's face. "They work in finance."

"Jealousy?" Red suggested.

"Possible. Except her friends state they were all doing well."

"Yeah, well maybe one of them thought she wasn't deserving, thought she got promoted out of turn. She was considerably younger. They were in their forties. Hell, I'd probably be pissed if I got overtaken by a kid in her twenties."

"But if they're all hot shots, I'd say it's unlikely," Jackson said. "Anyway, they all checked out. They all left together, without her, and went straight home. She'd had too much to drink, apparently wanted to walk it off."

"Some friends."

Jackson shrugged. "It happens. None of the other diners remember anyone suspicious. Nothing we could use."

"What about credit cards?"

Jackson shook his head. "Slow night, only a few transactions and they checked out."

"So he paid cash."

"Maybe. No one remembers a lone diner. No one paid her group any attention."

"Well, someone did." Red pursed his lips, removed his legs from the desk, and walked round to the other side to sit down. "If the guy was there, he looked like a regular. He fitted in. No one noticed him."

"And a regular guy can fly under the radar, mingle easily. That's how he does it." Jackson slapped a hand down on his desk. "We're looking for someone who fits into society. Someone with a job, maybe even a few friends. On the one hand he kills, has an aversion to the law, but he also lives a part of his life normally, like everyone else."

"Could have been someone she worked with. One of the group. Or a schizophrenic."

"Not a schizophrenic. I don't believe there's any distortion of reality for this guy. I believe he knows exactly what he's doing."

Red nodded. "You're right about him being local."

Jackson pulled up a fresh sheet in his notepad and began to scribble. "Here's what we've got," he said to Red, "I think he's a white male, probably late twenties to early thirties, strong, agile, social to an extent but really a loner."

"Family?"

"Little or none."

"Think he killed 'em?"

"His family? No. If he's local we'd have gotten something on that. He's from this area, so they're either dead already, or they've moved away."

"Why d'you think that?"

"Hunch. Plus, he can go about his business more easily with no one keeping tabs on his hours, his comings and goings. My gut tells me this guy is a loner, not one of her group."

"Good enough for me." Red yawned behind his hand, and rubbed his eyes, ran a hand through his hair, and stretched in his seat. "I'm beat." He laced his fingers together behind his head and leaned back, putting his feet up on his desk. "Still think it's a thrill killer?"

Jackson sighed. "I don't know. Yes…and no. There's an underlying motive, but he's a sadistic bastard. He enjoys the violence."

"The tongue?"

"That, the genitals, and the fact he mutilates them after they're dead. The two back in ninety-five...I believe it's the same guy." He locked eyes with Red, saw his furrowed brow, and could almost hear the cogs turning in his partners head. "What is it?"

"The fact her body was still warm."

"What about it?"

Red unlaced his fingers, removed his feet from his desk, and leaned forward in his seat, his face taut with concentration. "The jogger found her at four-thirty, Tuesday morning."

"Right." Jackson watched his expression with interest.

"If he'd been inside the restaurant and followed her out, killing her on her way home, her body would have been cold by the time the jogger found her. We know the jogger didn't do it because he'd only left the house ten minutes earlier, confirmed by his wife, and he had no blood on his clothes."

"Okay." They'd been through this already, but Jackson didn't mind going over it again. Maybe they'd missed something the first time.

"We know she'd been dead for only about thirty minutes, so, if time of death was four in the morning, we've got six hours to account for from the time she left the restaurant to when she died."

"Well, we know she went for a walk, she was drunk, and she was alone. Maybe she fell asleep somewhere, and maybe he didn't follow her. He might not have been in the bar at all; no one remembers a lone guy, so maybe it was purely random and he stumbled upon her sleeping it off."

"It's possible," Red said, "but it doesn't fit with the tongue. That kind of violence had to be provoked. It wasn't random. She said something to piss him off. He was in that bar, and he followed her out. Know what I think?" He didn't wait to be asked. "I think he tortured her for a while."

Jackson sighed. "No marks on her body to suggest it, no ligature on her wrists or feet."

"Mental torture. I think she felt comfortable with him, trusted him. She went with him willingly."

"She was drunk," Jackson reminded him, a headache beginning to kick around at the back of his eyeballs. "She wouldn't have had the same fear she might have had sober."

"That's true, too, but…if he was mad enough to hack off her tongue, he wouldn't waste six hours idly chatting. Somehow, he gained her trust before he killed her, and he took six hours to do it. There's a reason for that, and I want to know what it is."

Jackson scratched his head. "We've been over this. I don't know."

"Jackson," Red shot him a dry look, "you're the master of hunches, and maybe it's rubbing off. My hunch: he's testing himself."

"Red." Jackson stared at him in astonishment, his headache suddenly vanishing. "That's it. You're brilliant." He punched the air.

"What did I do?" Red stared back in surprise.

"You hit the nail on the head, that's what you did." Jackson smacked his hands together triumphantly. "He is testing himself, not us." He laughed out loud. "Why didn't I see it before?"

"See what?"

Jackson grinned at Red's puzzled expression. "You see how the murders have been escalating? Both in frequency and violence?" He didn't wait for Red to comment. "I figured he's been working his way up to something." He pulled open the file on his desk with the old notes from the earlier murders. "The ones in ninety-five…those were homeless, nobodies…their bodies could drift about for days, months, and no one would miss them. He was warming up, getting a taste for murder. He didn't care if anyone found them."

"And these latest ones?"

"These victims have families. He knew they'd be missed. He wanted them to be found. He wanted to know he could walk into a crowded area, somewhere like the Embarcadero, choose a victim, and kill them without getting caught, and then watch how the case unraveled. See what he could learn from the moves made by police."

"If we don't believe the victims were chosen at random," Red said, Jackson's sudden enthusiasm rubbing off on him, "then there's a common link, something that makes him snap, something that ties them all together."

"Yes." Jackson smacked his desk again. "We need to find that link." He grinned across at Red. "We're finally making progress."

Red seemed to be on a roll. "And if the victims were chosen by something they said or did, he upped the stakes each time, increased the violence, let us get closer. He tested himself to see how far he could go before we start closing in."

"And that tells me something else. Red, when he abducts his final victim, he's going to do it in a public place. He's been training for it, building up to it. He's going to try to snatch him or her from right under our noses."

"Think he's following the reports on the news?"

"I don't doubt it. The vicious bastard has enjoyed destroying those families."

"That's it." Red leapt from his chair, wide-eyed and

without a trace of exhaustion.

"What?" Startled, Jackson stared at him as if he'd gone mad.

"Jackson, you're fucking brilliant." Red grinned.

"Piss off, Dennis."

"Don't you get it?" Red flicked a paperclip that hit Jackson on the nose. "You just figured out the motive."

Chapter Seventeen

"You said he enjoyed making those families suffer; that's he's working up to something, wants to settle a score. He's after revenge." Red couldn't wipe the grin from his face. "All the others have been payback for something, but nothing significant. He won't stop until he's taken his final revenge."

Jackson didn't share Red's enthusiasm. "Well, that's fucking brilliant. Revenge against who?"

Red dropped back down into his seat, still excited. "That's our job to find out."

"And we'd better figure it out fast. I can't imagine what he's going to do to that guy when he catches up with him."

"He'll want us to see it," Red said. "He's going to want us to have a front row seat."

"Figures."

"He's been drawing us in since the minute he stopped killing the homeless."

Jackson picked up the paperclip that had hit him on the nose, and twirled it around in his fingers. "The last one's gonna be especially brutal."

"Why is he waiting? I mean, if he is the killer from ninety-five, why so long? Seven years is a long gap."

"I don't know," Jackson said, "we've still got pieces missing. Could be other bodies and we never found them." He knew most serial killers did not go seven years without feeding their fetish.

"Another of your hunches would be useful, Jackson. If

this guy has a score to settle, how do we find out who the poor bastard is?"

"Start with old news." Jackson got up from his desk.

"Huh?"

"Large companies that might have fired someone, corporate layoffs, scandals, drug busts, public divorces, that sort of thing." Jackson strode past Red on his way out of their office.

"Going to archives? Get the kid to help you. That's why you brought him in."

"No, man, I'm going to get coffee."

"What do you think he did with the tongue?" Red said, when Jackson returned with a fresh, steaming coffee.

"How the fuck should I know?"

"Souvenir?"

"Like I said, how–"

"Yeah, I know…how the fuck would you know? I'm just curious."

"Morbid more like."

Red laughed.

Chapter Eighteen

The season hummed with shoppers. The office hummed with staff. At eight o'clock on Friday morning, Jessica arrived at her desk to the low, continuous, indistinct sound of fingers tapping rapidly on keyboards, employees milling around, and the usual cheerful chit-chat that didn't include her.

With nineteen days to go before Christmas, her mood had disintegrated even further. She hated the holidays–and the painful reminder–more than any other time. Anderson's door was closed. As Jessica slid behind her desk, directly outside his office, she heard the sound of voices coming from inside. Two voices. One male: Anderson's smooth set of vocals; the other female: young, exuberant, happy. Anderson's boisterous chuckle. A tiny tinkling laugh. Perhaps he had a new Friday chick.

"Thank goodness it's almost the weekend," she muttered, aiming a hateful glare at his door before switching her thoughts to the approaching weekend, and her mother. With fingers flying over her keyboard, earplugs jammed deep into her ears, and her favorite music soaking into her skull, she couldn't drown out the thoughts plaguing her. Tomorrow would be her mother's birthday. She'd have to drive the long trip to Park Glenn, the residential home in Sacramento, where Marianne had spent the last two decades.

She hated the trip; hated being back in Sac, where all the bad memories attacked her like a plague of locusts waiting to swarm; where Cam's body lay in the ground along with her father's. Where the bastard's family, the brute who'd started it all, still lived. Jessica called it a residential home because she couldn't bear to think of it for what it really was: an asylum. An asylum for the insane.

This morning, Judd had already told her he didn't want to go, but she'd argued. "It's her birthday, Judd. We have to go."

"Then you go. I don't want to. It's not like she'll know."

Typical. His moods had become so much worse. A distance had crept between them. For the past couple of weeks, Judd had been slipping away, and Jessica felt more alone than ever. Things were no better at work. Anderson–the Letch, she'd branded him–had begun stopping by her desk each morning for a brief chat, a quick hello, a nod of encouragement.

Jessica so badly wanted to quit. She feared what might happen if she ever got called behind that closed door, into the lion's den.

She thought about her mother, and how Judd was right. Marianne wouldn't know they'd visited. She wouldn't recognize them, even when they held her hands, stroked her hair, talked with her for the thirty minutes or so that they usually stayed. *Hell, she won't even know it's her birthday.*

She snatched up the glass of water on her desk and took a gulp, washing down the lump in her throat. Crying in the office would do no good. She had to save her tears for when she was alone.

"She'll only escape her lunacy when death comes to claim her."

The nursing staff hadn't realized she'd been behind them the last time she'd visited. Their words had burned her throat when she realized they'd been talking about her mother. She remembered Judd's anger; how she'd laid her hand on his arm.

"But they're right," she'd whispered. Perhaps that's why he'd said this morning he didn't want to go, but Jessica had insisted.

The sound of Anderson's door creaking open made her open her eyes. She hadn't realized she'd squeezed them shut. Out of his office strode a striking young woman, somewhere in her late twenties, Jessica guessed, a wide smile stretched across her beautiful face, her long, brunette hair swishing gently from side to side with each step. Jessica stared. Anderson came out behind her, anxious to keep up. They headed to the front of the office, and disappeared behind the thick glass doors leading out onto the street.

Whatever. She pushed her earplugs in further. Ten minutes later, Anderson returned alone. Head buried in a mound of papers, she hadn't noticed him standing there until he rapped his knuckles on her desk. Startled, she jumped.

"Sorry." She yanked the plugs from her ears.

"Order a new name plate, Jessica."

"Yes, sir."

He turned on his heel headed for his office. "For Alexandra Sullivan."

Alex had had a stellar week and could barely wait for the weekend. Last night's date with Ben still had her tingling. He'd been romantic, funny, charming, and had even brought her chocolates. John had never done that. After her meeting this morning with Anderson Collins, she had a new job. It might only be on the bottom rung, but still, a job in one of the most successful real estate firms in San Francisco. *What would you say to that, Uncle Edward?* She pictured his face, his surprise, and his happiness that she hadn't given up on her ambition. Life looked good. The only blot, the only blemish, was that the cops still hadn't picked up John. *Just a matter of time*. Ben had said as much over dinner when she'd brought up the subject.

"A sting like that takes time," he'd said.

"You sound like you know what you're talking about," she'd replied, "I believe you. I'd just feel better if I knew."

"Sooner or later, he'll be behind bars," Ben consoled. "He doesn't sound too smart."

That's where Ben had been wrong. "John's incredibly smart," she'd said. "Wily, too, and cunning. That's what makes him so dangerous."

"You know, I'd feel happier if you changed your job," Ben had said, putting his arm around her shoulders as they shared a cozy booth at The Gold Dust Lounge. "Put another layer of separation between you."

She stood in front of the stove in her tiny kitchen, stirring homemade chili, thinking about Ben. His concern had brought a bubble of warmth to her stomach, a slow fizz that had become warmer and warmer throughout the evening, until it had gradually started to sizzle and pop, kind of like her chili on the stove. She chuckled at the resemblance of a date with Ben to a bowl of chili. *Have I got news for you.* She couldn't wait to tell him.

Her eyes glazed over ever so slightly at the memory of his dimples that flashed in and out when he talked. Even more when he laughed. Ben laughed a lot. *You'll be good for me.*

The chili started to splutter. Alex turned out the flame and grabbed a bowl from the cupboard. Her phone rang, and she dropped the bowl onto the counter to answer it. "Alex."

More breathless than usual, Sammy's voice broke her peace, bursting into her ear. "Hey, Alex. Have you heard?"

"Heard what?"

"Turn on your TV. There's been another murder." Alex dropped her spoon, aware her face had grown hot. "What?"

"Late last night. A woman got strangled. And guess where it happened?"

Alex didn't have to guess. "Embarcadero."

"It's all over the news. They're calling it a graveyard."

That could have been me.

"It's not safe to go out," Sammy continued. "Police say it's a serial killer."

Alex found a stool, sat down with a bump, felt cold fear sluicing down her spine, pounding in her heart. She thought her head might explode. Her lip quivered. A tear welled, and rolled down her cheek. *John. You knew didn't you? Knew I was at the Embarcadero.* He must have followed. Every murder had been on a night she'd been near. The pounding in her head grew louder. Sweat soaked through her blouse. Another tear dripped into her lap. San Francisco should have been her freedom after all she'd endured, but John still had the power to rob her of liberty. John had many connections. She'd never know when he might strike. When the murder on the news would be hers.

It's never going to end, is it? Quietly, she sobbed.

Chapter Nineteen

Beautiful. Jessica stared at the woman in the black leather chair opposite her desk. *So you're Alexandra.* She seemed quiet and withdrawn, not the woman Jessica remembered, who'd exuded such confidence when she'd strutted out of Anderson's office almost three weeks earlier.

Today, the day after Christmas, was not a good day for a new recruit, especially one Jessica had to train. "You'll have to forgive me," she muttered curtly, "I'm a little stressed."

"Sorry. I know I'm early," Alex apologized, in a quiet voice.

"I had a run-in on my way to work."

Alex nodded. "Sorry."

A jerk in a silver sports car had come within an inch of rear-ending her on her drive to the office. Jessica swung her jacket over the back of her chair, still bristling with the memory. He'd hugged her bumper, menacing, slowing down, speeding up, matching her every move. On the outer edge of his lane, he'd pulled alongside, their mirrors almost touching. Alarmed, she'd swerved across her lane, to the annoyance of the motorists there. He flashed his lights, stayed so close she couldn't get his plate. He honked and glared. No one seemed to notice; too caught up in their own boring commute. *Just like my life. No one gives a shit.* "Someone tried to run me off the road." She didn't know why she felt she had to tell the girl. Maybe she wanted someone to care. Anyone, but the girl didn't. Why should she? She didn't know Jessica.

"That's awful." Alex said.

Jessica thought about when she'd left the freeway. He'd blasted his horn until he'd disappeared from her sight. *Or until I disappeared from his.* He knew her exit. Knew roughly where she worked. Why else would she be on the road so early in the morning, with all the commuters? The murders never strayed far from her thoughts. The incident had shaken her more than she'd first thought, and she clutched at the glass on her desk, took a sip.

"Are you all right?"

"What?" Jessica set the glass down. "Yes. I'm sorry, just a little shaken."

Alex nodded, but said nothing.

Jessica took in her silky, dark hair, her delicate profile, long lashes, high cheek bones, full mouth. She sensed an overwhelming urge to warn her about Anderson, but squashed it down. She didn't want a friend. A friend would only get in her business. Eventually.

"You must be Alexandra." She forced a smile.

"Actually it's Alex." Alex appeared to be forcing one back.

"Well, Alex, welcome–"

At the precise moment, rounding the corner and coming from the general direction of the kitchen, Anderson appeared, a steaming mug of coffee in his hand.

"Well, isn't this nice." He stopped at Jessica's desk. Her stomach churned violently at the look on his face, a lecherous sneer, almost like he'd opened the pages of his favorite porno. "If it isn't my two favorite brunettes. What a way to start the morning." He grinned broadly. Jessica stared at the two even rows of gleaming, white teeth, and wondered what might be going through Alex's head. *All the better to eat you with*, had popped into hers.

"I see the two of you are already getting acquainted. Excellent."

Jessica wanted to vomit. As always, the silver-tongued bastard stood a little too close.

"Jessica, perhaps you can show Alex to her desk and I'll meet with her later."

Anderson turned into his office, sat down behind his large mahogany desk, and set down his coffee. He rubbed his hands together. *I've done well.* Extremely pleased with himself, he watched Alex get up and wait for Jessica to show her where to go.

She looked lovelier than ever this morning, more than when he'd interviewed her, and more than when she'd first caught his attention at the restaurant. He hadn't forgotten about her, or her soft, inviting curves, even when she didn't call for two months. *You're here now. That's what matters.* He'd become bored with Nicky. He took a sip of his coffee and watched Jessica get up. The similarity struck him immediately. She looked so much like Alex they could have been related. *Funny.* He ran his tongue over his teeth. *Wonder why I never realized before how lovely she is.*

Chapter Twenty

The harassment began subtly, not long after Alex started. So subtly, she barely noticed.

Yet, the hand resting lightly on her shoulder, his proximity so close behind, a rub or squeeze of her arm when he passed her in the kitchen, a gentle pat on the hand or a touch on the back during every conversation, none of it had ever felt right. The whisperings and nudges had evolved into uncensored stares and knowing looks. The other women turned their backs when she approached, shunned her, seemed hostile. She knew something had happened. Then one afternoon, after she overheard gossip in the ladies room, Alex turned to Jessica at her desk.

"What's going on?"

"You mean you don't know?"

"I wouldn't be asking if I did."

"The looks, the pats. Come on, Alex, you must have figured it out." Jessica turned away, apparently reluctant to get involved. The ugly realization dawned on Alex, that these had not been the innocent gestures of a caring, compassionate boss. The man had been stalking his territory, sniffing his prey, inching a little closer each day, getting ready to strike.

Alex wanted to be sick. The warmth suddenly slipped from what had started out as a beautiful, sunny, mid-April day. "No. I didn't."

She stared at Jessica, horrified that she'd missed it, but utterly aghast that no one had warned her. "Has he done this before?" she demanded. When Jessica didn't answer, Alex thought her blood would boil over. How could one woman betray another over such a fundamental fear? A sexual predator; something all women dreaded.

"Why didn't you say something?" she hissed, her teeth clenched, her face hot. "Why didn't you warn me?"

Jessica shrugged, turned her head, stared at the floor. "I don't get involved in other people's business. They don't get involved in mine."

"Other people's business?" A flash of anger added another layer of grit to Alex's voice, already trembling with shock, and fury. "This *is* your business, Jessica. This has been going on for three months, right under your nose. You knew what was happening, yet you said nothing. I could have been raped. Were you going to stand by and let that happen? And then tell me it's none of your business?"

She watched Jessica busy herself with nothing in particular on her desk, refusing to look at her, her voice empty and flat when she spoke.

"You're a grown woman, Alex. You can take care of yourself. Other women around here do it just fine."

Alex recoiled like a snake that had been beaten back. So, he'd done it before. *Other women around here do it just fine.* Jessica's words stung her ears, shocked her to her core. How long had this behavior been allowed to continue? Had anyone been forced to submit to his demands? Worse, had anyone ever been raped in his office?

Her voice lowered to a harsh, venom-filled pitch, Alex unloaded her abhorrence for what Jessica had done. "Let me tell you something, right now. You're wrong. It *is* your place. It's yours and every other woman's place to look out for one another in situations like this. We all have a fundamental right to feel safe, Jessica; at home, on the street, and certainly in the office. No one has the right to take that away from us. Do you hear me? No one."

She couldn't tell if her words had sunk in; Jessica refused to meet her eyes.

"How could you let this go on, right under your nose?" she went on. "Men take away our sense of safety all the time. Every day we live under the threat, the intimidation, that we might get attacked. And you knew what he was doing. You saw it happen, you've seen it happen with others, yet you did nothing. You sat back and watched." Alex drew a long breath, blinked slowly, and, with much of her anger released, stared pityingly at the morose form in front of her. "When were you going to do the right thing? After someone has already been raped? Jeez, Jessica, when did you stop being human?"

When a monster raped and murdered my brother, she wanted to scream. Instead, Jessica said quietly, "They were all willing, Alex. He's never raped anyone. You've never been in any danger. And you can always say no."

"I intend to," Alex snapped, "even if it costs me my job. Only, unlike you, I'm not going to sit by and do nothing. Because one day, a woman will be raped. A woman that you could have helped." Alex turned on her heel and stalked away.

Back at her own desk, Alex's stomach pitched unsteadily, tossing its contents like a small boat on a rough sea. *What can I do? Where do I start?* She had never reported a sexual harassment before and had no idea how to begin. With Anderson the sole proprietor, she didn't even know to whom she could complain. *Ben, he'll know what to do.* A lawyer, he had to have some ideas.

She thought about Jessica, how she seemed to teeter on the periphery of life, not really a part of it. *Something must have happened to her. Maybe she's been raped or attacked.* A rush of unexpected sadness hit Alex, and she hoped she hadn't been too harsh. *Maybe no one's ever protected Jessica. Maybe she has scars that haven't healed, that don't allow her to reach out to others.* The more she thought about it, the more sense it made. Alex decided that when the temperature settled down, she'd go back to Jessica and offer an apology; see if she could get a glimpse inside of her head, draw her out, maybe even help her deal with whatever had happened.

At the very least, I might make a friend. Jessica had made no attempt to become friends.

Alex saw him, out of the corner of her eye; her boss, smiling, advancing, a cat on a mouse. Suddenly, she wished she had worn a different blouse, one less flattering. She sucked in her breath and folded her arms over her chest as he approached. He bore down on her before she could move, his breath thick, heavy, the strong smell of coffee and cigarettes seeping up her nostrils, nauseating her further. "As usual, you're looking lovely this morning, Alex."

Anderson's smooth voice curled over her shoulder, his blue eyes blazing a hot trail down her blouse. She tightened her arms.

"How is everything? Are you finding your way around?" Like the serpent he was, his hand slithered onto her right shoulder, strong fingers applying subtle, meaningful pressure. They fanned out like a hand at poker, splayed out to their full extent, fingers like brandishing irons aimed toward her breast. She could feel the heat in their tips, along with the warm air of his sigh, and the mixed stench of coffee and desire on his breath. Her stomach lurched. *Help me, Jessica.* She shut her eyes.

"I'm fine." She shifted in her seat, opened her eyes, kept her words clipped. If she didn't yield, maybe it would end, he'd leave, go back to his office. Then she could call Ben.

His grip tightened, ever so slightly, but enough so she noticed. *He's sending a message.*

"Well, that's good. I'm glad you're enjoying it here. I like having you here." Even without looking, she sensed his smile, that lecherous, ogling grin. Alex suddenly shot up from her seat, sidled out from under his grasp, and headed out of the office, clutching her stomach. "I'm feeling queasy," she called over her shoulder, "seems I've picked up a particularly nasty parasite."

Since her arrival at Collins Real Estate, three and a half months earlier, Jessica had shown neither warmth or friendship, but Alex felt certain she saw the corners of Jessica's mouth curve up when she marched past her desk.

"I owe you an apology." As Alex soaped her hands at the bathroom sink, Jessica arrived at her shoulder.

"That's funny." Alex reached for a paper towel to dry her hands.

"What is?"

The slight softening she thought she heard in Jessica's voice instantly disappeared. "Well, I was actually thinking of apologizing to you." She tossed the wet towel into the trash.

"For what?"

"For going off on you like that. I don't know what it's been like here, what you've had to deal with, or anything. For all I know, he might have done the same thing to you."

She heard hesitation, and then, "He hasn't. Not yet. But I'm afraid he will."

They surveyed each other in the mirror. "Why don't you like me, Jessica?" If Alex sensed an opportunity to break through the blockade Jessica had built around her, pry open her secretive shroud and reach the prisoner trapped inside, she wanted to grab hold of it. Large blue eyes, so much like her own, stared back; a vacant facade, the frontage to disguise a well of pain. Alex didn't know how deep the well ran, but she sensed grief, agony, sorrow, even torture. What the hell happened to you? she wanted to say. But she didn't. She waited, her eyes never leaving Jessica's in the mirror.

"I'm sorry." Jessica finally looked away. "I should have said something, I know."

"Why didn't you?" Alex asked, her voice far more gentle than it had been in the office. Jessica shook her head. "I was afraid."

Alex nodded. "I can appreciate that."

"You can?" Jessica glanced across at her. Alex noted the surprise.

"Yes," she nodded again, "believe it or not, I can."

"But...you were so mad back there. I thought you hated me. I - wouldn't have blamed you."

Alex saw a slim chance. "Well, I don't hate you. In fact, I understand." She paused.

Jessica said nothing. She hadn't turned away, hadn't tuned her out yet.

Alex took a calm breath, and continued. "I know what it's like having to face something you're afraid of. I've had to deal with things that made me scared, and I haven't handled them very well. In fact," she laughed a dry laugh, thinking about all the years she'd wasted with John, too afraid to stand up sooner, and walk out, "I've made quite a mess of things in my life. So I'm not mad at all. I don't know what I might have done in your place." She did know what she would have done, now that she'd found her own courage, but she didn't know Jessica's place, so she had no right to be mad, she told herself.

"I loved what you said back there," Jessica said, that same small smile Alex thought she saw a few minutes ago playing with the corner of her mouth, "about the parasite. I know you meant him. He is a parasite, and he makes me sick."

Alex nodded. "Me, too."

A few seconds of silence, and then Jessica suddenly asked, "How old are you, Alex?" Alex blinked in surprise.

"Twenty-eight. Why?"

Jessica giggled shyly, and pointed in the mirror. "Look at us. I already have a twin, but I'm wondering if I'm really a triplet."

Alex gazed at their reflections. "I guess we do look alike."

"But you're a year younger," Jessica said, serious again, "so we can't be." Another few seconds of silence. "I better get back. It won't be long before he notices I'm gone."

"Okay." Alex headed out of the door, behind Jessica. "Jessica?"

"Yes?"

"Do you think we could be friends?" Alex held her breath.

They entered the main office, and, as Alex turned left to head to her own desk, while Jessica walked straight ahead to her seat outside Anderson's office, she heard her tiny reply. "I'll try."

Back at her desk, Alex sensed an uncanny element of peace. Despite the repellent boss she still had to handle, and the fact she might well lose her job, a quiet calm had settled in her stomach, replacing the nausea she'd had a few minutes earlier. She might not realize it herself, but Jessica had done two things for Alex. She'd reminded her she was not alone, and she'd given her a purpose. *We're both loners. Maybe we've ended up here through totally separate circumstances, but we're here, together, at similar points in our lives. Maybe our paths crossed for a reason.*

She didn't know if someone had let Jessica down, or how they might have hurt her, but she recognized pain, fear, and lack of trust; all the things she come to learn herself. *Maybe she's my reason for staying, my basis for being out here alone.*

Deep in her own thoughts later that evening, Jessica crossed the sterile hallway with Judd toward the reception at Park Glenn. She'd never had a friend. Could Alex really become a friend? Would she have to reveal hidden elements of her past? Could they be friends and still have secrets from each other? She didn't know.

The nurse on reception, a stout Irish woman in her early sixties, had a cheerful face and a disposition to match. Instantly recognizing the twins, she greeted them warmly in her broad Irish brogue. "Well, if it isn't me favorite two yung 'uns, cummin' to pay me anudder visit. S'luvely ta see da two o' ya's, an' wid da both o' ya looking sa well."

Jessica smiled at the plump woman. "Hello, Eleanor. Good to see you, too. How's Mother?"

"Grand." Eleanor grinned. "Ya'll not find her in her room." She waived away the twins' worried expressions. "She's 'avin' a grand day, so I put your Mam in the dayroom, that's all it is."

Stunned, Jessica thanked Eleanor, and quickened her

step in the direction of the dayroom, at the end of the long corridor. "She's never out of her room," she whispered to Judd. "Wonder what's made the difference."

"Just be thankful," Judd muttered back, striding alongside Jessica. He lapsed back into silence.

They found Marianne sitting on a bench, by a barred, open window, staring down onto a manicured lawn, a few feet below. Jessica bent, kissed the top of her head, and sat on the bench beside her.

"Hi, Mom," she whispered. Marianne didn't move. Judd did the same, taking the spot on her right side, flanking their mother. "How have you been?" Jessica wondered what the hell a 'grand day' was to the Irish. As usual, Marianne stayed mute and motionless. Nothing about her seemed any different.

Over the top of Marianne's silvery-blonde head, Jessica frowned at Judd. "I don't know," he mouthed, and shrugged.

A few silent seconds passed, then Marianne turned to face Judd, and opened her mouth.

Jessica's heart almost stood still, and then shattered into a million, fragmented pieces.

"Where's Cameron?" Marianne asked. "Did you bring my boy?" The thin, hollow-faced woman, who'd once been a beauty, studied the two adults sitting one on each side. They visited regularly, but she didn't know why. *Are they my children?* They called her Mom. *But shouldn't they be small?* The young woman on her left had slipped a hand into her own. Marianne studied it for a moment, didn't recognize it, and uncurled her fingers. "Where's Cameron?" she asked again. "When is he coming back?"

Jessica shot an alarmed glance at Judd. "Mom," she asked gently, "what do you mean by coming back?"

Judd shook his head.

Jessica looked into her mother's face, saw the pale blue eyes fill with water, and then the frail lady turned her gaze back out of the window.

"Cameron came last week," she whispered, and then became mute.

Forty minutes after they'd arrived, Jessica kissed her mother again, stood up and prepared to leave. "We'll be back soon," she said softly. The woman continued to gaze onto the lawn.

In the far corner of the dayroom, a man in a dark jacket and dark beanie witnessed the event. An idea formed in his head. What an interesting conversation. He watched them leave, gloomy, morose.

Neither glanced in his direction, not even when he got up to follow. Too consumed in their own little lives. They hadn't noticed the first time, either. He tailed them to the parking lot, keeping a safe distance behind, watched them climb into an old, red pickup.

He slid behind the wheel of his Mercedes. He knew the truck belonged to Judd, even though she was driving. She owned a shitty little grey thing; he remembered it from the day they moved into their apartment. When the pickup's engine shuddered and finally spluttered into life, he turned the key in his ignition, listened to the soft purr, and swung his baby out onto the road behind them.

"What was that all about?" Jessica asked Judd, on the tedious drive home. "What did Mom mean?"

"I don't know. She's crazy, Jess, she's stuck in 1982."

Chapter Twenty-One

That's it. Screw it. Alex snorted furiously, madder than a Matador's bull. Hot, angry tears pricked her eyes. The sultry heat of August added a flush to her already reddened face when she stormed out of Anderson's office, ran past Jessica's desk, and grabbed her purse.

"I don't need this shit. Nobody needs this shit." Another four months had passed and working for Anderson had been the equivalent of walking a tightrope; treading with the utmost care along a thin line of perpetual tension. Even after she'd mentioned her fears to Ben, she'd had to continue working. Ben had told her to leave, to quit, to find another job, but Alex knew it wouldn't be that easy. She wouldn't go back to retail. Anderson, she had decided, would not cost her the opportunity to achieve her dream. Or had she stayed to protect Jessica? In truth, she couldn't be sure.

"Wait," Jessica urged, when Alex stormed toward the door, long hair flying out behind, small feet thudding over the carpet, loose papers on Jessica's desk lifting with the sudden draft. "What happened in there?"

Alex whipped past without stopping. "Call me later, Jess. I can't stop. I'm on my way to see Ben."

In his office, Anderson sat stone-faced, staring at his coffee. Frustrated by Alex's failure to yield to his more subtle attempts, he'd been forced to step it up. Still she'd resisted. The more she resisted, the more he liked it. This morning, things had come to a head.

What's so fucking wrong with a little casual sex? He spread his hands out on his desk, wondering how it had blown up in his face. He'd called her in a few minutes earlier. She'd gone in all defensive, playing the hard-to-get card. *But you knew what was coming.* He sneered. *You've been here long enough, you knew what I had in mind when you walked through my door.*

"Teasing bitch," he snarled under his breath. "You're so fucking fired."

Jessica ran out after Alex, caught up with her in the parking lot before she reached her car. "Alex, wait," she yelled, "please."

Alex turned, saw Jessica bearing down on her, and threw her purse into the back seat of her car, fighting back tears of anger.

"He was like a dog, Jessie," she cried, when Jessica drew nearer. "A fucking wild dog, sniffing me like I was some kind of animal. He trapped me in the chair, had a hand on each arm so I couldn't get out. And when I didn't give in, when I told him to leave me alone, he turned nasty. Said I'm not a good fit, that I don't have a job."

"He fired you?"

"He said I have a bad attitude, and if he'd known it sooner, he'd never have hired me. I wish he fucking hadn't. I wish I'd never set eyes on that slimy, lecherous piece of shit."

"Oh, Alex, I'm so sorry." Jessica rested a hand on Alex's shoulder. "I had no idea it had become so bad."

"Well, I'm out of a job, but I'm not out," Alex shot back.

"What are you going to do?"

"Sue him. That's what I'm going to do. Ben said I didn't have enough before, but I do now. I'll get him for unfair dismissal if I can't get him for harassment." She yanked open the driver side door and stepped behind it, so it acted as a shield between her and Jessica. "I've got to go. But I'll be in touch."

"Promise?"

"Yes, I promise." Alex smiled at Jessica. Over the past few months, they had slipped into a guarded friendship; guarded on the part of Jessica, but still a friendship of sorts. Alex knew little about Jessica's life, except that she had a brother and no other family, apart from some distant uncles she'd never met.

"I know they live in Australia," Jessica had told her. When Alex asked if she knew their names, Jessica shook her head. "My mother never kept in touch with her brothers."

Again, the question hung in the back of Alex's mind, but she didn't think it possible. She'd have to ask her uncle Edward next time they spoke. Could it be possible he had a sister?

The astonishing similarities in their appearance still made her wonder, but surely someone would have told her.

"I'm afraid to go back," Jessica whispered, letting go of Alex's driver door. "I won't be able to make it without you, Alex. You're strong. You always know what to do. I don't know what I'll do if he does the same thing to me. I…I…," she lowered her gaze. "I've never even had a boyfriend."

"Jessica, listen to me." Alex hooked a finger under her chin, brought her head up until their eyes leveled. "He won't do anything to you. He'd be stupid to do that. He's in enough trouble already with what happened today and it would be too obvious if he did anything to you."

"It would? How? He's always had girls. No one seems to care."

"Someone cares, Jessica. I care. And I'm going to do

something about it." Alex smiled. "Remember when I yelled at you for not doing anything about this a few months ago?"

Jessica nodded.

"Well, I'm to blame for what happened today. I wasn't afraid of him, but I did nothing. I let it go on. I should have stood up to him back then, before it got so bad."

"It's not easy to prove sexual harassment, Alex. Especially when he's the boss, and so many of the girls are willing. You're going to have quite a fight on your hands."

"You sound like Ben."

In a mood far gloomier than usual, Jessica left the office at five o'clock and decided to stop off at the grocery store on her way home to buy herself a treat and try to cheer herself up, something that would remind her of happier times. Thirty minutes later, she returned to her Taurus, tossed the bag of Milky Way treats onto the back seat, and began backing up out of the parking lot. Her phone rang. *Damn.* Expecting it would be Judd with another excuse why he wouldn't be home until late, she took one hand off the wheel and fished around in her purse to find it, while she continued to reverse.

"Shit." She'd looked in the mirror in the nick of time and stamped on her brake. *That was close.* She couldn't have missed by much more than a hair. Immediately behind her rear bumper, another car had pulled up alongside, driving along the narrow lane into which she'd been attempting to reverse. *Where the hell did you come from?* He hadn't been there a minute ago. *Didn't you see me pulling out?* Not that it mattered; he had the right of way, and she'd taken her eyes off the road.

"Phew." She held up a hand, signaled an apology, and waited for the driver to move. When he didn't, her agitation grew. He had her boxed into her spot, unable to move forward, and blocking her reverse. She signaled again, gesturing for him to precede. He didn't. An alarm bell rang in her head. *He wants to teach me a lesson. Fuck.* She had nowhere to go, nothing to do but sit and wait. News of the recent murders flitted through her head. *Shit.* She remembered her phone. She'd dropped it onto the front seat, but hadn't ended the call. Fortunately, Judd was still on the other end when she held it to her ear, shouting with impatience.

"Jessica, what the hell's going on?"

"Judd," she exclaimed with relief, "Thank goodness it's you. I've got a maniac right behind me and I can't get away."

"What?" he demanded. "What are you talking about? Jessica, is everything all right?"

"I almost rammed a Benz at the store," she said. "Nearly backed into this guy, and now he won't move. He's blocking my way. Judd, what should I do?"

"Don't get out of the car," he ordered. Jessica noticed the alarm creeping into his voice. "Lock the doors and call the police."

"The police? Is that really nec–"

"Just do it, Jessica."

She peered into her rearview mirror and tried to get a look at the driver. He had on a cap and sunglasses and she couldn't make him out. The coupe looked familiar, as did the big chain hanging from the mirror.

"Judd, I think I've seen him be--"

"Jess." Exasperation floated into her ear. "I said call the cops. Don't mess with this guy. You don't know who he is."

Suddenly, the Benz began to move. Slowly, the driver edged forward, moved away from the back of her car, reached the end of the row, and disappeared. Jessica breathed out a relieved sigh and waited a few seconds to be sure he'd gone.

"It's all right, Judd, he's gone. Just some asshole who shouldn't be out on the road."

"You're sure you're okay?"

"I'm fine. I'll be home soon."

"I won't be in when you get home, Jess, that's why I called. I'm going to be late tonight, so keep the doors locked and stay inside."

"Again?" She tried to swallow down the instant irritation that arose in her chest, and the unease about Judd's questionable behavior. He had no job, yet he stayed out all the time, and always came home late. "Where this time?" She tried to sound casual.

"Just out, Jess. You'll be fine, just do what I said." Before she could protest, he'd hung up.

A few minutes before six, Jessica pulled into the driveway of their hilltop home, parked, and climbed out of her car. She reached into the back seat for her belongings when a flash of silver streaked past. She heard a loud roar as the driver gunned the engine, and lifted her head in time to see the tail end of the Mercedes disappear over the crest of the hill.

Alarm prickled her skin; lifted the hairs on her arms; and caused an unpleasant tingling in her scalp, like someone had begun raking through her hair with prickly, metal nails. For a moment she stared, eyes glued to the hill, half expecting the driver to return. Until Judd's words came flooding back. *Keep the doors locked and stay inside.* She grabbed her things, slammed the car door shut, and raced to the front door, fumbling with the keys in a desperate attempt to get inside the apartment. Inside, she slammed the door shut, locked it, dead-bolted it, and tried to calm herself. *It could be nothing, could just be a coincidence.*

She pushed her hair off her face, ran to the living room window, and carefully peered through the blinds. He hadn't come back, but she waited a few more minutes, watching, just in case. Even as her head tried to sort through the logic, tried to rationalize and make sense of what had happened, every inch of her body told her the silver Mercedes had been no coincidence. After the incident at the grocery store, she realized, he hadn't driven away at all, but had rounded the corner and had lain in wait. *He must have followed me.* Focused only on getting home after she'd nearly rammed the Mercedes and her relief when it had eventually disappeared, Jessica had driven with tunnel vision, not bothering to check in her rearview mirror. She hadn't noticed the sports car rejoining the road behind her, keeping a tail on her Taurus. *Stupid.* She pressed a hand to her chest, trying to still the thumping. *Why?*

The pounding of her heart sent a rush of blood to her head making her forehead ache, her ears hurt, and her eyes sting. *Dammit, Judd, why couldn't you just be home?* She took another tentative peek through the blinds. Nothing. She sat down and tried to think. *Why would anyone be so mad over such a minor incident, even if he is in a Mercedes?* She thought about the Mercedes, the silver sports car, and a stirring deep in her consciousness brought about a brand new wave of alarm. *This isn't the first time. He's followed me before.* A cold fear trickled slowly up her veins like someone had poured ice-water into them, freezing her to the spot where she sat. Unable to move, she remembered the big silver chain; the same one she'd seen dangling from the mirror of the silver sports car a couple of days ago on the grounds of Park Glenn, and how she'd thought it odd to hang such an ugly thing in such a nice car. *Nice car.* The banging in her chest became so loud it sounded like someone knocking on the front door. Afraid she might be sick, Jessica somehow managed to get herself off the chair and into the bathroom, where she kneeled on the floor, hanging her head over the toilet. *Why didn't I see it? How could I be so dumb?*

The racing in her head brought nausea to the back of her throat, where it stayed. With one hand on the sink, she pulled herself up, ran the faucet, and splashed her face with cold water. *I've got to call Judd.*

She went back to the living room, dug into her purse, and pulled out her phone, dialed his digits, and waited for answer. One ring–two–three–his voicemail came on. *Shit.* She snapped the phone shut, and thought about calling the police. *What do I say?* Her fingers grew damp under the phone, sweat built up on her brow.

"Wait a minute," a little voice said in the back of her head. "There hasn't been a murder for months. Try to calm down, think this through."

Jessica clutched the phone to her chest. *But he harassed me on my way to work.* The memory of her drive to the office, the day Alex started, came flooding back with the recollection of the chain, but worse; the nice car. *I remember thinking that the day we moved in.* The nice little sports car parked just down the street. *Someone's been stalking me for months.*

"But he'd have made his move if he wanted to kill you," the little voice said. "It's all a coincidence. Nobody wants anything to do with you; they never have, and they never will."

Judd. Why couldn't you just be home? Anger at Judd, at the abandonment, took root, competing with the fear beginning to recede. Logic, a powerful weapon, had begun to put things into perspective. *That's right, I just pissed him off. So many crazies. He'd have made a move if he wanted to kill me.*

"That's right," said the voice in her head, "and you don't want the cops poking into your business, finding out about your crazy mother. They'll only think you've inherited the gene."

Once more, she peered out of the window. No sign of a Mercedes.

It's going to be a long night. Despite having managed to placate her initial fear, Jessica's breathing remained a little ragged. Logic and panic hadn't finished their contest. She slumped onto the couch and curled into a ball, wrapping her arms tightly around her legs, knowing every noise tonight, every click, creak and moan, in the dark, empty house would keep her awake, until Judd came home.

Chapter Twenty-Two

What time is it? Jessica pushed herself into a sitting position, groggy and disoriented, rubbing at her eyes and squinting at the clock. *I must have dozed off.* The TV had become a blank screen filled with fuzzy white dots. Jessica stumbled from the couch to the TV and switched it off. She shivered in the pre-dawn cold. Two-thirty, and Judd still hadn't come home. She knew he hadn't because he'd have woken her, either with his key in the lock or with a gentle shake.

The eerie silence seemed more ominous in the early morning hours, like the precursor to something bad, something frightening. Old memories played tricks with her mind. *Everything bad always happens at night.* The terror of an eight-year-old came rushing back. Not wanting to disturb the silence, to awaken the evil, she padded barefoot and silent out of the room, climbed the stairs, and entered the bathroom, where she wiped her face, and brushed her teeth, all the while keeping her ears trained for the sound of a key in the lock.

Where the hell are you, Judd? What are you involved in? She tiptoed softly to her room, left the door ajar, and crawled into bed, pulling the sheet up under her nose, just as she had as a child, on all those long, fearful nights back in Sacramento. In the dark, her thoughts seemed louder. Her ears picked up the whooshing sound of blood being pumped through her veins, faster than normal. Frightened by the shadows, she closed her eyes and lay still, waiting, listening.

Tick-tick-tick. The clock on the nightstand seemed agonizingly loud; loud enough to wake the dead. Her heart pounded beneath the sheet, so hard she feared it might burst.

Then she heard it; the rattling of the front door, like the wind had picked it up and given it a good shake. She stopped breathing, stared at the open bedroom door, ears pricked for every sound. A key entering the lock, a creek, a latch catching, another turn of the lock, and the sound of boots on the wooden floor, coming closer, moving down the hall, the closing of another door, and then silence.

She lay back against the pillow, shut her eyes, began breathing normally. With Judd home, she could finally get some sleep.

Jessica groaned, flung out an arm, and shut off the beeps. At six-thirty, morning had come far too soon. Her head felt heavy, like someone was dancing around inside in hob-nailed boots. *Shit, I only just went to bed.* Four hours of sleep left her feeling like a drunk. She remembered Judd.

She threw back the sheets, stumbled out of bed, and lurched clumsily down the hall. At Judd's room, she peered inside the open door and saw his bed already made. Surprised, she continued down the hall, past the bathroom, down the stairs, and into the kitchen. *Damn.* The apartment being small, it took her only a few minutes to realize Judd had already gone.

The alarm went off, waking Alex at six-forty-five. Unemployed, except for few nights at Harry's, she'd allowed herself some extra time to lie-in. With things to do, she hopped out of bed, showered, dressed, and called Ben. "He'll know how to get things started," she told herself, waiting for him to pick up.

"Alex." Ben answered on the third ring, sounding harried. "I'll have to keep this short and to the point."

"Bad time?" She was disappointed he didn't have time for her, and anxious to set things in motion, afraid her momentum might be destroyed by the odds stacked against her.

"Not bad, just busy. I'm due in court all day."

"Got time for lunch?" She hated pleading, hated the needy way it made her sound.

"Uh." He hesitated. Maybe he heard something in her voice. "Okay, sure." Or maybe she just had a way of making him feel like a pubescent teen. "Twelve-fifteen, okay?"

"Twelve-fifteen's fine. Meet me at The Elite Café."

Ben gathered his case papers together, stuffed them into his briefcase, and wondered what could be so important. As he let himself out of his Pacific Heights townhouse, he frowned.

He had an obstinate client, a difficult case to present, and, knowing who would be presiding over the case, harbored doubts about his chances of winning. He had to keep his head straight this morning, not let it get caught up on Alex.

He opened his garage, and a smile climbed over the frown. *What a beauty.* His eyes lingered on her curves, her body, her sleek appearance. He loved every inch of her, inside and out. Beep-beep. The keyless entry flipped up the locks, and he slid behind the wheel of his brand new Mercedes. He fired up the engine, revved her up, slid her into reverse and effortlessly backed her out of the garage. Into drive, he took off down the road, loving the soft purr of her engine, like a powerful, contented cat.

With only a short drive to the courthouse, the distraction was short-lived, and his mind wandered back to Alex. *It's going to be a long morning.* He was anxious to get through to lunch and discover what she had to say.

As expected, his morning began at a disadvantage. The judge, recently divorced, seemed less than enamored with his client, an attractive woman suing her wealthy husband for half of his assets as well as claiming spousal abuse. Judge Lane Samuels showed his dissatisfaction for her tardiness, when she claimed traffic had caused her to be five minutes late.

"The rest of us managed to get here on time." He had just warned Ben that if his client didn't arrive within the next two minutes her case would be dismissed.

Ben presented as best he could, when she arrived in the nick of time, but Samuels seemed indifferent to her claims, hell-bent on sustaining the defense attorney's objections while overruling his own.

By noon, the uphill battle had worn him down, his chances of success had continued to diminish, and he had another awkward case in the afternoon. When he arrived at the Elite Café, a few minutes later than agreed, he saw Alex already seated in a corner booth, waving to get his attention. He strode over to where she sat, gave her a tired smile, a peck on the cheek, and slid into the seat opposite.

"Tough morning?"

"You could say that."

"Well, I hope I'm not about to make things worse."

"Alex," he covered her hand on the table with one of his, "you could never make things worse." He breathed in her scent, the smell of freshly washed linen, and frowned at her blue polo-shirt and faded, blue jeans.

"Day off?"

"You could say that," she quipped back.

"Any particular reason?"

"I quit."

"I'm glad." Ben picked up the menu. "I've been telling you to do that for a while. I'm glad you finally took my advice to get yourself out of there and into something that'll make you happier."

"No, Ben, you don't understand." Alex pulled the menu away from his face. "He went too far this time. He told me I no longer have a job because I wouldn't give in to his demands."

"He what?" Ben dropped the menu onto the table. "When did this happen?"

"Yesterday."

"And you didn't say anything before now?"

"I tried to call, but you didn't pick up. I figured you were busy. That's why I called this morning."

"Oh, Alex." Ben swore. "What happened?"

While Alex relived the events of yesterday afternoon for Ben, he sensed an aura of fatigue, listening to her claims, her emotions rising when she talked about Anderson and then softening when she mentioned Jessica. He cringed at the detail of Anderson's hand creeping near her breast, his breath in her ear, and the finale in the lion's den.

"Can anyone back you up?" he said, when she'd finished.

"Jessica saw me go in," she said, "but I don't know what she heard."

"Sexual harassment claims are hard at the best of times, Alex, but without anyone to back you up, it might be nearly impossible." Ben sighed, hating the situation, hating the fact he had another afternoon in court when his mind wanted to be elsewhere, and hating the fact Alex might not be able to right this wrong.

"What will I have to do? I'm not letting him get away with it. Tell me what I need to do."

A waitress took their order.

"If you make a claim, it will have to be thoroughly investigated."

"I expected that."

"You'll have the burden of proof that it actually happened. You'll have to convince the Court–"

"I don't ha–"

"Let me finish. They'll dig into your past, and it will be unpleasant."

"You mean about John?"

"Yes, that's exactly what I mean. They'll claim you must have known about the drugs."

"But I turned him in," she cried.

"I know, but they'll still use it against you." He squeezed her hand. "I don't mean to be harsh, but you were married to a drug-dealer and they'll use it against you. They'll try to taint your character."

"But–"

"Can you prove you knew nothing about it? Can you prove you didn't lead that animal on? Can you even prove he touched you?"

"Ben." Alex snatched away her hand. "I'm the victim. How can you say these things?"

"Because a defense attorney will, Alex, that and a lot worse. I know you're the victim, honey, I believe you." He winced at her wounded expression, as though he'd just called her a liar. "But the law also has to protect the accused. Innocent until proven guilty, even if we know he's guilty. A jury would have to decide, if it ever got to trial. And, I hate to say it, but few of these cases, sexual harassment cases, ever end up in Federal court."

The waitress set down their plates.

"So, I'm supposed to sit back and do nothing?" Alex snapped.

Ben picked at his food, not really in the mood to eat. "If anyone else will back up your claim, you might have a case. Before you do anything, you need to see if there is anyone willing to testify."

Alex sighed, and pushed her plate away. "Then I might as well give up now."

"Wait a minute." Ben flinched at the defeat in her voice. It wasn't the Alex he knew, the woman he admired for her strength and courage. "You had the guts to do the right thing about John. Don't give up on this yet. Maybe we'll find a way." He slid her plate back in front of her. "You invited me to lunch. Eat something."

As they left the Café, thirty minutes later, Ben gave her a hug. "Talk to Jessica. See what she heard. I'm in court all afternoon. Call me tonight and we'll see where we go from there."

Back in court that afternoon, an idea formed in his head. As he got up to cross-examine, he put it out of his mind, knowing he needed to make a phone call first.

After lunch with Ben, still low and depressed, Alex decided to call Jessica.

"Alex," Jessica kept her voice low, so her words wouldn't be overheard. "I miss you. Is everything all right?"

"Jess," Alex ploughed straight in, "I'm going to need your help."

"What can I do?"

Alex quickly relayed her lunch-time meeting with Ben, told Jessica she needed a witness to have any chance of winning. She noticed the more she said, the quieter the other end of the line became.

"...I'm going to need you to testify in court. We're the only ones who objected to his behavior." Alex waited. She could only hear Jessica breathing. "Will you help?"

For a long moment, Jessica gripped the phone and said nothing. She drew one deep breath after another, her mind whirling with emotions. *I can't go back to court. I can't.* Her heart hammered, the phone slipped in her sweaty hand, her mouth went dry. She tried to speak but nothing came out. The bastard had to be brought to justice, had to be made to stop. *But I can't go back into a courtroom.* Even though it had been so many years ago, she remembered the scrutiny, the interrogation, the mean attorney sitting next to Bodie who accused her poor father of so many awful things. The way he dug into the privacy of their lives, hurled out his filthy accusations, tried to shift the blame.

Anderson became Bodie, the monster whom she'd have to battle, the one who would twist things around, dig into her private life, bring sordid allegations against her, and Alex.

She gasped, a rasping sound that sounded a million miles away. "Alex." She couldn't breathe. "I can't. I...can't go back inside a courtroom."

No one in her life, other than Judd, knew about the ordeals they'd suffered or the details of their horrifying past. No one knew about the murder, the suicide, and the mental illness in her family. They had moved to escape it, and now, if she did what Alex had asked, it would all come tumbling out. The slender hold she had on normality already seemed to be slipping away. "I'm sorry."

Alex barely heard the whisper. She sensed the fear, the dread, the absolute terror. It no longer mattered. Whatever Jessica had been through in her past, she wouldn't make her relive it. *She's suffered enough already.*

"It's okay, Jess. I understand." She kept her voice soft and kind. "I'll figure it out one way or another. Don't you worry. We won't let him get away with this."

Jessica squeezed her eyes shut, tried to squash the pain and the memories, and the tears threatening to leak out. *It's not fair. Why do I have to be me? Why did my father have to be so weak? Why can't I do this one thing for Alex?*

"Jessica? Are you all right?"

The deep, smooth, familiar voice, sounding way too close, shocked Jessica back to the present. Her eyes fluttered open to see Anderson, an amused expression on his handsome face, leaning on her desk, his face a few inches away from hers. The blue eyes twinkled with the hint of laughter. "Boyfriend trouble? Need a tissue?" He dropped a box on her desk and strode away.

"I'm sorry," Jessica managed into the phone, and dropped it back in its cradle. Anderson had already strutted back into his office and closed the door.

At seven o'clock that evening, when she arrived for her shift at Harry's, Alex still felt defeated. Without Jessica's help, her chances had dwindled from slim to none.

"Something on your mind?" Sarah quizzed.

For a moment, she considered asking her advice, and then remembered Anderson came here for lunches or dinners when he met with clients, or girls. *Shit.* She hadn't thought about that. That could cause Harry problems, and possibly cost her the job, her second job. *Damn you, you son-of-a-*

bitch.

"Alex?"

"What?" She looked back at Sarah. "Oh, no, sorry. It's nothing. I'm just a bit frazzled with these murders."

When her shift ended, she walked the two blocks to her apartment, thinking about Ben, about Jessica, about Anderson. *There has to be something.* She let herself in, and saw the red button flashing on her phone.

"Long shot," Ben's voice floated into her kitchen, "make him think this won't go away…threaten to file the grievance…he might agree to an out-of-court settlement…better than nothing."

Alex wondered. *Not ideal. Would it even work?* She listened to the message again. *But what other options do I have?*

Chapter Twenty-Three

Anderson leaned back in his chair with a satisfied smile. *Great ass*. He watched Nicky Drew wiggle it out through the door of his office, past Jessica's desk, and out of sight. He sighed and reached for the coffee she'd brought him earlier. This morning, Nicky'd been incredible, and afterwards she'd even remembered to reapply her lipstick. She'd told him about the previous time, when she thought Jessica had noticed.

"I think she suspects us," she'd said, ten minutes earlier, lifting her head up from between his muscular thighs.

"No, she doesn't," Anderson had reassured her, pushing her head back down again and rolling his eyes almost to the back of his head. Nicky could do the most amazing tricks with her tongue. He wondered if the stud she wore in it had something to do with that.

Sitting alone now, sipping the lukewarm coffee and opening his mail, his face rapidly lost its afterglow, turning more murderous with each word he read. He almost choked on the bitter brew he'd been swirling around his mouth. A letter from a familiar law firm, signed for this morning, had been delivered to his desk. *What*? He blinked, stared, blinked again, as though the words had been playing a trick.

They hadn't. His face grew hot, his tie felt tight, and his fist curled into a ball. Alex had hired a lawyer to threaten a lawsuit. She claimed others knew of his conduct. Enraged, he read the letter again, just to be sure. He slammed it down on the desk.

Why, you bitch. You fucking little bitch. How dare you threaten me? Who do you think you are? So, you think you can sue me. Well, little miss fucking frigid, we'll see about that. Like the steam in a pressure cooker, his rage mounted. His eyes bulged, his nostrils flared, and he banged his mug down hard on his desk; so hard the rest of the cooled liquid inside shot upwards and out and splattered itself in a wet, dark mess across his desk.

"Damn that bitch," he spluttered, even more furious than ever.

"I need you. Right away." He spoke brusquely into his phone, summoning the harlot, Nicky Drew, back into his office. "Come back in here. Immediately."

Wow, that man has an appetite like no other. Nicky smiled happily and skipped her way across the floor and back into his den, oblivious to the amused sneer on Jessica's face.

Jessica had heard the bang, heard the cuss, and figured out what had happened. *Plus*, she guessed, *a man in his forties probably couldn't go two rounds in such quick succession.* She watched with amusement, waited for the inevitable, and smothered a giggle when it happened. Anderson barely looked at Nicky's fresh, pretty face when she reentered his office, breathless and giddy.

"I'm going out," he growled, a total contrast to the sweet nothings he'd whispered in her ear a few minutes earlier, when she'd given him the blow job of his life. "I won't be back for a while. I need you to clean up this mess." He thrust a roll of paper towels into her hand and stalked from his office, seething, with Ben's letter still gripped in his hand.

Her fingers had become stained with newspaper ink and

her back ached from hours spent hunched on the floor. Alex leaned back and stretched out her shoulders. The classifieds in the *Chronicle* offered nothing of interest. *Thank goodness for Harry.* She rolled her head to work out the kinks. Harry had given her extra shifts, starting with one tonight. *But it won't be enough.* A part time job in a restaurant would only keep her going for a while. With bills mounting and rent due, Alex couldn't ignore her dilemma. *I need a job.*

Her stomach muscles tightened and she wondered if Anderson had read her letter. She'd been more confident yesterday, when she'd got Ben to write it. This morning, the confidence had begun to wane. *What if it doesn't work? What then?* Ben had warned her the bluff might fall flat, that Anderson was no fool and not a pleasant man with whom to tangle. *It has to work.* She folded the paper, pushed it aside, and began to get up when her eyes fell upon an article at the bottom of the front page.

...again San Francisco feels fear...has the killer returned?...late last night...another brutal attack...once more near the Embarcadero, victim struck from behind...

Her eyes flew over the story, picking out words. *...survives...injuries...young woman...helping police with inquiries...maniac...links to last year's unsolved murders not ruled out...*

Alex had to read it twice. The murders seemed to have stopped, in fact there hadn't been one reported for months. *So he's back. He's still out there.* She read the article once more, this time more thoroughly. Once again, no one had seen anything. *How could there be no witnesses in such a busy city?* The victim, a young woman, had survived the attack and had been able to help the police with a brief description. *Thank goodness for that.* The attacker had approached from behind and attempted to stab her. She had heard his footsteps, turned her head, and saw him a split second before he attacked. The detective on the case, a Mac Jackson, had commented that her actions had eliminated the attacker's main advantage–the element of surprise. The glance behind had probably saved her life. Alex read the details about what had happened. The woman, on her way to her car after finishing a late-night shift at a local bar, had put up a fight, screaming loudly while the man had tried to overpower her, jabbing at her throat with his knife. She'd struggled with him, kicking and punching, and had been able to plunge her car keys into his face before he'd yelped and run off. She'd described him to police as a white male, somewhere between twenty-five and thirty, around six-feet-two, of muscular build, around one-hundred-and-ninety to two-hundred-pounds, with a blue, woolen hat pulled low over his ears. She hadn't noticed any visible tattoos, piercings, scars, or other distinguishable marks. The one thing that stuck out, she'd said, was the smell of his breath. It reeked of beer, and she wondered if he might be an alcoholic.

Detective Jackson went on to add to the report that the public should be on the lookout for a man with a distinct facial injury, a gouge in his left cheek. The gouge had been what made him abandon the attack and run off, leaving his victim lying on the ground, shaken, but alive.

That had to have been awful. She eyed the statistics. *One hundred-ninety to two-hundred.* That fit. *Twenty-five to thirty.* Close enough, give or take. *Six-feet-two.* Alex shuddered. A lot of men would fit that description, but she could only think of John. *I need to call Narcotics*. Although she had thought of him less often, she hadn't forgotten, and Narcotics hadn't called. *They must have something by now*. Another thought crossed her mind. *Should I still be walking home from Harry's?*

"It's two blocks," she said out loud, as if that would be enough to convince herself the decision to do it again tonight made sense. Some might call it reckless; Sarah did, so did Ben.

To Alex, it had nothing to do with being reckless, or brave, or bold, but everything to do with independence. *Maybe you can only understand that if you've been robbed of it once, and I refuse to be robbed of it again.*

In the large living room of his fancy apartment, an ugly, raw, red welt across his face and the bitter taste of beer on his tongue, he read the morning paper; about the one who got away. *...helping police with their inquiries...maniac...links to last year's unsolved murders not ruled out...*

He stared at the paper and wanted to laugh, but his face hurt too much. He touched his cheek where she'd gouged him with her keys. *Bitch.* He winced, and remembered, and a slow smile spread across his lips, stretching the wound and making it sting. He didn't mind. He'd enjoyed the fight. He never raped them; he didn't have to. He got off on the struggle. Thrilling. Perhaps even orgasmic. Sometimes, he wondered if he enjoyed it too much. He loved it when they squirmed, and fought for their lives. He loved the terror in their screams at the sight of his knife. Even the men screamed. *Pussy's.*

The knife always did that. They saw it coming. He made sure of that. This one had a pair of lungs and a will to live he hadn't counted on. She'd almost risked him getting caught, although he'd run off before that could happen. "I should have just killed the bitch," he muttered, holding his ice-cold beer bottle to his cheek. She'd flipped his advantage and had surprised him. Usually they didn't hear him coming up behind them; and if they did, he seduced them with his charm, before he went for the kill. They never figured it out, until it was too late. He loved hearing the last breath leave their bodies. He called it their 'dying sigh'. He loved it so much, he even wrote about it.

I need to update my journal. He reached for a pen. *I think I'll call her the screamer.* He wrote it down under yesterday's date. *Now, she warrants at least half a page.* He wrote quickly, making sure he covered all the details so he could relive them later, then threw the book aside and knocked back a mouthful of beer. *I'll have to be more careful.*

He would not be caught until he'd finished what he started. Eventually the police would catch him, he knew that. He could only get away with it for so long. He didn't mind getting caught; as long as he first achieved his aim. *The police. They're so fucking stupid.* He took another swig. *Except Jackson.* He thought about the detective, his drive, his determination, and how he'd never give up. If anyone caught him, he knew it would be Jackson, the only one with the resolve, the fortitude, and the skill to see it through. Jackson had proved himself once before, many years ago. He remembered it well.

He raised his beer to Jackson. "Salut." He emptied it down his throat. In another life, they might even have been friends. In this life, the law divided them, so it would never be possible. He tossed the paper aside. The report amused him. They always did. *So the police think the murders are linked.* A chortle started deep in his gut, worked its way up his throat and reached his lips. He winced when he let it out. *Of course they're linked, not that you bunch of assholes would ever know. You have no idea about all the others.* He laughed at the cops. How could such a bumbling bunch of idiots ever hope to keep a city safe? *They don't. At least, not this fucking city.*

He'd been killing for years. The police had no idea how many he'd killed; hell, even he had no idea. Best of all, no one suspected him. The rest of the world saw a regular guy, living quietly in a nice neighborhood with his own set of problems, along with everyone else. He'd become a master of disguise.

He yawned, stretched out on his bed, and thought about his trail of destruction. Until recently, he'd killed only bums, nobodies, down and outs, homeless people, folks no one cared about or would ever report missing. That had soon become boring and he'd needed a bigger thrill. Murdering someone with a family who loved them, someone who would miss them and grieve for them, provided that thrill. *I know all about grief.* He knew the depths, the nadir–the lowest human point a person could reach. He'd been to rock bottom and climbed his way back. The time for payback had come.

He sniffed, threw the empty beer bottle on top of the paper, and closed his eyes. *Crazed maniac. I'm not crazy, you incompetent bastards, I'm insane.*

He drifted into a pleasant doze, where he saw himself closing in on his intended; the one for whom he came back. After that, it wouldn't matter. His purpose would be accomplished.

Soon. He smiled, and sank deeper. *Soon.*

The evening at Harry's had been slow, giving the girls time to chat.

"Do you think it's someone who lives around here?" Alex asked Sarah. "I mean, we could be standing next to him in the grocery store and not even know. He could be one of our customers, watching us right now."

"Alex. I don't want to talk about murder. I'm nervous enough as it is."

Alex scanned the room, checking out the patrons; the elderly couple sitting next to each other in a window booth, holding hands and sharing a dinner; a father and son eating at a corner table; several business associates in the middle of the room; a group of chattering girls; a small birthday party near the bar. They all looked normal.

"He could be anyone. We wouldn't even know."

"I said I don't want to hear it."

"Remember the woman last year, the one who had her throat slashed?"

"Of course," Sarah said curtly. "Do we have to talk about this?"

"Just hear me out. I remember the reports mentioned the knife made such a clean cut the police said that it had to have been very sharp. They said it had an eight-inch blade, like a chef's knife."

"Are you saying you think it's someone who works in a restaurant?"

Alex shrugged. "I don't know, but it would make sense. Think about it. All the murders happened either late at night or in the early hours of the morning. Perfect for someone coming off a shift."

"What's your point?" Sarah turned to clear up a table that just vacated.

"My point is," Alex hurried after her, "that we would have no idea. He could watch people all night long, pick out his victims, vulnerable ones, those who're alone, like you when you go out to drink."

"Or you, Alex, when you insist on walking home by yourself."

"The police said he doesn't rob them or sexually assault them. What else could it be about?"

"Look, Alex," Sarah said, with an irritated sigh, "I don't know, but I've heard enough. I don't know why you want to play detective, but I don't want to fill my head with thoughts about murder when I'm working a late shift and I still have to get home. If you must talk about it, wait 'til I am home…and then call me." She stalked off to fiddle with something behind the bar.

"Sorry," Alex called out, her words bouncing off Sarah's back, "I just can't stop thinking that I know what it's about."

"Well tell it to the police." Sarah disappeared into the office behind the bar.

Revenge. Hatred. A crazy psychopath with a grudge. She thought about John. *It is you, isn't it?* "It's about vengeance." Her words echoed around the room.

Thursday evening had already rolled around and Jessica had still not managed to talk to Judd. Anderson had been a bear when he'd stormed out, growling at her along with everyone else. Again, she had come home to an empty apartment, and now the light had faded from the day, the air had grown cold, and the nights shadows had come tapping on the window. *Damn you, Judd.* She turned up the volume on the TV, and tried to forget about this morning's paper.

Just for once, why can't you be home? The news flashed onto the screen, and Jessica groaned. As she reached for the remote to switch it off, she heard a name that jolted her again. She'd read it in the paper this morning, and it had shaken her then. His face seemed older, more lined, more harried, but recognizable, even after more than twenty years.

What are you doing in San Francisco? As she listened to the news, about the most recent murder, she thought about the man working the case. As long as she lived, she didn't think she'd ever forget Detective Jackson. Surprised to have read about him in the *Chronicle*, she realized he must have transferred to San Francisco. She smiled at the coincidence. Something about Jackson being near gave her a sense of security, a sense of peace.

Maybe he could help me again.

Jackson wouldn't have forgotten, she knew that. He knew her history, the tragedies of Cameron and her father. *He won't judge, he won't pity.* She checked her watch: eleven o'clock.

Probably too late to call. Tomorrow, I'll call the police and ask for Detective Jackson. Jackson would know what to do about Judd. He always knew what to do. He could find out things, like if Judd was in trouble. *Maybe he could keep an eye on him, find out where he goes.* She hadn't permitted herself to think too much about that, afraid to know, scared to discover that her rock, her beloved brother, the only family she had left, might have wandered down darker paths than before.

Chapter Twenty-Four

The rest of the week and the weekend passed uneventfully, and by the following Monday morning, when Alex had heard nothing from Anderson, she could barely contain her frustration. *He has to have read the letter.* She said as much to Ben when she called him that morning. "Why hasn't he reacted?"

"He might be weighing up his options," Ben said, "considering the alternatives. Give it time."

"What are the alternatives?"

"Well, there are really only two." Alex knew by the dry note in Ben's voice that he didn't think the bluff had worked. "Either he settles outside of court, or he ignores the letter and waits for your next move."

"When will I know? How much time does he have?"

"Alex," Ben warned, as gently as he could, "remember I told you this was a long shot. We don't have a next move, so he can take as long as he wants."

"And if he ignores us?"

"I think you know."

"Fuck. I hate this."

Since she'd stormed out of her job, she'd been consumed, thought about little else. "I can't believe he wouldn't even respond. I know his temper, Ben. I know the letter will have made him madder than hell."

"Well, madder than hell is one thing. But he's no fool. A man like Anderson Collins knows his way around the law.

He's a savvy businessman, Alex. He's not going to do anything rash."

"How come you know so much about him, Ben?"

Ben smiled into the phone. "I was wondering when we'd get to that. I don't know him, but my sister does. She knows all about him; his previous company with Kelly Kirkland; his divorce from his ex-wife Melissa; how he lost half of his assets in the settlement. So, you see, Alex, he isn't about to turn over a large settlement to another woman, even if it means risking his reputation."

Alex drew a sharp breath, and snapped sarcastically, "What reputation?"

"Anderson Collins doesn't care," Ben continued. "He relies on charm, wits, and inflated promises. Sometimes he wins, sometimes he doesn't. But he plays hard, plays dirty, and there are as many people who dislike him as there are those who are enamored. Somehow he always manages to stay within the boundaries of the law, Alex, like I said…he's savvy. But he didn't become successful on morals and ethics."

"How does your sister know all this?" Alex was amazed Ben hadn't told her before.

"My sister began dating Kelly Kirkland about six weeks ago. I told her about your situation the day after you walked out, after I finished my day in court."

"You told her? Why?"

"Because I think she can help."

Alex's hope rose a little for the first time since she'd had Ben send the letter. "How, Ben? What do I have to do?"

"Not with Anderson, with your situation. My sister can get you a job."

Her hopes instantly fell flat, although not entirely. "Oh." She couldn't disguise the disappointment. "I thought you meant about the harassment."

"I know, honey, I'm sorry."

Alex hadn't meant to sound so ungrateful. A shard of shame washed over her. "No, I'm sorry, Ben. I didn't mean to say that. You've been really good to me. I'm thankful for your help, whatever it is."

She could hear his tone had lightened a little when he spoke next. "Well, there's a temporary opening in Kelly's firm. It came up unexpectedly. Real estate, prime location. You already have a shoo-in."

Appreciation temporarily lifted Alex. "Oh, Ben, that's terrific. And temporary's great. When do they want me to start?"

He chuckled. "Well, you have to interview first, and it's not a sure thing, but Sue thinks he'll take you if I recommend you. And I did. Your interview is this afternoon, at three."

She listened while he went on to tell her how one of the sales guys had taken off without warning, something about caring for a sick relative for a couple of months. "You'll be helping the team cover his area, and I hear it's prime."

"Ben?" she couldn't help but wonder, and had to ask. "You said Kelly used to be partners with Anderson...what do you know about Kelly's firm?"

"It's a reputable company, Alex, and nothing like Anderson Collins. That's the reason they split. Their moral values didn't match. Kelly is a good guy."

Alex arrived for the interview on time, confident and eager. Kelly arrived to escort her to his office, and she noticed she didn't flinch when he placed a hand on her shoulder. Something about his appearance; his wavy, light-brown hair; his eyes, dark as licorice; and the many laughter lines creasing his mouth, instantly put her at ease. During her eight months with Ben, she'd met his sister only a handful of times. She liked Sue Ryan, and she took to Kelly Kirkland on sight.

Kelly studied Alex while she answered his questions. He knew more than she realized about her nightmare. Now that he'd seen her; her beauty, her innocence, it came as no surprise. *So, the dirty swine's still up to all his old tricks. Someone needs to take him down.*

He listened while she spoke, summed up her ability, and made his decision. By four o'clock, Alex had returned to her apartment in a more positive frame of mind and with a new job. Kirkland and Associates, on Van Ness Avenue, had a large team of associates, sales agents, brokers, and finance professionals filling numerous offices on two floors of a four-story building.

"It's for three months," she told Ben, calling him the minute she arrived home. "Or until Russell Ross returns." *And I hope you don't.* Guilt stabbed her, aware she'd come by the position purely through misfortune. "I start tomorrow."

Alex sensed trouble immediately. A particularly melancholy Jessica answered the phone when she called her next to share the good news.

"What's wrong?" she asked, her heart already sinking.

"Things have become worse since you left yesterday," Jessica said. "I know about the letter and his attitude's been awful. You've made him madder than hell. He's not used to losing, Alex. He's not going to let this go."

"That's good," Alex said, "I don't want him to let it go. I want him to know he can't get away with it. Maybe I'll get my day in court after all."

"Alex." Jessica paused. "If he comes after you, it won't be in court. I'm afraid for you. He's calling you a coward and a liar. He's making up all kinds of nasty rumors about how you walked out after *he* rejected *your* advances, how you did the same to the other guys in the office. He's going to try to sully your reputation so that no one else will employ you."

For a moment, Alex couldn't speak. "Jessica," she struggled to take in what she'd just heard, "that's absolutely ridiculous. No one's going to believe that. The other guys in the office know I didn't do that. They'll say something."

"Don't be so sure." Jessica's voice had dropped to a whisper. Alex could barely hear.

"They don't want to cross him. No one does. He's rich and successful. He's got a lot of clout in this business, Alex, and he could make their lives hell."

Alex gritted her teeth, and spoke far more sharply than she'd intended. "Then you have to say something, Jessica. You know none of it's true. I know you don't want to, but if this gets to court, and he slanders my name, you need to do the right thing. I'm going to be counting on you."

Ben took Alex to dinner that night to celebrate, but the glow of her new job had already been extinguished.

"Something wrong? Nervous about the new job tomorrow?"

"No, Ben. I'm looking forward to that." She picked at her nails, remained silent for a minute. "What's the relationship like now between Kelly Kirkland and Anderson Collins?"

Ben sighed. "Why? What does it matter?"

"Humor me."

"They're fierce rivals. All the old hostilities are still remembered." He eyed her from across their table. "What are you up to?"

She avoided his gaze. "Nothing. Let's order dessert."

Jessica slumped on her couch, eyes staring blankly at the TV, having spent another long, lonely evening without Judd. Once again, he'd been out by the time she arrived home. Something about meeting some guys, he'd said in his message. *What guys?* Judd didn't have any friends. He didn't socialize. He didn't have a job. *So where are you going?* She doubted he'd be home before morning, he usually wasn't, and that revived her nagging suspicion. *Where do you go after dark? What do you do all these evenings?*

Her thoughts switched to Detective Jackson. When she'd called, a few days ago, he hadn't forgotten, although he had been a little taken aback by her call.

"What are you doing in San Francisco?" he'd asked, surprised.

"I could ask you the same thing," she replied.

Jackson had agreed to keep an eye on Judd. "I'm sure he's fine," he'd said, attempting a reassurance that barely scratched the surface. "I'll let you know if there's anything to worry about."

Too late for that, I've been worried for months.

"I'm busy with a case," he'd warned, "I won't have much time. Hope you understand."

She did–the woman who'd survived her attack–but she didn't feel any better. "Please don't mention this to Judd," she'd pleaded. The distance between them had already grown wider than she liked.

Nothing on the TV could shake the sense of foreboding. Nothing grabbed her interest. She switched it off and the apartment became silent. Too silent. Her thoughts seemed louder in the eerie quiet. *Could you really be mixed up in murder?* The police reports had warned the public to be on the lookout for a loner; someone with a personal vendetta; a white male, they suspected. *The age and profile could easily fit Judd.* Even if her gut told her one thing, her heart would never accept it.

What about the Mercedes? Could he be the murderer, in which case it couldn't be Judd, or had she attracted the attentions of some other crazed lunatic? Her head ached with trying to sort it all out. Then there was Alex. Her words from this afternoon came flooding back: 'I expect you to do the right thing. I'm going to be counting on you'.

Jessica buried her face in her hands, and wept. For what seemed an eternity, she sobbed, doubled over on the couch, her head between her knees, her fingers pressed into her eyes. The pain of the last two decades tore through her, searing her insides with its razor-sharp edges, pounding against her ribs with every shudder, burning her throat, stealing her breath, and stinging her eyes until she had nothing left. Finally, when the sobbing subsided, she pushed herself up from the couch, and went over to the window, where she peered out through the slats. *See, there's no one out there.* Darkness had wrapped the street in its clutches, but from the public lighting, and the glow from the moon, she saw no evidence of a lurking maniac in a Mercedes. The slats fell back into place when she stepped away, willing Judd to come home so she would know that if another murder happened tonight, it wouldn't have been because of him.

He saw her move the blinds; watched her peer through the slats; and he smiled with contentment. He knew he had her scared out of her wits. Not only that, he knew she was alone. *Should have stayed at the window a little bit longer.* A sneer contorted his lips. If she had, she might have seen the shiny, silver Mercedes cruise slowly past the apartment one more time, before cresting the hill, and disappearing into the night. Waiting.

Chapter Twenty-Five

Jessica awoke with a start. *What time is it?* She glanced groggily at the clock on her bedside table. *Shit.* She threw back the covers, stumbled out of bed, and hurried into the bathroom, already late for work and fearful of what Anderson might do.

As she stood in front of the mirror, brushing her teeth, and staring at her tired, pale reflection, something unexpected came over her, and she sat down on the edge of the bath, and stopped brushing.

"Fuck Anderson," she muttered under her breath.

Could it be courage? She wandered slowly down to the kitchen. *I don't know what that feels like. How would I know?* Something seemed lighter in her heart, even though sickness, worry, still rolled in her stomach. *Maybe it's defiance.*

She stifled a nervous giggle, forced herself not to think about the rent, and what would happen if Anderson fired her for arriving late with no good reason, and fixed herself a pot of coffee. Today, this morning, she would get to talk to Judd. On her way to the kitchen, passing his bedroom, she noticed the door had been closed. Judd had left it open when he'd gone out last night, which meant he'd come home. At what time, she had no idea, but it didn't matter. He hadn't left. She'd heard the sound of snoring on her way to the kitchen. While she waited, she scanned the morning paper, telling herself that wasn't the reason. All the same, she couldn't deny the relief at finding no further murders had been reported.

Might as well check the jobs. She flipped to the classifieds. *Who knows, after today?*

"Morning sleepy." She looked up at the sound of bare feet slapping lightly on the cold, tiled floor, about twenty minutes later.

"Morning. What are you still doing here?" Judd wandered over to the coffee and poured himself a cup, yawning and scratching his head.

"Taking control." A piston fired in her belly.

"What?" He sat down at the table, opposite, and stared at the paper. "Are you looking for another job?"

"Maybe." She raised her eyes to meet his, ignoring his surprise, determined not to miss this chance. If she didn't ask now, she might have to wait days before she saw Judd again.

"I thought you hated things changing."

"Well, Judd, it's time for change. I stayed home to talk to you. I want to know what's going on. Why you're out every night. Why you won't get a job. Why you're so secretive. And I'm not going back to work until you tell me."

He coughed, looked at her in surprise, sipped his coffee. She saw the shutters come down, locking her out.

"I don't know what you're talking about. I'm not up to anything. And why do you care if I work? I give you my share of the rent, don't I?"

"Where does the money come from?"

"That's my business." His voice had become like granite. Inwardly Jessica winced. He never used to take such a harsh tone with her. *When did I lose you?*

"Judd," she tried not to sound accusing, "I'm just worried. I just want to know you're not in any trouble."

"I'm not."

He pushed back his chair and moved away from the

table. He couldn't bear the look in her eyes, the hurt on her face. If he stayed any longer, he'd tell her. He couldn't; not yet. If she found out too soon, it would ruin everything. He loved her too much to lie, but he couldn't tell her the truth. Not if he wanted to keep her alive.

"I have to go."

Without another word, he left the kitchen, the scorching from her eyes burning his back.

Don't ask, Jessica, don't ask. He prayed that when he came tonight, she'd already be deeply asleep.

Alex pushed open the glass door, and stepped into the foyer of Kirkland and Associates, energized and excited. The place had a dynamic smell, even the lobby. She sniffed, breathed it in, let it wash over her. Best of all; no Anderson Collins. No sexual predator.

"Ahhhh." She let out a contented sigh, and became aware of a pair of eyes watching her with amusement. "Sorry." She walked across to the reception. "Nervous, excited, all those things."

Within a few minutes, she found herself whisked off in all manner of directions, subjected to handshakes, greetings, a flurry of names she'd never remember, in and out of an assortment of offices, more handshakes, and, finally, deposited at the work station of Russell Ross, next to a heavy-set woman Alex guessed to be about five years her senior.

"Julie Lovelady," the other woman said, smiling, and holding out a chubby hand.

"Alex Sullivan." She returned the smile, gripped the hand, and completed the introduction. "Tell me what to do."

Alex sped through the morning, listening, observing,

digesting. By lunch time, she had already built a rapport with her mentor, and felt comfortable enough to probe, ask a few questions.

"Why did Russell leave so abruptly?"

Julie snorted. "Russell can be odd."

"Kelly says he's one of your top sales guys."

"Not one of, Alex, Russell is *the* top sales guy."

"You don't seem to like him."

"Oh," Julie shot her a grin, "was I that obvious?"

Alex wondered if the animosity stemmed from competitiveness. Already aware the real estate world could be cut-throat, she decided it was probably quite logical that the two most highly regarded agents in the same office might not always get along.

"Russ is an extrovert." Julie must have sensed a need to explain, and Alex listened with interest. "On the surface, he's gregarious, friendly, vibrant, the kind of guy everyone likes."

"But?"

"He has a dark side. Just something about him that's not quite right. You know the type?"

Alex nodded. "Seems like every place has one of those types."

After showing up more than two hours late, and having been subjected to another austere mood and the even deeper scrutiny of Anderson Collins all afternoon, Jessica had reached the point where she no longer cared what he did. Feigning a headache, she grabbed her belongings, and waltzed out of the office, leaving him thunderstruck and furious.

Behind the wheel of her car, she sighed, snapped her phone shut, shifted into reverse, and, instead of going home, took off early for the long trek alone to Sacramento. Judd would have ruined her afternoon, even if Anderson hadn't done so first.

Judd's message, even briefer than usual, told her he wouldn't be going tonight and she'd have to go to Park Glenn alone. Jessica eased her aging Taurus onto Lombard Street, where she joined a throng of other equally tired commuters. Like a trail of multicolored, metallic ants, they snaked their way through the congested streets toward the busy interstate eighty. *Damn you, Judd.* If he knew how much she hated making this trip alone, how she hated being back in Sacramento–the place that stored all her bad memories–he wouldn't make her do it.

He knows I hate it. Anger simmered near the surface. *Not a good thing before a drive.*

She forced her thoughts elsewhere, pushed a CD into the stereo, and settled back into her seat, hoping the music would soothe her.

Immediate panic filled Jessica when she got to Park Glenn and couldn't find her mother in her room. She checked the dayroom and came up empty. *Please don't tell me she died.* Her heart pounded in her chest, sending a ringing into her ears, a weird sensation into her head. *Am I going to faint?* She stopped for a second, leaned up against a wall in the long corridor that led back to the main reception, and tried to collect her thoughts. *Maybe Eleanor took her outside for a walk in the grounds.*

"Eleanor's not on duty today," a young nurse she'd never seen before said, when she reached the reception and asked about her mother.

Jessica ran passed her and back outside. *Could she be out here all by herself? Could she have slipped past all the staff?*

She searched the grounds, ran back to the parking area, racked her brain, trying to think where a bewildered woman, living more than two decades in the past, might possibly go.

"Oh, Mom," she wailed under her breath, a gentle breeze blowing strands of hair across her sweaty cheeks. "Where are you? Please don't have come to any harm."

She stopped dead in her tracks, three hundred feet from the entrance to Park Glenn. Arm in arm, a man and a woman strolled across the lawn, back toward the building.

Mom. Temporarily stunned, she stared, transfixed, glued to the spot. She watched them walk together; her mother in a filmy outfit that billowed out around her as she moved. The man, youngish it seemed, and tall, didn't have on the white uniforms the nurses all wore. She couldn't make him out. They'd disappeared into the lobby before Jessica pulled herself out of her trance.

Her mother hadn't been outside in years. Jessica began to move, slowly at first, and then faster, until her feet flew over the lawns, and she careened back into the reception.

Frantic, and aware she looked disheveled, she asked a nurse returning to the front desk, "Where's my mother? Where can I find my mother?"

"Miss, are you all right?"

She brushed aside the nurse's concern. "My mother, she was just outside. Marianne Croft. Where is she? Was she with Judd?"

"I'm sorry Miss, I don't know any Judd," the nurse said, a frown replacing an earlier smile, "but Marianne Croft is back in her room. Are you her daughter?"

"She never goes outside." Jessica tried to calm down, tried to regulate her breathing so she could speak more clearly, and make sense of the situation. "Yes, I am her daughter, and I'm sorry, I panicked when I couldn't find her. She's never outside, you see. Did she…did she take a walk with my brother?"

The nurse's smile returned. "Ah, yes, a nice young man. Said he was her son."

Jessica's pulse began to settle, but her confusion only grew. *Why would you go without me? Why make me drive alone, Judd?*

"Did he leave a name?"

"Yes, I think so, let me check." The nurse turned to pull open the book laying on the counter, and Jessica saw a page of names.

Impatient to get to her mother, to Judd, she told the nurse, "Never mind. Did he take her back to her room? I need to talk to my mother."

"No, he left her here with me, I just took her back myself." She looked over Jessica's shoulder and shrugged. "He must have already left. Are you sure you're all right, Miss?"

Jessica had already turned her back, to race back outside and confront Judd. Furious, she ran faster and faster, over the grounds, calling his name. Not until she reached the parking lot, and leaned up against her own car, panting, and soaked with sweat, did she realize his truck had gone. It dawned on her that his truck hadn't been there when she'd arrived. *Wait a minute*. As she turned her eyes to the road, and heard the sound of squealing tires, she caught the flash of something familiar, and a silver Mercedes careened out of the car park and onto the road, speeding off in the opposite direction.

Wild-eyed with fear, Jessica ran back into Park Glenn, more anxious than ever to reach her mother. She didn't even stop at reception. Winded, frightened, bewildered, Jessica stopped in the doorway of Marianne's room to catch her breath. On her bed, a look of tranquility on her face such as she'd never seen, Jessica stared at her mother.

At that moment, as though she'd never been ill in her life, as if she knew her own daughter, Marianne looked up. She smiled, a rare beam of pure elation. "He came, Jessie, he came."

"Who came, Mom?" Jessica crossed the room, and took her mother's bony hands in her own. She watched the beam slip away, the light flicker out. "Who, Mom?" she whispered, but Marianne had slipped back into the past.

On her way back out of the home, Jessica stopped by the front desk. The same nurse as before looked up, smiled, spoke kindly. "Feeling better, dear? Did you find your mother?"

"Yes, thank you. You said you had a name," Jessica asked, as calmly as she could. "One of my brothers just visited our mother, Marianne Croft. Please…could you tell me which one?"

"Of course." The nurse smiled. "He said he was Cameron Croft."

Chapter Twenty-Six

Jessica made a hasty call on her way to her car, got the answer machine, left a message, and snapped her phone shut. Park Glenn quickly disappeared in her rearview mirror. She sped back to the freeway, and floored her car, desperate to get home, her mind in turmoil. Someone was playing a very sick game. At nine o'clock, when she pulled onto their driveway, relief flooded through her at the sight of Judd's red pickup. *Good.* Maybe he had some answers. Without knocking, she barged straight into his room. He lay on his back, eyes closed, his light still on.

"Judd." She shook his leg.

He opened his eyes. "I'm not asleep. How's Mom?"

"You tell me," she almost yelled.

He attempted to sit up. "What do you mean?"

She stared angrily into his deep blue eyes; eyes like her own, yet sated with secrets. "I want to know where you were tonight, Judd. Tell me the truth."

"What's gotten into you?" He stared back. "Has something happened?"

"Why do you ask?"

"Because you're acting weird. What the hell's wrong with you, Jessie?"

Jessica exploded. "I'll tell you what's wrong with me. I went to see Mom, tonight, only I couldn't find her." He opened his mouth to speak, but she didn't let him. "I searched all over the grounds, panicking, thinking she was dead, wishing you hadn't made me drive there alone, and when I did eventually find her, Judd, you know what she said? She told me he came to visit. I asked her who. And she said nothing."

She drew a breath, and this time Judd didn't try to interrupt. "She was gone again, or maybe she was never there to begin with, because I stopped at the reception on my way out and I asked the nurse which of my brothers came to visit, and she told me, Judd. She told me Cameron came to visit, and that's what Mom meant, she meant Cameron came to see her." Aware she'd begun shouting, and rambling, Jessica stopped. "But he couldn't have. Cameron is dead."

She looked at Judd, and realized his face had gone white. His posture had changed to one of alarm. Bolt upright on the bed, he gripped her hand. "What do you mean, Cameron came?"

"That's what the nurse said, and that's what Mom said." She sighed, suddenly overcome with exhaustion. "You should have seen her, Judd. For that one split second, I've never seen her look so happy."

"Jessie," Judd shook her by the arm. "Did you see him?"

Jessica shook her head, too tired, too spent from her outburst, the fears, the panic, the terror of the past few months, even to register the distress in Judd's voice. "No, only from the back. I didn't see his face. He wore a baseball cap. But," her voice grew more resigned, "I saw a car speeding off when I went outside to look for you, a silver one, a sports car. I've seen it before, it's always the same one."

"What do you mean, Jessie? What car? What are you talking about?"

"Someone is following me, Judd. They have been for a while. I'm going to bed."

Without another word, she got up from where she'd been sitting on the edge of his bed, and left his room. Judd lay back on his bed, thinking, waiting. He heard her move about in the bathroom, heard her bedroom door closing, heard her bed creak, and then silence. He lay still, listening. She'd sleep more soundly knowing he was home. He waited, and waited. When he'd heard no more sounds from his sister's room in over an hour, he made a call. A few minutes before eleven, when he thought she'd be fast asleep, he opened and closed the front door quietly, and crept down the driveway. Down the road a few feet, a car sat waiting with its engine running, and Judd hurried over. He got in the passenger side, and still had his hand on the door when the car sped away from the curb. The driver looked across at him, irritated. "So what's so urgent you had to get me out of bed in the middle of the night?"

"Something's come up." Judd settled back into the seat. "She saw someone tonight at Park Glenn. I had a feeling he might go there."

"How the hell could he have known?"

"I don't know. Somehow, he figured it out."

"Does she know?"

"No. She had no idea."

"Shit. I don't like this, Judd. We're putting her in danger. Your mother, too."

"I know."

A short silence. "Jessica called me tonight."

Judd turned his head, stared at the driver. "She did? What did she want?"

The driver kept his eyes on the road. "Did she tell you about the car? The one she says has been following her?"

"What?" Judd cried. "You know about that? I didn't

know until tonight. Why am I only finding out now? And why did she call you? She isn't supposed to know anything."

"Calm down. I didn't tell her anything. But I'm beginning to think keeping her in the dark isn't such a good idea."

Judd ignored him. "What did she say when she called?"

"She left me a message. Told me about the silver Mercedes she saw at Park Glenn this afternoon. She believes she has a stalker, Judd. He tried to run her off the road, and she says it's the same one she almost rammed at the grocery store. She asked me to call her back."

"You can call her back, but she can't find out," Judd warned. "We're too close. We can't lose the trail now. I can almost taste him."

"What we're doing is dangerous. We're gambling with people's lives. I should never have let you talk me into this. I should have known better."

Judd choked back a sarcastic laugh. "But you didn't know better. If it wasn't for me, you wouldn't know anything at all. In fact, if you hadn't waltzed into the bar that night, you still wouldn't know. And how did you know I'd be in the bar that night? I've been trying to figure that out." He looked across at Detective Jackson, who didn't take his eyes off the road.

"Hunch," Jackson replied.

"My ass," Judd shot back. "She told you, didn't she? Jessie put you up to it."

"How would Jessica know where I might find you? She told me you never tell her anything."

"I see." Judd turned to face front, a wry grin on his lips. "When did she tell you that, Jackson? When she called and asked you to put a trace on my ass?"

"You can stay at my place tonight," Jackson said,

changing the subject. "Tomorrow, I'm going to look into getting your mother moved."

Hours later, after he'd finished pleasuring himself with a few of his favorite girlie magazines, he tossed his empty beer bottle onto the bedroom floor, on top of the pile of clothes he'd thrown down there earlier. Almost a week had gone by and his cheek had started to heal, although it stung tonight from the makeup. He couldn't risk the pretty little nurse seeing the long jagged scar. Once again, he wished he'd stayed until he'd finished the screaming bitch off. Marianne hadn't noticed it, and if she had, she hadn't said anything. She had just been so happy to see him, her beloved Cameron, whom she hadn't seen in so many years. *How many has it been now?* He counted back. *Jeez*, he whistled under his breath, *more than twenty years.* She hadn't seen him in all that time, and when she'd strolled with him this evening, she'd acted as though it had only been yesterday. *Of course,* he realized with a sneer, *I could have been Elvis Presley and she would have believed that, too. Wow.* He wondered if he might try that next time. The idea amused him enormously. He'd enjoyed their walk and their little chat. For a kook, she'd been remarkably lucid, a pleasant surprise. Years ago, when he'd first read about her in the paper, first began collecting the stories and planning his revenge, he'd wanted to one day meet her.

Her pathetic old man blowing his brains out all over the living room floor had really done a number on her. He smiled as he thought about that. She was crazy as a loon. He liked crazy people. He sensed a connection. He rolled onto his back on top of the bed and covered himself with a sheet. Thoughts of crazy Marianne mixed with the bitter smell of beer from the empty bottle lying nearby filled his senses. A smile formed on his thin lips and he drifted into a deep, contented sleep.

The next morning, Jessica rose early, showered, dressed, and made her way to Judd's room, hoping to see him before she headed into work. *Damn.* She swore at the empty room, his bed unmade as if he'd just climbed out.

Noise traveled so easily throughout the small apartment, she knew he'd already left. As she let herself out of the apartment some twenty minutes later, she noticed his truck on the driveway. Judging by the morning dew all over it, it had been there all night. *That's odd.* She frowned, and toyed with the phone in her pocket. *Where would you be without your beloved truck?* As easy as it was to hop on a cable car, a tram, or a bus to get around town, Judd never did that. He never went anywhere without his truck. Unable to think of a good explanation, she pulled out her phone and dialed his number. *Of course.* Irritation puckered her lips. She didn't bother to leave a message.

A flurry of activity greeted Alex, when she arrived at Kirkland & Associates for her second morning. "What's going on?" she said to a frenetic Julie.

"Only the biggest opportunity ever." Julie bustled with excitement, showering Alex with flyers, photographs, details of a magnificent looking property in the Presidio. "We've just been asked to present a proposal this afternoon for Barclay Sanders' home."

"The author?" Alex looked at her in amazement.

"Yes, that Barclay Sanders." She tossed Alex a set of property particulars. "Count the zero's," she said, chuckling with delight.

"Wow." Alex whistled. "How does that equate in commissions?"

Julie giggled. "Ah, a girl after my own heart. It equates in that it would have been Russell's and now it's ours. If we win, that is. Guess I shouldn't assume."

"Ours?"

"Yes. I want you to help me."

Alex could barely breathe. A win like that would be enormous. *It would put me on the map.* Big enough to garner plenty of attention. Enough even to reach the ears of... "Can I ask you something?"

"Hit me."

"How many firms are competing?"

"Besides us, probably three or four. We'll have some significant rivals."

"Is Anderson Collins among them?" She remembered Ben's words over dinner.

"Ohhh." She watched Julie's eyes twinkle with glee. "So you've heard the rumors?"

Alex nodded. "Oh, yes. I've heard all about them."

"Anderson is one of our biggest competitors, and the most ruthless. He'll be prospecting, and he'll stop at nothing to win."

Exactly what I was hoping. "Then we'll have to make sure we don't let him." She gave Julie a knowing smile. "Let's get started. Tell me what you need me to do." *I can't stop you lying, I may not be able to stop you slandering my name, and it seems I can't get you into court, but I can still take you down, you arrogant bastard. And what better way than on your own turf?*

At that moment, Alex's mobile rang. She saw Jessica's

number on the display. "I better take this," she apologized to Julie, excusing herself for a minute.

"Alex." Jessica's voice sounded peculiar; unnaturally loud, shrill.

"What's wrong, Jess?"

"I need to talk to you. Can you meet me after work?"

She heard the sharp pants for breath, the struggle to maintain her composure. "I'm working tonight, it's Wednesday. Is everything all right?"

"No."

Her heart sank. "Is it Anderson?" This wasn't the time. With Julie just a few feet away, it also wasn't the place.

"No," Jessica squeaked. "It's much worse. Call me before you go to Harry's."

Alex heard the line go dead, and closed her phone, wondering what could be going on in Jessica's life that was worse than Anderson. She'd suspected a dark past, secrets, maybe something sad, but how bad could it be?

Jessica wondered if she could really go through with it. *Can I trust her?* The secrets had been buried for so long, they belonged to another era, another life, not the one she had now. *But that's not true. Someone knows. How else would they know about Cam?*

Whoever had been at Park Glenn yesterday knew all about her brother. They must know all about her father if they'd figured out where they could find her mother. How they'd found out, she had no idea, but she suspected it had something to do with the silver Mercedes.

To dig deeper into that, she needed to talk to Jackson; but he hadn't called back. That left her with only one other option. *Please, Alex, please call back.*

Alex rejoined Julie and poured over the property specifics, her mind back on her own agenda; a smell of triumph in the air. Side by side, they worked up numbers, bounced around ideas, discussed marketing plans, advertising, prospective purchasers, preparing the home, and coming up with a winning strategy that would oust the competition.

"No gimmicks," she told Julie. "Just honest, insightful, and outstanding. That's what it takes to win."

"Anderson won't see it that way," Julie mused. "He'll come in with a spectacular bid; one that any seller will find hard to resist, even a millionaire like Barclay Sanders. Somehow, he'll have market evidence to back it up."

"So will we." Alex grinned at Julie. "I don't doubt he'll be ostentatious, he'll be glitzy, he'll be brazen. That's what I'm counting on."

All afternoon, jerking this superlative win out from under Anderson's nose fueled Alex, driving her, inspiring her to tap into a creativity she didn't know she had. She worked like a demon, guided by Julie, putting everything she had into preparing a principled, yet unpredictable presentation that would expose Kirkland's strengths and electrify Barclay Sanders. When she got home that evening, worn-out but buzzing with excitement and anticipation, Jessica popped back into her thoughts. Before she called, Alex made a quick call to Narcotics to get an update on John. *Should have done this ages ago.* She waited impatiently for an officer to come on the line and fill her in.

"Can't give you any details," the officer said, "except we're closing in."

"How long does it take?" She tried not to be rude. "It's been ages since my initial report."

"Takes as long as it takes, ma'am." She sighed at the indifference in his voice. "We'll be moving in soon. I'm sorry, but that's all I can tell you."

"Will you let me know?"

"Yes," the officer confirmed. "Someone will call."

"And you'll keep my name out of it?"

"Best we can."

Jessica answered before Alex even heard the phone ring. "I don't know where to begin," she said, launching headlong into an almost incoherent ramble the moment she heard Alex's voice. "Everything's happening so fast. My brother has been acting so weird, the police haven't called me back, someone's pretending to be Cameron, and I know I'm being followed. Alex, I don't know what to do."

Taken aback by the outburst, it took Alex a couple of seconds to make sense of everything she'd just heard. "Slow down, Jess," she said, "try to stay calm. Now, what do mean by the police?" *What on earth could Anderson have done that warrants the police?*

"Detective Jackson, Mac Jackson."

"I don't know who that is. You said you're being followed? Who's following you? Is that why you called the police?"

"Yes, but that's not all." Jessica sounded fatigued

"Take a deep breath, Jess," Alex advised, "and tell me, as calmly as you can, what's going on."

She heard Jessica breathe in and out a couple of times, trying to do as she suggested. When she spoke again, her words came out more slowly, an effort noticeably forced. "I can only tell you this once, Alex, so please listen hard," Jessica said. "I know you don't have much time."

"Take all the time you need," Alex kindly offered. *Harry will understand.*

Another deep, shuddering breath, and Jessica began. "My family has a dark past. My brother and I moved here from Sacramento, after we lived in foster care for ten years. Judd is all I have." A brief pause, and then a launch into forbidden territory. "My eldest brother was murdered when I was eight. A year later, my father killed himself, and my mother was carted off to a mental home. She's still there."

Alex said nothing, while Jessica stopped to take another breath. "Judd has been in trouble with the law; drugs; theft; alcohol; the usual things. For the past few weeks, I've seen a change in his behavior. He stays out late, often all night, he doesn't have a job, and some of those nights have...some of those nights have coincided with the murders, Alex. That's why I called the police."

"What did they say?" Alex heard her own voice come out as little more than a whisper. Horrified, she wondered how Jessica had kept this all to herself for so long.

"The detective, Mac Jackson, is the same one as before."

"Same one as before...what?"

"He dealt with Cameron's murder back in Sacramento. He transferred here some time ago, I guess. He was the same cop that came to our house the night my father shot himself. So, when I learned he was here, I called him about Judd, because I didn't know what else to do. But he hasn't called back. I just wanted him to watch Judd."

"I'm sure he'll call, he–"

"You don't understand." Jessica stopped, and when she continued Alex heard the hysteria beginning to set in. "It's not just about Judd. Someone is visiting my mother in the mental home, pretending to be my dead brother. Someone knows about us, Alex, and I can't get Jackson to call me back. And whoever knows, whoever is doing this to me, is right here in town…and I think he's coming after me."

"How do you know that?" Alex was aghast.

"He drives a silver Mercedes. I saw it leaving the asylum the night he saw my mother. The same car tried to run me off the road the day you joined Anderson's firm. And there've been other incidents, too."

"A silver Mercedes?" *Lots of people drive a silver Mercedes. Ben drives a silver Mercedes.* "You're sure?"

"I'm positive."

Alex's mind scrambled. "Are you saying Judd could be involved with the murders?"

"I don't know." Jessica sounded desperate. "I can't believe he could, but I don't know. I can't ignore the suspicion, that he's been out almost every one of those nights that someone got attacked. He doesn't have any friends, or a job, yet he brings home money. What am I supposed to think? He's been in trouble before, he's angry at everyone for what happened to our family. Maybe he's lost it, Alex. Maybe the crazy gene runs in our family."

And all the while I suspected John. Alex didn't know where to begin. Jessica's wounds ran so deep. She needed professional help. Someone trained to deal with death, with murder, madness, and psychological damage.

She could hear Jessica's ragged breathing, like she'd run out of air, waiting on the other end of the phone for rescue, salvation, whatever lifeline Alex could throw her.

"Jess, I don't even know what to say. I had absolutely no idea." Her mind reeled, spinning with all kinds of thoughts, suspicions, possible scenarios. *What the hell do I tell her?* She tried to think calmly. "Okay." *Maybe I have a good place to start*. "Jess, you said you called the police. Did say anything about your suspicions that Judd might be involved in the murders?"

"No. I just said I thought he might be in trouble. I asked Jackson to watch out for him, let me know if he found out anything I needed to know."

"Good. Let's keep it that way."

"But–"

"One thing at a time, Jess. You said he's all you have left, and if you want to keep him, don't jump to conclusions." She could only imagine the depths of Jessica's anguish. "There could be another explanation."

"Like what?"

"I don't know. I need time to think. But I don't think you should give up on him yet." An idea formed in Alex's head that she knew was probably both stupid and dangerous. On the other hand, the law hadn't come through for her, either. She understood the agony of waiting, of looking over one's shoulder, of living with fear, wondering when the next strike might come.

"I'm willing to listen to anything, Alex."

"I don't think you should mention your fears about Judd to anyone, and certainly not the police. If Jackson calls you back, tell him about the guy following you, that he pretended to be your brother, but leave Judd out of it. Tell him you overreacted. That you don't need him to watch your brother."

"Why would I do that? What if he is in trouble? I can't ignore–"

"Hear me out. You won't be ignoring him, Jess. If he is in trouble, if he is somehow involved, you'll find out. We're going to do a little detective work ourselves."

She held the phone away from her ear for the second that

Jessica screeched, "Are you crazy?"

"Probably," she said, "but do you have a better idea? You want to know what's going on, don't you? Your brother trusts you, doesn't he?"

"Yes."

"Well, think about it. The cops are busy. They're dealing with unsolved murders that are piling up. If you hand them your brother and tell them you think he's involved, they'll haul him in faster than a speeding bullet, especially with him having a record. And while they focus their attention on him, a real killer is out there, prowling for another victim."

Alex realized what she'd said. Jessica must have, too. "You believe he's innocent, don't you?"

"I can't possibly know that, Jess," she said, unwilling to lie to her friend, "but, if he's at all like you, then I don't believe he could be guilty of murder."

She heard something sounding like relief in Jessica's voice. "So, what do we do next?"

"We follow him. Next time he leaves the house. We find out where he goes, who he sees, what he does."

"How will we do that, Alex? He knows my car. I can't afford to rent one."

"So, we go in mine. He doesn't know me. You keep out of sight. He won't suspect a thing. We watch him, and if there's any trouble on one of those nights..." Alex shuddered, "well, then we'll know for sure."

After she'd hung up, Alex hurried to get ready for her shift, her thoughts crashing around in her head, banging into one another, wondering if Jessica had been right. *Maybe I am crazy. Only an idiot would do something like this.* She had absolutely no idea how to play detective, well aware she could be getting both of them in way over their heads. *What the hell am I doing?*

She grabbed her keys and headed for the door to walk the two blocks to Harry's. *Helping a friend, that's what.*

As Alex worked her shift that evening, her mind kept working its way back to everything Jessica had said. Back and forth she went, distracted, tempted to tell Harry, wanting advice, questioning her own wisdom. *What if Judd's crazy? What if he is involved? What if he sees us? We'll be dead, too. No one would know.* She wished she could ask Ben, but that was out of the question. He'd go straight to the police. *Wouldn't it just make more sense to go to the police and let them handle it?*

She served her customers with barely an acknowledgement, ignored quizzical gazes from Harry, pushed on through the evening, hearing Jessica's desperation over and again in her head, beseeching, despondent, hopeless. *Jessica's already a victim, she has nothing left to lose if Judd's gone.* Alex might not know the extent of Jessica's grief, but she remembered the pain and the emptiness of being alone. *I'd want her to help me*. Even though she hadn't when Alex had asked, she understood there'd been a good reason. If she'd gone to court, tried to stand up against Anderson, his attorney would have tried to discredit her as a witness. *This would have all come tumbling out.* Alex knew she'd made her decision; to stick by her friend. The plan would go ahead.

Chapter Twenty-Seven

Summer moved gently into fall, Alex and Julie worked diligently on Barclay's presentation, finally turning something quite magnificent over to his representatives for the author's consideration. The protracted wait for his decision weighed heavily on Alex, who had become more anxious than ever to sock the winning punch to Anderson.

So far, nothing had come of her letter. Even Jessica said he no longer mentioned it in the office. Alex knew he hadn't forgotten. A man that vindictive didn't forget.

With the buzz of the presentation over, at least until they heard from Barclay's people, Alex turned her thoughts back to the prospect of following Judd. For the past ten weeks, he hadn't given them a chance to put a tail on him, coming and going from the apartment when Jessica was not around. Alex had been preoccupied, allowing the idea to slip gradually from her thoughts, and she sensed Jessica might have had second thoughts.

"Think he suspects something?" she'd said to Jessica, a few weeks ago.

"I don't know," had been the reply. "Our paths have barely crossed."

"Well, one good thing," Alex had told her "There haven't been any more murders."

She thought about that during a quieter moment in the office this morning, wondering if the lull in attacks could mean the killer had been caught; perhaps not for murder–that would have made the news–but brought in for something else. *Like drugs.* No longer on the streets. Naturally, her thoughts turned to John. *Why didn't I say anything to Jessie?*

A few months ago, when Jessica had trusted her with her deepest secrets–those awful terrors from her past–Alex hadn't said a word about John. She'd let Jessica pour out her heart, give voice to her most acute fear that her brother might be involved, spill such galling, intimate details of her family's past, yet had said nothing about her own history with John. *And I suspected him, too. I could have eased her fears.* Yet she didn't. *Why didn't I speak up?* The thought had occurred to her before, but she'd just pushed it away. She knew why. *Shame. I was afraid she'd judge, that she'd think less of me.* Yet she'd had no trouble telling Sammy the previous year. The puzzling thought made her question herself, and, this morning, she began to examine her motives. *Is it easier to let someone else assume guilt, let someone else be flawed, than to face up to disgraces in my own past, with my own choices?* Jessica had the air of a victim. Alex didn't. *Would she think less of me for being married to a drug dealer, a possible killer? Would she think I harbored the same habits? Would she still look up to me if she knew I wasn't perfect?*

Alex began to see something she hadn't noticed before. She might be determined, capable, kind, even audacious to an extent–the letter to Anderson was evidence of that–but she lacked the depth to her soul that Jessica possessed. Jessica might have kept secrets, but she knew where she came from. She'd been humbled by her experiences, she'd faced demons that Alex couldn't even imagine, and she'd still risk what little she had left to right a wrong. She'd risk a friendship, her own brother. *Jessica never hides from the truth.* Alex tried to find excuses. *Maybe when you've been on the bottom for so long it doesn't matter what others think. Maybe you have nothing left to lose, no place else to fall.* She couldn't convince herself she hadn't been a coward; something Jessica was not.

Jessica had resigned herself to the strange familiarity that had settled over their lives. Alex had been so busy; Judd had been someone she rarely saw; Anderson had left her alone; there hadn't been another murder. Tedium and monotony had begun to replace fear. She hadn't stopped thinking about the Mercedes, even though she hadn't seen it for a while. Neither had she given up wondering about the stranger at Park Glenn. Judd had refused to discuss it any further, after that night it had happened, and even Detective Jackson had blown her off when he'd called back, a few days after she'd left him a message.

"You're probably suffering from too much stress," he said. "Understandable with all that you've been through. Anxiety's a strange thing, Jessica, it plays with your imagination. It can make you envisage all manner of things; even that you're being followed."

"I understand," she'd tried to be polite, "but I'm not imagining it. Despite what you think, I'm not crazy. Not yet." Back in Sacramento, Jackson had been a good detective, she remembered. What had brought about the change to where he no longer cared?

"It's an affluent area and there are probably hundreds of similar sports cars on the streets, Jessica. Can you even be sure it's silver? Could it be grey? Are you certain it's a Mercedes?"

Eventually, she'd begun to wonder if she had made a mistake, Jackson had been so persuasive. The memory of the ugly silver chain kept coming back, and she knew she hadn't.

"What about the man at Park Glenn? The one pretending to be my dead brother?" she'd persisted, "Are you telling me that I imagined that, too?"

"Of course not, although it is possible the nurse made a mistake. She may have simply misunderstood what the young man said."

She'd heard the tiredness in Jackson's voice. Jessica hadn't cared about that. She hadn't cared if he'd been up all night. He had to believe her.

"No one other than Judd and I knew about Park Glenn, about our mother," she'd said, "no one up until now. And now somebody else does. They know about that, they know about Cameron, and they must know about Dad to have found my mother. They know everything. Detective Jackson, I'm not making this up. That silver Mercedes is tied into all this, and I believe they're coming after me."

Shocked to realize how close Jessica had gotten to the truth, Jackson had reexamined his decision over and again to risk her life in trying to trap a killer. The constant doubt, and the worry, had kept him up nights; nights he'd spent at the station, pouring over every scrap of evidence, no matter how small, looking for something–anything–that would tie in to his killer.

For the past two months he'd wanted to have Marianne moved to another location, somewhere safer. Judd had refused. "We don't have enough. We need solid proof."

"You could get your sister killed," Jackson warned. "Your mother, too." The gamble to use Jessica as bait, and without her knowledge, went against all his instincts.

"All we have is a suspicion, and two anonymous notes. We have to have more, or he'll walk."

Jackson had reluctantly agreed. Even if both he and Judd knew the identity of the killer, they had nowhere near enough to prove it in a court of law. A move too soon would jeopardize everything. Robbie would crawl back into the woodwork, until he felt it safe to emerge, and rekindle his plan. All their progress would be lost. Initially, when he questioned Judd's own motives for keeping Jessica in the dark, he'd had no intention of following through with Judd's plan. Until Judd's response convinced him the risk was worth the danger.

"I'm trying to save her sanity," Judd had explained. "If she knows our brother's killer's family is coming after her, it will finish her off. Until you've seen a loved lose their mind, Detective, I don't expect you to understand. But I won't let you tell her. I won't let it happen to Jessie."

Jackson didn't bother to tell Judd that he couldn't prevent him from telling Jessica that her life was in danger. Instead, he thought about it, weighed his options; thought about his alternatives, and realized he had none. He didn't even tell Red, knowing Red would probably not have agreed. Thankfully, Red hadn't questioned the nightly appearances of Judd down at the station, helping Jackson with what he'd termed clerical duties.

One advantage Jackson still had were his friends on the force, back in Sacramento. After he'd ended his call to Jessica, he'd called in a favor and arranged to have a patrol car cruise by Park Glenn at least once a day for the next few months, looking for any more unusual activity. He'd also arranged for the nurses to contact him directly if Marianne Croft received any visitors. His efforts had seemed to appease Jessica, and she'd hung up sounding a little less stressed.

In the bathroom mirror, he surveyed the damage, turning his chin first to the left, and then to the right.

"Not bad," he told his reflection. The wound had practically healed, and a dark shadow had spread across his face. The unshaven look suited him, gave him a roguish appeal. "You should have done this before, handsome." Under the new stubble, the jagged mark from the keys barely showed. *Soon be time to get back out there.* Back in his bedroom, he picked up a girlie magazine, thinking about the weeks he'd wasted being cooped up, waiting for his face to heal. Lying low and hiding bored him. That made him angry.

He threw himself back on the bed, flipped through the pages of his magazine, picked out a tried and true favorite, and spent the next five minutes whipping himself up into a frenzy and enjoying the ecstasy. When he was done, he tossed the magazine down onto the floor, laid back on the bed, and stared at the ceiling, thinking about the others. He wondered if they ever thought about him. "If only you knew," he muttered to the ceiling.

He despised them. All of them. "No better than the cops," he sneered. "No fucking clue." Sick of the pretense, of having to fit into a society that offered him nothing but took everything, he needed to get back out there, back to business, back to the next level of his game.

The thought of games brought Marianne to mind. He rolled off the bed, rubbing the stubble on his chin, and made his way back into the bathroom.

Time I paid you another visit. He peered back in the mirror. *Wonder what you'll think of the new beard, Momma dear. What do you think of your big, handsome boy, all grown up?*

He took a long shower, and dressed in a pair of

handmade, luxury, denim jeans, a white silk shirt, and black Gucci shoes. *Why not?* He grinned, and splashed on a generous amount of expensive cologne. *You're worth it, Mother.*

He had expensive tastes, and loved to indulge; the racy sports car he'd bought a year ago had been his latest extravagance. *Time for another spin.* With a cackle of the insane, he left the apartment.

Later that afternoon, a crisp and sunny Wednesday in late October, he neared the grounds of Park Glenn. The commute had been awful. He flipped on his indicator signaling his intent to turn left at the same moment he spotted the patrol car parked in front of the hospital. *Fuck.* His face twisted into an ugly scowl and he glared. The presence of the black and white police unit brought up bile from his stomach. He hated the law. He hated any kind of authority.

"Fuck it," he spat angrily, flipping off the signal indicator and steering straight. He'd planned an afternoon of entertainment with Marianne, but it would keep. She wasn't the target.

He thought about Jessica, the one he wanted. *Figured it out, yet? Did you think you and your fucking nitwit of a brother would really get away with killing my father?* He raced against the light, swerved through a red, and whipped a u-turn, heading back toward the freeway, hating the wasted journey. The patrol car outside Park Glenn had surprised him. *What on earth could a bunch of old crazies be up to that would make the pigs come out?* Without a signal, he veered to the ramp, taking him onto the busy interstate, and gunned his engine, the powerful car lurching forward. He hoped one of them had fled the asylum, making a futile bid for freedom.

His mood vile now, enraged that he'd driven the ninety

miles for nothing, he decided he would take his revenge on a sleeping city. *Things have been too quiet, time for a little action, time I shook things up.*

As he mentally plotted out his evening, he began to feel better. Tonight, he would get back to business. He would trawl the streets of San Francisco again, and read all about himself in tomorrow's newspaper. As he swerved lanes, wove in and out of traffic, heading back towards San Francisco, he smiled.

Chapter Twenty-Eight

"Feel the buzz?" Julie asked Alex.

Alex nodded. "Must be decision day."

"About time. What's it been…two months?"

"Something like that. Guess when you're rich, you don't have to hurry."

The excitement seemed to have rippled throughout the office. All morning, Alex found both herself and Julie answering questions about how they felt, did they expect to win, how would they celebrate…and on it went.

"I can't handle this," Julie moaned. By eleven o'clock, she'd picked up her purse and sauntered out of the office.

"Wait up." Alex took off after her, desperate to escape the weight of pressure, and the mounting tension inside her. Today, just like Julie, just like all of Kirkland and Associates, she would either win or fail. Only, for her, it was personal. She followed Julie into The Coffee Bean, on Sutter Street, ordered a black coffee and sat down at one of the tables.

"You sure seem nervous," Julie said, seating herself opposite.

"I am." *So anxious I could almost throw up.*

"It'll be huge for Kirkland." Julie sipped her coffee.

Alex nodded, her mind not on Kirkland at all, but back in Anderson's office, with his huge perverted hands trapping her in the semi-circle of her chair, the sickly stench of his coffee-and-tobacco-soaked breath inches from her face. Disgusted by the memory, she screwed up her nose.

"Wow, you've got a face like sour milk," Julie said, with a snort of laughter, peering at her from across the table. "That bad?"

Alex stared at her, stared at her coffee, and laughed.

"That's better." Julie continued chuckling. "Pressure's a bitch."

"Isn't it just," Alex agreed. She picked up her mug, sipped the liquid, and decided to make a toast. She raised her mug in the air, to an amused look from Julie. "Here's to us, to winning, to putting Kirkland on the map, to Russell for being gone," she giggled at Julie's snort of laughter, "but most of all, here's to beating our adversaries, whoever they may be."

They clinked mugs, and lapsed into a comfortable chatter.

"It's one o'clock," Julie said, suddenly checking her watch. "I had no idea we'd been here so long. I haven't had this much fun in ages."

Alex's stomach lurched. "Think the decision is in?"

"Only one way to find out." They grabbed their things and left The Coffee Bean, linking arms in the warm afternoon air, for the short stroll back to the office.

"They're back," Alex heard someone yell, and the office immediately erupted.

A sea of faces, arms, fists punching the air, hands clapping, slaps on the back, and cheers confronted them…and Alex knew. Her face split into the widest grin, so wide she could feel her muscles stretching, aching, pulling…but she couldn't stop. An ear-splitting whoop beside her and Julie joined in the jubilation. The entire office seemed to be celebrating. Kelly waved from a corner, and Alex figured they'd get the details soon enough. She could wait. For now–for this wonderful, heart-stopping, breathless moment–she wanted to be all alone in savoring her own private victory; in toppling an arrogant, unscrupulous, manipulative man who had so easily discounted her as a worthy opponent; a man who believed women were nothing but playthings. She'd done it in his arena. She began to laugh; so hard each roar shook her body. Tears pooled in the corners of her eyes and ran down her cheeks. *Who knew success could taste so good?*

"I had my doubts," Kelly admitted, working his way through the crowd, and finally reaching her, still laughing, and Julie. "Right up until the last minute. Seems Barclay isn't into gimmicks. He wanted something creative and honest...and you delivered. I'm very proud of you both."

The atmosphere in the office remained upbeat for the rest of the day. By the time Alex got ready to leave, Julie had become pensive. "I'm really going to miss you, you know," she said, when Alex grabbed her jacket. "Russ will be back soon, and I have to be honest, I'm not looking forward to it. Too bad you can't stay."

Amid the hype and the focus on the presentation, her assignment had passed in a blur.

Alex had forgotten her time was almost up.

"Do you think there's any way he could keep me on?" she asked Ben, the phone hooked under her chin, while she got ready for another shift that night at Harry's.

"You can only ask," Ben said, in his typical, pragmatic way.

Alex had a slow, boring night at the restaurant. Few customers came in.

"Probably a blessing with Sarah out sick," Harry said, perched on a bar stool next to her. "So, big shot," she'd told him about her success today, "what comes next?"

"Don't know, Harry." For every step forward there seemed to be another one back. "I'm hoping they'll keep me on."

He patted her arm. "They will if they're smart. And you'll always have your old gig here, any time you want it. I got lucky when you called us that day."

"Oh, Harry." Alex put her arm around his waist. "You've been so good to me. I'm the one who got lucky. I don't know what I would have done if I hadn't found you, if I hadn't had this job."

"You'd have been just fine." He stood up, as though embarrassed at the emotion she heard cracking his voice. "Why don't you get off home. It's already nine. I can manage the rest of the night without you."

"Are you sure?"

"I'm sure."

Alex slid off her stool. "I'll just clean up that last table," their final customer had just departed, "then I'll go."

"Leave it," Harry ordered, "I'll take care of it. You go enjoy the rest of the evening with that fancy boyfriend of yours. And you tell him, if I were twenty years younger he'd have some serious competition." He grinned, and shooed her out the door.

Alex stepped out onto the darkness of Fillmore Street, waved goodbye to Harry through the window, and began her short trek home, phone clamped tightly to her ear, chattering to Ben and arranging for him to come over. Over the sudden roar of the engine, she didn't hear what Ben said. She turned her head, saw the black car mounting the sidewalk, and let the phone slip out of her hand. Shocked, she couldn't move, couldn't get out of the way, felt the sickening thud and the loud crack of her own bones breaking when the car barreled right into her.

Harry arrived first on the scene. By the time he got to Alex's body, lying in a crumpled, broken heap on the sidewalk, the driver had already sped off. He placed two fingers at her neck, found a pulse, and snatched up her phone from where she'd dropped it. On the other end, he heard a frantic male voice.

"Sorry." Harry disconnected the line and dialed 9-1-1. "Hit and run, Fillmore, hurry, she's still breathing."

Paramedics and police arrived promptly, whisked Alex's body away, and questioned Harry for whatever detail he could provide. "I didn't see much," he apologized, "only heard the squealing tires, the impact." He shuddered, sickened to his stomach. He remembered the voice he'd cut off. He opened the phone and looked for the last number dialed.

"Ben?"

"What the hell's going on?"

Ben sounded frantic. Harry spoke quickly. "This is Harry Hammond, Alex's boss at the restaurant. She's been in an accident. She's on her way to the hospital, Ben. I'm going there, too."

At the hospital, Ben and Harry sat in the waiting room, side by side, anxious while the doctors worked on Alex.

"What happened, Harry?" Ben asked, his head in his hands, his body hunched forward, elbows resting on his knees.

"I don't know." Harry closed his eyes, remembering the thud. "I closed early, she waved goodbye through the window, I saw her talking on her phone–"

"That's my fault. She might have heard the car if she hadn't been on the phone."

"She called you," Harry reminded him gently. "I heard a crash, and then I found her. I'm sorry I had to cut you off like that."

"You did the right thing."

"You must have heard the crash on the phone." That hadn't occurred to him before. "That must have been awful."

"I don't understand," Ben said. "She was on the sidewalk. How could she have–" He sighed and shook his head, "Harry, did you see anything? Anything at all?"

"A car speeding off in the distance, that's all. I'm sorry, he took off so fast I couldn't get the plates."

"Was there anything you could tell the police?"

"Not much. A dark vehicle, blue or black, I don't know which."

"Model?"

"I couldn't tell. I only saw the tail end before it disappeared. Just an awful hit and run."

"Probably a drunk." Ben rubbed his eyes.

"He took off without even stopping."

"How do you know it was a he?"

"I assumed, by the way he drove. Like a maniac. I'm so sorry, Ben, I wish I could have helped."

"You did. I'm glad you were there to call the ambulance as fast as you did." Ben shook his hand. "You might have saved her life."

"I wish I hadn't closed early. Then it wouldn't have happened."

"Don't," Ben said. "This has nothing to do with you, or me. I just hope they catch this guy."

"Ben?" He almost didn't want to ask.

"Yes."

"Do you...do you think it's possible this wasn't an

accident?"

Ben squeezed his eyes shut, tight. "I don't know."

"She told me about Anderson," Harry went on. "He's a customer here, although he hasn't been in for a while. He wouldn't be welcome if he did show up. I don't tolerate that kind of behavior against women."

"Did she…did she tell you about John?"

Harry shook his head.

"John is another bad seed from her past. I don't know, Harry. She was on the sidewalk. I think it's entirely likely this was no accident. If we're looking at attempted murder, I know two people with motive."

"Anderson Collins," Harry said.

Ben nodded. "And John Donnelly."

Fillmore Street would be a crime scene, crawling with pigs, which meant driving back the way he came was out of the question. He couldn't risk going anywhere near the area in the hit and run vehicle they'd all be trying to find. With a much better plan in mind, he drove stealthily, in the stolen black Acura, toward Baker Street.

When he reached the top of the hill, a few feet from the Baker Street apartment he saw the grey Ford Taurus on the driveway and the red pickup nowhere in sight. *Typical.* He cackled quietly and crowed with pleasure, muttering away to himself with the sheer brilliance of his plan. A few feet from their home, he switched off the engine, climbed out of the Acura, and took a quick look at the newly banged up fender. *Fantastic. Quite a dent for such a small thing.*

He slipped off his gloves, shoved them deep into his pocket, and slinked off into the cool night air, back in the direction of Fillmore Street and his precious little baby, parked just a short distance from Harry's, where he'd recently dined.

He wondered how Jessica would take the news when it reached her in the morning. The lights off in the apartment told him she must be in bed. He knew her pattern pretty well by now, well enough to know she never went out. *How I wish I could be there.* He quickened his pace. *How I wish I could see your sniveling face when you discover your friend is dead.*

The night is still young. He marched through the streets, until he finally reached his baby, gleaming under the moonlight, waiting like a faithful spouse for his return. He slipped behind the wheel of his best girl and headed off into the night, prowling for yet another, unsuspecting victim. In his mirror, he could see flashing lights in the distance. After a nice long nap, the police would soon be upping their game. It wouldn't be in time to prevent what he planned for tonight. San Francisco, and it's myriad bars, eateries, and night spots, provided perfect pickings. He slowed the car, trawling the neighborhood, searching for the right one, malice glinting back at him every time he checked his mirror, reveling in the knowledge that tonight's assault would be especially brutal.

Much later, in the early hours of the morning, before the veil of darkness had lifted, he swung his Mercedes towards home, satiated and calm. The evening had been extremely productive, and soon there would be a sinister discovery. He smiled, thinking about his victim; a narcissistic, arrogant, young bartender, aggressive and cocky. He'd watched the boy prance around the bar, owning the room, pursuing the women, acting like a jerk. Taking the stupid, young punk out had been easy. He'd lost the bravado the second he saw the knife. They all did. He'd enjoyed killing this one.

"Where's your bravado now?" he'd jeered in the kid's ear, one hand choking his airway, the other stabbing him repeatedly in the groin, before the razor sharp blade plunged deep into his chest. He thought about the sound of the blade grinding against the bones, and how much he'd enjoyed pulling it out to stab the boy again, and again. Finally, with a malicious sigh of satisfaction, he'd stood back and let the young man's lifeless body drop to the ground. After he'd wiped the blade on the dead man's jacket, he'd moved out of the shadows, careful not to step in the blood, and strode briskly along the busy Embarcadero to the retreat of his car. *What a satisfying kill.*

A little while later, lying on his bed in the early morning hours, he wondered what his folks would think of his life so far. Not that it mattered; he was never going to know. He toasted them anyway, for the hell of it, raising the bottle in his hand, tipping the final dregs down his throat, and tossing it onto the floor. He would enjoy reading about his kill in the morning.

As lethargy kicked in and his eyes began to droop, a plan hatched in his mind. Before he slipped into the darkness of a sound and dreamless sleep, a callous smile formed on his lips.

Chapter Twenty-Nine

Jessica got up early, the smell of something delicious wafting through the apartment, awakening her senses. She reached the kitchen, her stomach growling, and noticed the coffee already made and Judd standing at the stove, busy frying.

"I didn't hear you come in." She pulled up a chair and sat down, picking idly at the corners of the *Chronicle* lying on the kitchen table.

"You were already asleep when I got in. Sorry, I got back later than I expected." Judd turned, gave her a quick smile, flipped something in the pan. "I'm making breakfast. Thought I would do something nice for you for a change. I think I've been a bit of a jerk."

Jessica bit back a retort, just happy to have him home, even if it turned out to be short-lived. "Thank you."

"Got plans today?" Judd asked.

"Not really. Work. Nothing special." She hesitated. "You?"

"Same."

Her silence must have prompted an explanation. She didn't know about his job.

"Nothing special, either." He grinned, heaped two plates full of pancakes and fried bacon, and set them down on the table. "Voila." He sat opposite and tucked in, engaging her in conversation. "Still job hunting?" He pulled a strand of bacon fat from his mouth.

"Kind of." Jessica slurped her coffee. "Judd?"

"Uh-huh?"

"When are you free for another visit to Mom?"

"Soon."

The small talk continued for the next fifteen minutes, and it almost seemed normal, how things used to be between them. Judd smiled when she pushed away her empty plate, stood up, and thanked him for breakfast. She disappeared to get ready for work, and he was glad she hadn't asked any questions, glad she hadn't heard about the murder last night.

An hour later, Jessica arrived to an extremely subdued office. Anderson sat behind closed doors. Nicky Drew sat morosely at her own desk, and Jessica wondered for a second if they'd had a falling out. No sounds came from Anderson's office. *He must be having a bad day.* She slipped behind her own desk, glancing at all the grave faces, soaking up the somber mood. The solemnity washed away the pleasures of breakfast and the few rare minutes spent with Judd. She began to shift uncomfortably. What could possibly have happened?

Before anyone had a chance to approach, the door to Anderson's office opened. He stepped out, saw her at her desk, and motioned her to step inside. Her heart sank. Her moment had arrived. With Alex gone, she had no one to protect her.

She shuffled in hesitantly, eyeing him coolly. "What is it?" She chose not to sit, remembering Alex's ordeal.

"Sit down, Jessica."

"I'd rather stand." Anderson had an unusual softness to his voice, one she'd never heard. He seemed different, concerned, and she trusted him even less. "What's this about?"

Anderson moved around his desk, sat down heavily in the chair, and leaned his elbows on his desk. Jessica watched, a growing sense of alarm tugging at the corners of her heart. Had something happened to Judd? *It can't have. I just saw him.*

"What? You're making me nervous," she finally said.

"Jessica, there's no easy way to say this," Anderson began.

She felt her mouth go dry, her throat close up, her breath catch in her chest. What other blow could life deal? What did she have left to lose?

"I'm afraid I've got some bad news about Alex. She's been involved in an accident." Anderson stopped when he heard her catch her breath. He saw her eyes had widened with shock. "She's alive," he continued, "but critical. She was hit by a car, late last night."

Jessica looked as though she might pass out. Alarmed at the idea, he thought he'd better get her out of his office. "She's in the hospital. I understand if you need to go, if you want to see her, it's okay to leave."

Jessica didn't move. Anderson thought she'd begun to sway on her feet. Her face had gone deathly pale, and he saw a bead of sweat on her brow.

"How did it happen?" Jessica finally managed.

"Hit and run, the paper said. Probably a drunk driver."

Before he could get out another word, she'd bolted out of his office. Bemused, he watched her race past her own desk, and out through the doors.

She ignored the cheerless glances, the sympathetic eyes, didn't cast another thought to Anderson still in his office. She didn't stop until she reached the Ladies, where she wretched over the sink, then splashed cold water onto her flaming cheeks.

Something is wrong. Something is so horribly wrong. Her thoughts swirled: Alex under the wheels of a car, the harassment, the letter, the threat of a lawsuit. *Anderson did this.*

She had to get away, out of the building, and far away from Anderson. She blotted her face, tore out of the ladies room, out of the building, and across the parking lot to the safety of her car.

Fresh tears coursed down her face. *I should have testified. I should have helped her. I'm such a coward.*

She hurled herself inside her car and slammed the doors shut, locking Anderson and the rest of the world outside. *I could have prevented this if I only I hadn't been so weak.* Her father's face flashed before her eyes and she cursed him again. *Damn you for making me who I am. Damn you for being so weak, and passing it to me. Damn you for making me.*

Unable to see through the blur of tears, she fumbled with the keys in her hand, tried to jam each in turn into the ignition. "Come on, come on," she cried in frustration, finally ramming the correct one in, and turning it to start up the engine. Sobs shook her body, and, depleted for a minute, she pressed her head up against the steering wheel, and let the agony out. She sobbed so loudly she didn't notice Anderson approaching. The light rap on the side window and the sound of his voice made her screech like an animal, cornered, fighting for its life against the worst predator it could imagine.

"Jessica? Are you all right in there?"

"Get away from me, you animal, get away," she screamed hysterically, stamped her foot on the accelerator and careened out onto the road. She took off so quickly Anderson had to jump out of her way.

"What the–" he stared after her in astonishment. Realization sank in. "She thinks I–" he gaped after her, open-mouthed. *She thinks I mowed down Alex.*

"Oh, shit." The disbelief hit him like a slap to the face. "Why would she think I–" . It all came flooding into place; the letter, the lawsuit Alex had threatened against him, his own fury, the damning remarks he'd made. He stared at the sky and realized he would soon have an even bigger problem. If Alex had told Jessica about the sexual harassment, she had probably told others, too, and he knew he could probably expect a visit from old Johnny Law before too much longer. Once they began poking about his business and delving into his affairs, they would almost certainly uncover the details of his sordid behavior, not to mention his bullying, his manipulation; and then the floodgates would be flung wide open. *So, the frigid little bitch is going to get her way after all.* He laughed at the irony, before the full fury hit him. Suddenly, he was not sorry at all for Alex's misfortune.

Jessica reached San Francisco General Hospital, on Potrero Street, in tears. At the front desk, she asked about Alex. The nurse explained Alex had been brought back from surgery and taken to the recovery ward, where Jessica would be permitted no more than a few minutes.

He won't get away with it, Alex, she vowed, on her way to the ward, *I'll make it up to you. I'll go to court. I'll do whatever you need. As soon as I leave here, I'll call the police and tell them everything I know.* Upon reaching Alex's bedside, she winced at the sight before her. Alex lying so still she looked dead, eyes closed, cuts and bruises covering her swollen face. A drip had been inserted into her good arm and a cast had been applied to the other. Something had been inserted under her blankets to protect her legs.

Jessica stared at the young, blond-haired man at her bedside, holding her good hand, the fingers of his other hand touching her hair, whispering something she couldn't hear. She turned to leave, but he looked up before she could go.

"Don't leave. She'd want you to stay."

Jessica turned back to the bed. "I don't want to intrude."

"You're not." He smiled. She liked his kind, handsome face. "You must be Jessica?"

"Yes."

He looks tired. He must have been here all night. "How is she?"

"Not good." He smiled again, a sad, watery smile. *Like he's bracing himself for the worst.* "She has two broken legs, internal bleeding, a broken right arm, several cracked ribs, and there's a blood clot in her right leg the doctors are watching."

"What happened?" Jessica whispered, wondering what Ben knew, deciding this was not the time or the place to raise the subject of Anderson.

"Hit and run. That's all I know."

Jessica nodded.

"I knew instantly it was you," Ben said suddenly. "Alex has told me a lot about you. She says you're one of the bravest people she knows. I'm Ben, her boyfriend." He held out a hand.

"Me?" Jessica's eyes filled with fresh tears. Her heart almost broke when she grasped Ben's hand. "Oh, Ben, Alex is the brave one. I'm just a coward. I'm not brave at all."

"We can't stay long," he said, "the nurses keep moving

me on. They don't want us to tire her. I spent the night in the lobby so I could see her first thing this morning, when she came out of surgery." He stood up, stretched, and rubbed his eyes. "But I'll have to go home. I've got things I need to do."

"Can she hear us?"

Ben shook his head. "They have her pretty doped up. She'll be out for a while."

"What about her family?"

"They're in New Zealand, I'll have to call them today."

A nurse came to move them on.

"Ben?" Jessica wondered if she should ask. "I need you to do me a favor."

"Sure." He looked at her in surprise.

"This might sound an odd thing to ask, but, when you call her folks, would you ask them something for me? Would you ask them if they know someone in California named Marianne?"

"Of course." Ben smiled. "I'll be back later. Maybe I'll see you here, too?"

They made their way to the lobby together. Ben left the hospital for the first time since Alex's admittance. Jessica stayed behind and sat down heavily on a bench. She needed time alone to regain her composure. *Could we really be related?* The thought had flickered in and out of her mind a number of times; Alex's accent, her mother's brothers, their similarities in appearance. Before, she'd always brushed it off, deciding it might be better not to know. She blew her nose on a ball of tissue she pulled from her purse.

"I recognize that feeling. Tough visit?"

"What?" Surprised, she looked up to see a dark haired stranger standing in front of her. He sat down on the bench beside her. "Someone close?"

She blew her nose again, her eyes welling up with a fresh batch of tears. "My best friend. My only friend." She didn't know why she told him, but he seemed kind, and it thawed her defenses.

"I'm sorry." He handed her a clean tissue. "What happened?"

"Hit and run. It happened last night."

"Yes, I read about that in this morning's paper. How is she?"

"Critical."

"I'm sorry," he said again.

"Thank you." She wiped her eyes and shot him a sideways glance. "What about you? Are you visiting someone?"

"Yes." He looked away.

She thought she saw something familiar flit across his face. "Someone special?"

He sighed, "My mother. She's dying."

"Oh, I'm so sorry," Jessica said, instantly understanding. Although her own mother hadn't died, she been lost for years.

"She's been ill for a while, but it's tough to lose someone you love."

"Yes, it is." Jessica stood up. She had too many memories of her own loss, too much raw pain, to revisit the past. "Well, I wish you the best. I've got to get going."

"Sure. Will you be able to drive?"

"I feel calmer now," she smiled at him, "and I really need to call the police."

"The police?"

She saw his eyes pop with surprise. "I know who hit her."

"Really? Who do you think it was?"

Jessica didn't see the harm in telling him. She was about to tell the police anyway, and before too long, once it hit the papers, it would be public information. "A man named Anderson Collins."

"Who's he?"

"You mustn't be local," she said, a hint of sarcasm in her tone, "or you'd have heard of Anderson Collins. He's one of the biggest realtor's in the area, a marauder, and an attempted murderer." The mention of him relit her anger, and she went on when she'd meant to stop. "He's my boss. At least, he was. He's the one who mowed my friend down."

"Your boss?" He seemed surprised. "Why would your boss–"

Jessica interrupted. "He used to be her boss, until he sexually harassed her and she threatened to sue."

"I see. So, you think he mowed her down out of revenge?"

"Yes. To stop her bringing a lawsuit against him."

"Well, that makes sense." He got up off the bench and stood beside her. "What about you? Does this mean you're out of a job?"

Jessica hadn't thought about that, but, suddenly, it didn't matter any more. "Yes. I'm not going back. I'm going to the police and I intend to watch them put the bastard away."

He could see how much she hated her boss. *I never thought she had it in her*. He was surprised at her resolve and determination. He'd always considered her the weakest of the bunch; the one most likely to go mad, like her mother. *Even better*. She stood straight, defiant, and bold. He wanted to laugh.

"I admire your courage," he said, fighting back the urge to snicker. "That's an honorable thing to do for a friend."

When she looked at him again her eyes shone unsteadily, a flicker of total surprise. *Just as I expected.* A spurious smile curved his lips. *She's never had a compliment in her life.*

"I… Thank you." She cautiously returned his smile.

He watched a slight smile play around her lips. *Sensuous lips*. He sensed a stirring in his groin. *Wonder how they taste. I'll be sure to let her brother know*.

"I'm not so sure I'd do anything as noble as that," he said, watching her smile grow. "I think you're a very brave young lady."

He had to fight hard not to snort with amusement at the red stain seeping slowly up her neck, and into her cheeks, flooding her face with an unnatural glow. Her embarrassment added to his pleasure, and showed him a weakness he could tap into. *This is perfect.* He wanted to shout it out loud. *I'll have this little sexpot eating out of my hand before she even knows what happened.* When she hoisted her purse to her shoulder, he allowed his gaze to drift quickly over her body. *A lithe body even in those dowdy clothes.* The clothes were a joke; frumpy, old, like a middle-aged woman. *Who ya trying to kid? That perv in your office?*

"I better get going." She blushed again when he lowered his eyelids, and gave her his best smoldering look.

She's gotta be a virgin. He felt his erection grow even harder, and decided he'd better let her go before she noticed, and bolted out of his reach.

"Maybe I'll see you here again," he said, folding his hands in front of the bulge in his pants, "when you next visit your friend. I'm here all the time, visiting my mother. I don't know how long she has left." *That should do the trick.*

"Yes. Maybe." She turned to leave.

"Don't forget to make that call."

He watched her leave, striding out of the hospital, a woman with a purpose. He turned back, wandered down a different hallway than before, in the opposite direction from Alex's room, and looked in on the yellow-haired woman, back in her bed after having had her stomach pumped to rid it of all the drugs she'd ingested.

"Fucking loser," he muttered, poking his head into her ward, making sure she didn't see him. "Should have been you that died, not Dad."

Robbie Allure's mother had been in and out of rehab and abusive relationships since he'd been a child. He hadn't come to see her today. He didn't care about his mother and hadn't for years, ever since his father had been murdered in prison. She'd taken up with one loser after another, lost in a drugged and drunken haze, and stopped caring about him.

On his way back out of the hospital, he remembered with bitterness her voice when she'd told him that she had never wanted him anyway, how she had only had him to keep his father content. His father had wanted a son more than anything else in the world. After he died, his mother decided she wanted her fun, and she'd had it.

"Hope it kills you this time," he muttered, sliding behind the wheel of his Mercedes.

His thoughts turned to Jessica as he drove out of the grounds, keeping his eyes peeled for cops. After last night's discovery, he expected them to be out in force.

What a great idea. He'd thought of it in the early hours of this morning, falling asleep on his bed, the beer loosening his mind. He seemed to do his best work after a dozen or so beers.

"Not long now, Dad," he said, glancing up at the sky. "Won't be long now."

What a fucking, marvelous bonus. He couldn't have planned it any better. The office pervert, about to be tossed into the ring of suspicion for last night's little incident, would come in quite handy if his plan for pinning it on Judd didn't pan out. Judd would be implicated the minute the cops found the stolen Acura outside his home, probably still smeared with Alex's blood.

He slapped his hand up and down on the steering wheel, barely able to contain his glee, and started singing at the top of his voice: "I killed a man last night, slit his throat open wide, I stabbed a man last night, he winced at the sight of my knife."

Much later, he arrived at the river. He hadn't been back there since his father died; saving it for a special moment; a moment drawing ever closer. The old familiar sensations returned as he got near; the deafening sound of the waves cascading over boulders, the hiss of the white foam that shot up into the air, the roar that filled the canyon. He remembered his father's spine-chilling stories, his rafting adventures, how he'd outfoxed the menace of the river where lesser men had drowned. Bodie Allure had lived life on the edge, taken the biggest risk, and always walked away with his life; until his path had crossed with the Croft's.

Robbie Allure parked, got out of his car, and stood on a large, jagged rock jutting out over the water. He took a swig of beer and welcomed the cool spray landing on his face. He stared at the raging waters a few feet below where he stood. Bodie had been his idol.

"After I'm done with her, I'll bring her here, Dad," he said, "let the rocks finish her off."

He stayed for a while, thinking, remembering, staring at the swirling water, picturing her beautiful head being smashed against the rocks, hearing her scream for her life until there wasn't an ounce of air left in her lungs.

The sun started sinking, bowing itself toward the horizon, and bathing the landscape in a fiery orange glow of early evening. Robbie turned to leave.

Chapter Thirty

Public hysteria had mounted and Jackson knew Red sensed the hostility directed toward them; the questions, the accusations, why hadn't they found the killer?

Police patrolled the streets in force. Undercover officers mingled in the bars, looking for anything or anyone odd, anything or anyone unusual. Jackson knew Robbie had brought things to a head, had prepared himself to strike, and he'd kept a closer watch on Jessica. As he and Red cruised slowly down Baker Street Friday afternoon, perusing the neighborhood for a silver Mercedes, something unnerving caught his attention. "Slow down, Red."

Red pulled alongside the curb, behind a black Acura. Jackson got out and walked around the vehicle. He scanned the street, returned to the black and white, and instructed Red, "Run the plates. Looks like it could be the one from last night. Front fender smashed in."

While Red called it in, Jackson wondered why he hadn't known it sooner. His instincts should have told him. He remembered the hateful eyes in the courtroom, all those years ago in Sacramento. The note he'd received, two weeks after the attack on the woman who'd survived, had never made sense. A page ripped from a notebook with letters crudely glued on to make a threat or a warning: **She's going to die. You can't save her.**

Who was going to die? he'd wondered. Cranks came crawling out of all kinds of places in the throes of public hysterics, and both he and Red had believed it had not come from the killer. He'd made no demands, no requests. He'd filed the note away. Not even when Red had mentioned revenge had he put the pieces together. In fact, not until Jessica had asked him to tail Judd, and had mentioned her stalker, had he finally realized who he was after. The plates came back.

"Match," Red said. "Reported stolen last night."

Jackson nodded, and spoke tersely to Red. "This is the work of our killer. The hit and run was a message."

"A message? What kind of message?"

"He's closing in. I've suspected it for a while. He's sending a message to Jessica that he can get to her and anyone she loves at any time."

"Jackson," Red's voice came out a mixture of surprise and impatience. "What the hell are you talking about? What does the hit and run have to do with the murders? And who the hell is Jessica?"

Jackson turned to face him. "I couldn't tell you before, I had to know for sure, and I haven't exactly followed the rules. I didn't want to drag you into it before I knew."

"Knew what?"

"Look," he sighed with frustration; frustration that he hadn't figured it out sooner–before he'd had to put Jessica at risk and involve her brother–frustration that Robbie had almost claimed another victim while he'd been dicking around, and frustration that he didn't have time right now to explain it all to Red. He went for the short version. "The kid who's been helping me nights–Judd Croft–he's Jessica's brother. This is their apartment. The kid who got mowed down last night is her friend. More than twenty years ago, I worked a case in Sac, involving a murder of a young boy."

"I heard something about that," Red said.

"Well that boy was their elder brother. We got the guy, me and my partner. He died in prison a few months later. Red, the killer is his son, Robbie Allure. And no, this isn't a hunch."

"You should have told me, I'm your partner."

"I know, I'm sorry." He looked over at Red's light-lipped expression. "I didn't want to drag you into what I was doing, it goes against all the rules."

He proceeded to bring Red up to speed about Jessica's stalker, how she'd asked him to put a tail on her brother, which he'd done a few days after she'd asked. How he'd confronted Judd in a bar, questioned him about the rough-looking guys he'd joined for a drink.

"I knew the guys," he said, "they'd all done time. Judd told me about a note someone stuck to his windshield."

"What kind of note?"

"Similar to the one we got before, but more violent. The guy walked right up this driveway and pinned it on his truck."

"Who were the guys in the bar?"

"He knew them from juvy, wanted their help."

Red snorted. "You let a guy from juvy help on our case?"

"Like I said, I haven't been following the rules. If it wasn't for him, I might not have figured it out. He figured the guys might be able to help him find Robbie, figured he's probably been in trouble before. I made him tell me everything he knew, and I agreed to let him help."

"So, the Acura? Robbie did that?"

"Yep, to pin the blame on Judd. If we take him in, he'll have a clear shot at his sister."

"Seems he already does," Red snapped, and Jackson

knew he was pissed to have been kept out of the loop. "If he knows where they live, he can get to her any time he wants."

"That's why we're going to tell her, today."

"You mean she doesn't even know?" Red blistered, "Man, how could you be so reckless? This is insane."

"You don't know the full story," Jackson said, "I'll fill you in on the rest later. Right now, I need to make a call."

Forensics showed up, after Red called, to examine the car. Jackson got on the phone to Judd. "Where are you?" he demanded.

"On my way home, why? What's up?"

"Get here fast, and don't stop anywhere. Come directly home."

"What's wrong?"

Jackson heard the panic in Judd's voice. "Jessica's all right. Just get here, Judd. I'll explain it when you get home." He snapped the phone shut, praying Judd wouldn't get picked up by another cop before he made it home.

"Where do we find this Robbie Allure?" Red said.

"I don't know yet, but I know one thing. With Jessica in his sights, he won't be far away. He's come back to finish what his father started with the Croft's." Why he'd targeted Jessica, Jackson didn't yet know.

"And all the other murders? Honing his skills?"

"That and the fact he's a psychopath, just like his old man."

"You think he killed the bartender last night?"

"I'm sure he did."

Jackson welcomed Red's silence for the next few minutes, while he waited anxiously for Judd to show up. He called Jessica's number, but got no answer. He left a brief message, asking her to call, hoping she wouldn't be alarmed.

"Jackson, I think I might have something."

He looked at Red's calm, determined, vigilant face. "Yeah? What's that?"

"The guy last night…he was a bartender. All the victims had been in a bar. That's gotta mean something. This guy–"

"Hold that thought," Jackson ordered, seeing a grey Taurus heading up the hill toward the apartment. He could already see Jessica's frantic expression at the sight of the police and the team of forensics outside her home.

She swung onto the driveway, stepped out of her car, and looked wild-eyed at Jackson, bewildered. He noted the fear in her face. "What's going on? Where's Judd?"

"He's on his way, he'll be here in a minute." Jackson put a hand on her shoulder. "We need to get you inside. There's something you need to know."

Jessica obeyed his order, her eyes darting from Jackson to Red to the forensics team processing the smashed in Acura. "Whose ca–"

"In a minute. When Judd gets here."

A shout came from inside the Acura, and Jackson looked back at the forensics officer, holding up something small and white. "Cocaine."

Jackson's mouth tightened into a thin line. *This is going from bad to worse for Judd.*

"Bastard knows exactly what he's doing," Red hissed in his ear, making sure Jessica didn't hear.

Jessica took a seat at the table, Jackson and Red took the couch. In silence, they waited for Judd. Jessica clutched her stomach, wishing the nausea would pass.

"You all right?"

She nodded, wishing she'd never called the cops to put a

tail on Judd. *He's stolen a car. He's in possession of cocaine.* She didn't even want to know what else he might have done. *I should have taken care of things myself.* She wished she had. *We're family. Families take care of their own.* She didn't want to talk to either of the detectives.

From across the room, Jackson watched her face. The wetness in her eyes and the emptiness of her expression took him back to the Sacramento home, and the eight-year old child he'd watched huddled against her brother, clutching her teddy, when he'd attended the suicide of her father. He could only imagine the terror raging inside her now, while they sat in silence, waiting for Judd.

Less than ten minutes had passed when Judd arrived home. He parked his pickup on the driveway behind the Taurus. He glanced at the police units swarming his home; the forensics team surrounding a black Acura that looked like it had been involved in a smash, and ran inside the apartment to find his sister, his mind on Jackson's call. *What the hell is going on here?*

"Jackson?" he hollered, hoping against hope the detective didn't have bad news about his sister or about her stalker. *I should have told her. Jackson was right.*

"Judd."

He heard Jessica's voice before he saw Jackson standing in the doorway of the living room.

"In here," Jackson ordered.

Judd followed him into the living room, so relieved to see Jessica, unharmed and seated at the table, that his eyes filled with tears. He scanned the three faces staring at him, waiting for someone to explain, wiping sweaty palms down the front of his jeans.

Judd sat next to Jessica. Jackson took the reins, joining

the twins at the table. "Judd, the Acura outside your place is the same one used in last night's hit and run. It was reported stolen last night. A small amount of cocai–"

"That's the car that hit Alex?" Jessica cried in disbelief. "How did it get–how cou–?"

Jackson held up a hand. "Jessica, let me finish. I'll explain everything in a minute." He turned his eyes back to Judd. "We found cocaine inside the vehicle. We believe it was planted deliberately, and the vehicle intentionally left to make it look–"

Jessica interrupted again, her voice rising with frustration. "But, if that's the car from the accident, then it's not Judd. Judd didn't steal that car. I know who did. I already called the police this morning. How come you don't know?"

Jackson stared at her in confusion, "What are you talking about? How could you know?"

"Anderson Collins stole that car," Jessica explained, looking from one face to another in earnest. "He's the one who hit Alex. He tried to kill her. Why haven't you arrested him?"

"Who's Anderson Collins?" Jackson looked to Judd, who just shrugged.

"He's the man you should be looking for," Jessica almost shouted. "He sexually harassed her until she quit a few months ago. He was her boss and she threatened to sue him."

Jackson cursed the dismal flow of information between different sections of the SFPD. "How do you know this?" He knew he'd have to check it out, even in his certainty that this Anderson wasn't the killer.

"He's my boss, I still work there. I saw it, I saw the harassment. I know about the letter."

Jackson looked over at Red. "Call it in, check out her

story and see if there's any news."

He turned back to the twins while Red made the call. "Jessica, listen to me. I'm pretty sure it wasn't your boss who ran down your friend."

"Why? Who else could it be?"

Jackson glanced at Judd, who looked at the floor. It was going to be up to him to crash Jessica's world. He began as gently as he could. "I believe the car outside has been left there on purpose, to frame Judd."

He saw Jessica send a fleeting look of apology to her brother for suspecting he'd stolen the car. He saw Judd's unflinching face, tight-lipped expression, and rigid posture as he waited for the detective to deliver the shattering news to his sister.

"Who left it there?" Jessica's eyes went back and forth between Jackson and Judd.

Jackson took a breath. "Jessica, I don't want you to be alarmed. We have this under control." He noticed Judd's involuntary shift at his lie. "I believe the man who stole the car, the man who hurt your friend, is the same man who's been stalking you all these months." He flinched at Jessica's gaping expression, the widening of her eyes, the paleness that had settled over her face, like a sheet of horror, like she knew what he was going to say next. He heard her breathing become shallow, like a dog panting in the summer heat.

"Jessica," he drew another breath, knowing he was only prolonging the agony, but wishing he didn't have to say it at all, "I'm sure the man we're looking for is Robbie Allure." Her face registered nothing. He wondered if she remembered the name. "Bodie Allure's son, Jessica. The man who murdered your brother."

Red finished on the phone. "They're investigating

Anderson Collins for claims of sexual harassment. Apparently, there's been more than one."

Jessica stared at Jackson, at Judd, her breath coming out in short, sharp pants. Her mouth had gone dry; too dry to speak, and her head felt funny–filled with a pain that intensified by the second. Her ears hurt, too, with the sound of blood, rushing blood, draining from her face. She saw their mouths move but couldn't hear a word. Her heart hurt in her chest and the floor seemed to be caving in under her feet. She sensed herself falling, falling, hovering between this life and the next, somewhere strange, watching three strangers conversing around a table. Her pulse quickened, her skin became clammy, and everything grew dim. She could no longer see Judd. The room faded, and she couldn't see Jackson. Then the pain racking her body simply melted away, her mind relaxed, and she let it all go.

Chapter Thirty-One

Robbie drove back from the river in silence, an empty twelve pack on the back seat, the last half-empty beer can between his knees. He kept his eyes peeled for cops and sped down the interstate, gripping the steering wheel hard enough to turn his knuckles white. Consumed with bitterness and hatred, he pushed down harder on the accelerator, making the Mercedes lurch forward.

"Careful," a voice in the back of his head warned, "don't wanna draw unwanted attention." With police out in force, he made a conscious effort to keep his speed under control, an effort that made him madder.

His mind wandered back to the day in court, when he watched his father, stoic as ever, dragged away, not knowing he would soon be dead. "You killed him," he spat, beer spurting out of his mouth. "And now it's time to pay."

Another car in front of him slowed; he swerved to avoid a collision, cut back in front, and made a vulgar gesture to the driver behind. "Fucking idiot." His mood turned ever more vile, more hateful by the minute. He sensed the hatred building within himself; for the cops, for the injustices in his life, for his pathetic excuse for a mother, for the loss of his beloved father, but mostly for the Croft's: the core of all his rage.

Killing had been a release for some of that pent-up rage, and he'd started soon after he'd turned fourteen and had the strength to overpower a man twice his size. He drew closer to home and thought about the twins. *Did you think I wouldn't come for you? Fucking fools.* His mouth twisted into an angry scowl at the years he'd had to wait, the time it had taken to track them down, following them around, figuring they'd moved to San Francisco and having to uproot, too. Traffic slowed, brake lights came on, and Robbie saw interstate-eighty jammed up ahead. He cussed, drummed his fingers against the steering wheel with impatience, took a swig from the can. His mind wandered back to Marianne. *Damn, I would have enjoyed one last game before the big finale.*

Traffic moved, he huffed out a breath, stepped on the accelerator, heard the squeal of his tires and ignored the honks from other drivers. Anxious to get home, he began to get careless, stopped looking out for cops, darted in and out of lanes gaining seconds wherever he could, not caring about anything except getting off this wretched interstate and home. Finally, The Marina came into view and he turned into his garage and checked his watch. *Fuck, what a waste.* Nine o'clock. He didn't have the energy to go back out again later, and, instead, dragged his hulking, exhausted body up the stairs and into his apartment. One quick stop at the bathroom, and he made his way on to the bedroom, where he threw himself face-down onto his bed, spread out his arms, and ran his hands over his expensive silk sheets.

Time's up Jessica Croft. A week to Halloween. Perfect. He sighed, stroking the luxurious fabric. *This is it. This is where I'm going to rape you, terrorize you, choke you to within an inch of your pathetic life, make you pay for everything you've done. And then I'll take you back to the Great American River for my Dad, let the rocks finish you off.* He closed his eyes, visualized her flailing arms, legs, begging for her life, disappearing under the waves… He drifted to sleep.

Chapter Thirty-Two

"You seem pretty down," Kelly Kirkland said, appearing at Julie's desk on Saturday morning, his face grim. "Missing Alex?"

"It's just so awful," Julie said. "I still can't believe it, and right after a huge success. I mean, she didn't even get to celebrate." She stopped, looked up at her boss. "You don't...you don't suppose..." She couldn't bring herself to say it, it seemed so appalling.

"That Anderson had something to do with it?" He shrugged. "I hate to think it, but I can't say the same thought didn't cross my mind."

Julie sighed. "I'm finding it hard to concentrate, and there's so much to do. I can't take care of all these calls, prepare the home, or give Sanders the attention he deserves. I can't get my mind off of Alex."

"Would it help to know that Russell called this morning? That he's ready to come back?"

"He did?" Julie's face broke into a half smile. "He is? I mean, I can't say I'm thrilled, you know how I feel about Russell, I'd far rather have Alex."

Kelly gave a short laugh and patted her arm. "I know, but it's come at a good time. You need help, and help is arriving."

"When?"

"He's coming in tomorrow for a couple of hours, and then back full time as of Monday."

Julie felt her spirits sink at the prospect of sharing an office again with Russell. "Too bad," she turned to Kelly, "I'd much prefer to have Alex."

Kelly made a tut-tutting sound, and cautioned her to be nice. "We don't know what he's been dealing with. And talking of Alex, are you planning on going to visit? I know how you hate hospitals."

"I suppose I should." She sighed, imagining the smell of sickness, and chemicals, and death. Her stomach turned over.

"I think she'd appreciate it." He fished in his pocket and pulled out a handful of bills he handed to Julie. "Get her some flowers." He turned to head back to his desk, calling over his shoulder, "Oh, and if she's awake…tell her to get better quick; she has a job waiting for her."

Later that afternoon, Julie tried not to breathe in the smells that made her queasy, tried to ignore the woozy sensation that came over her the moment she stepped inside the hospital, and made her way to Alex's ward, clutching a bouquet of flowers with one hand, her stomach with the other.

"Name," a gruff looking man outside her room asked, preventing her from entering.

After scrutinizing her ID and giving her the once-over, while she swayed slightly on her feet, he let her pass. Her stomach rolled even further at the sight of Alex, hooked up to drips, a tube in her arm, her face looking like it had been used as a punch bag.

"Julie," she gasped, almost apologetically, handing the flowers to a beautiful girl who bore an uncanny resemblance to Alex, and backing out of the room. "Please tell her I stopped by, I don't feel that well, can't stop." With that, she dashed back the way she'd come, tearing through the lobby, knocking into a business man in a suit, standing with his back to her. "Sorry," she muttered, and kept going, not stopping until she reached the sanctity, and fresh smell, of her car.

Jessica handed the flowers to Ben, who put them in a vase. She glanced at Jackson, barely recognizing him in plain clothes. *He looks almost fatherly.* She suffered a momentary rush of anguish, and a longing for her own father.

"We'd better go," she said to Ben, and then to Jackson, "do you think he'll try to come here, to hurt her again?"

Jackson shook his head. "He won't do anything more to Alex. He's sent his message. Plus Bateman will be posted outside, checking anyone who tries to visit. He'll come back to the hospital, Jessica, if he thinks you might be here. He's going to expect you to visit Alex. You mustn't come here alone. Always make sure you have someone with you, at all times. I mean it. I don't want you taking any chances."

As Jackson, Jessica, and Ben left Alex and made their way back to the lobby, Jessica wondered how Robbie had ever managed to find them. "How did he know?" she whispered to Jackson.

Jackson put a hand on her shoulder. "Probably been tracking you for years, ever since the trial. With the internet, you can get all kinds of information these days. Are you all right there, Jess? You gave us quite a scare yesterday, when you passed out at the table."

Jessica caught her balance after a brief stumble. "Yes, I'm not going to do that again. It was just such a shock. I'd never have thought…I mean, how did he know we moved to San Francisco?"

"People can find out anything they want, and when they've harbored a grudge as long as he has, they find a way. The point is, he's here, and we have to find him, before he finds you."

They said goodbye to Ben, and continued through the hospital lobby, out to Jackson's car. "But why is he targeting me and not Judd?"

"I don't know," Jackson said. "Maybe he thinks you're weaker."

They reached the black and white, parked in clear view of the front of the hospital. Jackson opened the passenger door for Jessica. She slid in, closed her eyes for a second, and saw Cameron's face, twisted in terror as it had throughout all her nightmares. She heard Jackson get in the other side and close the door.

"I'm not surprised," she said. "Not really. I think I always knew this day would come."

"What do you mean?" Jackson started the engine.

"All those nightmares, for years, I saw an evil I didn't know, but I recognized it. Every night, I'd see Cameron, trying to scream, terror in his face, his throat crushed, helpless while his life was squeezed away, and then I'd be running, running for my own life," she began breathing more heavily. "Sometimes, Judd would be with me. We'd run and run from the evil, and I'd wake up, my sheets sopping." She turned to look at Jackson, and found him staring at her with the most compassionate expression she'd ever seen.

"I wet the bed until I was thirteen-years old," she whispered. "I always thought Bodie would come back from the dead. But I know now. The evil in my nightmares was never Bodie–it was his son; the boy in the courtroom with such hate, such murder in his eyes. Even then, I think I always knew he would come."

Jackson turned his eyes to the road, said nothing, pulled out of the parking lot and headed in the direction of the station. For a while, they rode in silence.

"He's more angry at me than Judd," Jessica said, breaking the silence.

"I've been thinking about that," Jackson said. "His violence has been greater toward his female victims. He seems to have a greater hatred for women."

"Why?" Jessica pressed.

Jackson sighed. "Could be any number of reasons. I'm sure his father's death had something to do with it. Maybe his relationship with his mother fell apart after that."

"Do you think his mother still lives in Sacramento?"

"She might." Jackson's mind drifted back to something Red had said about the victims. *All the victims had been in a bar.* He began to have an idea about how he might find Robbie Allure.

"What?"

"What?" Surprised, he glanced across at Jessica, and found her staring at him. "*What*?" he repeated, a little exasperated.

"I've been watching you these past few seconds. I can tell by your face, you're onto something. What?"

He turned his attention back to the road, unwilling to divulge. "This is police work, Jessica. I'm not going to get you involved."

"I am involved. I'm the target, remember?"

"I'll handle it."

"Oh, like you have so far?" she snapped. "I'm sorry. I didn't mean that."

She's right. Jackson's hunches hadn't come through this time, at least not concerning Robbie Allure. "I think I might know how we can find him," he said, "and until we do, I want you to stay away from all restaurants, all bars, in fact anywhere where alcohol is served. And I don't want you to be alone. Judd needs to be home with you every night. If you visit Alex at the hospital, someone has to go with you. Understand?"

"You'd better have a word with Judd about that," Jessica said dryly, "I haven't been able to get him to stay home, so I doubt you will."

Jackson laughed. "I followed him after you asked, and I'm glad you did ask. He's been a great help to me."

"How?"

"I'm sorry we didn't tell you sooner," Jackson said, "but that night when I tailed Judd, I discovered more than I had in the entire time I'd been working on these murders. Judd suspected Robbie right away. He showed me a note he got that was similar to one I'd received a few weeks before."

"A note? What kind of note?"

"A threat." Jackson didn't see the need to go into detail. "Anyway, it allowed us to put the pieces together and I realized who had been stalking you."

"So, you knew where he was going all this time? And you didn't tell me? You let me worry, believing he was in some kind of trouble?"

"I wanted to tell you, but Judd said he thought you…he thought it might be too much for you." He stopped himself in the nick of time from using the word crazy. "He'd been out all night looking for guys he knew, guys from juvy, who he thought could help him find Robbie. He never wanted you to know, so he let you think what you wanted, as long as you didn't know the truth."

"I'm a fine one to talk about the truth," Jessica said, "I've been kind of hiding from it myself."

"Judd's a good kid, Jessica. You should give him a little

more credit. I realized after that night how resourceful he is, and he's been coming down to the station at nights, helping me sort through the information we've collected on Robbie."

"If you find him, how will you know it's him?"

Jackson had thought about that. He hadn't seen Robbie Allure since he was a boy; nine-years old. *But if I see the eyes, I'll know.* He'd already been in touch with his old partner back in Sacramento. Hodges had run a check in the local data base for Robbie and nothing had come back. Jackson couldn't believe he hadn't been caught for some offense or another, prior to becoming a killer, and figured one of two things had happened: either Robbie had moved, or he'd changed his name.

"I don't know what he looks like now, but I do have an idea, something I need to work on."

Chapter Thirty-Three

Robbie rubbed his elbow. *Clumsy bitch.* Infuriated that she hadn't stopped to apologize, hadn't offered to replace the coffee she'd made him spill, and furious at the brown stain on the front of his white silk shirt, he was livid to have missed Jessica.

After he cleaned himself up the best he could with a paper towel and cold water, he went to check on his dope-head mother, to see if she'd kicked the bucket. He snuck his head around the door, careful that she didn't see him. *Shit.* She looked like she might be improving. A few minutes earlier, he'd gone up to the ward where Jessica's friend lay recovering from his handiwork, but the big, plain-clothes cop had thwarted his efforts. He'd changed his mind, delighted to see they thought she must be in some kind of danger. No one would suspect a serial killer of something as mundane as a hit and run, so he'd decided they must be expecting the office pervert–her former employer–to make another attempt on her life.

Fucking marvelous. He'd gone back to the lobby to wait, thrilled with the edge Jessica had thrown him, and decided to take a quick peek on the old lady. *Now, if you would just snuff it, the day would be perfect.*

After having his hopes dashed again, he trekked back out to his car, thinking about what he'd heard. They'd passed him in the lobby, Jessica and the detective, and he'd overheard snippets of their conversation. "I still can't figure out how he managed to find us," she'd been saying, and his ears had pricked up. He'd hung around to hear more. "How did he know we'd moved to San Francisco?" or words to that effect.

Well, I'll be jiggered. He stepped out into the bright afternoon. *How the fuck did you figure it out?*

He strolled quickly back to his car, parked way in the back of the grounds, and got in, revving the engine and peeling out onto the road. If her comment meant what he thought it did, that Robbie Allure had tracked her down, then the stakes would be much higher and the office pervert would be off the hook.

Jiminy-fucking-cricket. Gotta give the girl credit. He realized the cop posted on Alex's door might actually be for him, that they might actually believe he'd go back to the hospital. *I'll have to if I'm going to get to Jessica.* He didn't expect her to be alone if she visited her friend, the cops would surely have warned her about the danger. *Things are just getting interesting.* He was not the slightest bit concerned. *You're looking for Robbie Allure.* He hadn't gone by his birth name in years, the one thing his rotten mother had done right in her miserable life. *Good luck with that.*

Chapter Thirty-Four

Jackson dropped Jessica off at her apartment after making certain she wouldn't be alone, and drove back to the station, intending to spend the rest of evening working, anxious to made headway on his idea. He grabbed a coffee on his way to his desk, and dialed Hodges. "Your old pal, Jackson. Need another favor."

"Name it."

He asked Hodges to dig up the old reports from the murder investigation of Cameron Croft, looking for something in particular.

"Got it," Hodges said, calling back after twenty minutes.

"What was the name of the old lady?" Jackson hadn't been able to remember.

"Went by Diamond," Hodges said, "must be a stage name."

Jackson felt his hunch get stronger. "For what?"

"Worked in a topless bar."

"I knew it." As he'd suspected, Robbie's rage against his victim's was fueled by debauchery and alcohol, and his rage against women was fueled by his hatred for his own mother.

"What was the name of the bar?" He waited while Hodges searched, agitatedly tapping the end of his pencil against the edge of his desk.

"Destiny," Hodges finally came back.

"Thanks, man. I need you to do me a favor and track down a Diamond Allure from that bar, fast as you can."

"That was over twenty years ago, Jackson. She 'aint gonna work there now, at least…I hope not. She'd have to be in her fifties."

If she's even alive. "Do your best work, man. I need her real name. Appreciate it."

He hung up, took a gulp of coffee, and pressed his finger tips together, thinking. Maybe there'd be a warrant, something that would give her location. If he could find her, he might have a way to get to Robbie. Maybe she'd know something.

Late in the afternoon, Hodges came through. "Real name's Sadie. I checked her out; a few drug busts, old shop lifting offense, several years of reporting spousal and child abuse."

"Child abuse?" That shocked Jackson. Why would a son avenge a father guilty of child abuse.

"She married within a year of Bodie's murder," Hodges went on, "and the kid claimed the step-dad abused him. Mother denied it, but reported him for spousal abuse."

The picture began to get clearer, and Jackson understood even more the depths of Robbie's rage against his mother. "Who's the second husband?"

"Larry Cox. I checked him out. Rap sheet for spousal abuse against two of his three wives before Sadie. She defended him against the allegation made by her own kid, but reported him for knocking her around. Doesn't make much sense."

To Jackson it did. He imagined Sadie Allure had had a tough time with her husbands' preferences for young boys rather than her; Bodie with Cameron, and then Larry with her own son; and had chosen to live in denial. "What else can you tell me?"

"Well, she and Larry got divorced after five years."

"Think I better have myself a little chat with this Larry Cox," Jackson said, "know where I can find him?"

"Yeah, but he 'aint gonna tell you much." Hodges snorted. "He's been dead for the past eleven years. Buried in the Sacramento cemetery."

"Fuck." Jackson sensed his progress slip away. "What happened to him?"

"Barroom brawl. Found in an alley, stabbed through the heart and eyes."

And I bet I know who did that. "Shit. Pal, did you happen to run a check on Sadie Cox?" Maybe something would come up under her married name.

"Yeah, nothing came back, except the abuse. She's clean."

Jackson thanked his old partner and hung up, disappointed. He put his elbows on the desk and rested his chin on his palms. *What else?* There had to be something.

"How long have you known?" Jessica watched Judd, while he wiped off the table after a pizza dinner they'd just shared.

"Just over two months," Judd said truthfully. "Why didn't you tell me about your boss?"

"Because I thought you'd do something stupid."

"I might have."

"You should have told me that Robbie had found us."

"I know." Judd realized he'd had no right to shut her out, or put her life at risk.

"When I told you about the guy following me, you didn't seem to believe me. I even began to wonder if I'd imagined it. Jackson didn't seem to want to believe me, and I thought I'd gone crazy, which wouldn't be surprising with our family."

"That's why I didn't tell you, I'm sorry." He stopped wiping and reached for her hand. "I was afraid it would finish you off if you found out."

"I wish you had said something. I've been thinking the most awful thoughts."

"I know." He laughed. "That I was a drug dealer, a thief, or a murderer. I know you suspected me. You thought I was involved in those murders, didn't you?" He watched her hang her head in shame. "I can't say I blame you, though. I haven't exactly been stable in the past."

"I had no idea you had a job," she laughed, "at the police station of all places."

"It's only a civilian job, doesn't pay all that much, but where did you think the money came from?"

"You don't want to know. But it's just as well you're working. I'm afraid I no longer have a job. I quit when I thought Anderson tried to kill Alex."

Judd remembered what she'd said about her boss. "You should have quit a long time before that, Jessie. I'm sorry you had to go through all that. He didn't touch you, did he? Because if he did–"

"No, he didn't. And there's been quite enough killing, thank you."

A little way down the street, he sat in his Mercedes in silence, watching their downstairs lights go out and the upstairs ones come on. His engine purred quietly as he waited. Tonight, he'd had to park further away, to avoid being detected. He'd already spotted the red Ford Focus up ahead; noted the driver slumped in the front seat; head back against the support, waiting, doing nothing. He'd watched him check his mirror from time to time, and glance over at the apartment, then slump back down in his seat, trying to look inconspicuous.

So, I was right, she figured it out. And if they're watching her apartment, they're probably watching her office. He understood the reason the police unit had been outside Park Glenn. *They've got that under surveillance, too.* He chuckled. *All this for lil old me.*

He didn't stay long. He couldn't arouse suspicion, not with the net closing in. That did make the game more difficult, more risky, but it also made it infinitely more thrilling. As he cruised down the street, passed the Ford Focus, crested the hill, and drove down the other side, he wondered how he might lure Jessica to his place without alerting her new entourage. He already had an idea.

Bored out of his mind, Detective Red Dennis couldn't find a comfortable spot in the tiny car. He'd been slumped down in his seat for hours, with nothing but coffee that had gone cold, donuts he'd become sick of, and he needed to pee. Nothing had happened all evening. The twins had finished dinner and turned off the downstairs lights, which meant they'd probably gone to bed. He yawned and wished he could, too. Another vehicle drove slowly up the road towards him and he straightened a little to watch. The sleek model unceremoniously passed by and up towards the crest of the hill. He wiped the donut powder from his fingers, grabbed his pen, and, as he had with every other vehicle that cruised down the street that night, scribbled down the license plate before the car disappeared out of sight.

Probably nothing. He knew tons of rich folk in nice cars came by these parts. He sighed and leaned his bored head back against the seat.

Chapter Thirty-Five

Everything looked the same. Julie sat at her desk, head down. Russell stood quietly on Van Ness Avenue in the afternoon sun, immaculately dressed in a beige suit, white shirt, dark brown tie, and brown brogues, peering in through the window. *Hustle and bustle as usual.*

Suddenly a loud yell came from inside the office, and he waved. A young guy he barely knew, whose name he couldn't remember, had spotted him, waved a hand, and alerted the rest of the office to his return. He smiled and waved back, and watched Julie look up from her desk, heave herself up, and make her way over to the door.

"Good to see you, Russell." She held the door open. "How long you been standing out there, watching us work?"

Same old sarcasm. I missed it. "Only for a couple of hours," he quipped back. "Long enough to see how this place still needs me."

"Glad to see you haven't lost your modesty."

He followed her to her desk, and his own, located right next to it. "How's it been?"

"Crazy. We could use your help." She filled him in on the Sanders home, but left out all details of the presentation, planning to gloat over that later on, when she didn't need his help quite so much.

"We hired a temp during your absence, but she's in the hospital, so," she tossed him a list of prospective buyers, "you can help me whittle down this list." They'd received too much interest, and much of it from a nosey public not interesting in buying, but wanting to poke around inside a celebrity home. "How long can you stay?"

"Haven't decided." He picked up the list. "What happened to the temp?"

"Alex Sullivan? Hit and run, few nights ago."

"Oh. The one on Fillmore? I heard about that. Too bad."

Julie turned back to her own desk and immersed herself back in her papers, trying to ignore the irritation that always arose with Russell sitting in the next seat. *How I miss Alex.* She wished Alex were the one working alongside her, instead of her old enemy.

She had no idea how much time had passed, it couldn't have been much, when she sensed a presence in front of her and saw the shadow that had fallen across her desk. Startled, she looked up, and saw Russell standing directly in front of her desk, watching her, a dark anger simmering in his eyes.

"What is it?" she asked, a fluttering sensation in her stomach. *Why does he always make me so uneasy?*

He placed a hand on her desk, leaned over until his face was a few inches from hers, and hissed with contempt, "My mother passed away, thanks for asking."

Julie stared after his departing figure, mortified. Usually in conflict, and their working relationship taut at the best of times, he couldn't often render her speechless. "Russell, I'm sorry, I didn't even think…we've been so busy…I…"

Without turning around, he waved her off. "Forget it, Julie." He disappeared into the kitchen.

All afternoon, they worked in virtual silence, animosity hanging like a barrier between them. Finally, when Julie couldn't take the awkwardness any more and feared she might say something she'd regret, she made an excuse, and left.

I'll wait until Monday. After today, he's fair game.

* * *

Jackson checked his calendar. *October 26th. Coming close to the holidays*. He still detested the holidays, but now with even more reason. The anniversary of Cameron's death was a month away and he'd been wondering if Robbie had been planning on using it as the timeline for his assault on Jessica; some kind of sick tribute to his dead father. *I don't think you're going to wait that long.*

At his desk, he thought again about what Hodges had told him yesterday about Larry Cox. *If Robbie killed Larry Cox, why would he leave it so long if he was being abused.* Hodges had said his mother had been married to the man for five years and that Robbie had claimed the molestation and the beatings had started almost immediately. *I guess at ten-years old, he might have lacked the strength, but, if he was mad enough.* He pondered it a while longer, trying to get it to make sense; to lead him somewhere useful.

After the divorce, Jackson realized, *you'd have been about fourteen or fifteen-years old. A different story. Maybe a match for a child molester.* He knew enough about Robbie to know he would want to get even. Everything that drove Robbie had to do with revenge. Twenty years spent tracking the Croft's had told him that.

Hodges had described the injuries Larry sustained: stabbed in the eyes and a knife wound to the chest. *Brutal, like the others.* He'd had Hodges send over the report, and scanned the papers in the file until he found what he wanted. The weapon of choice had been an eight-inch blade. Larry's murder had never been solved. Jackson had no doubt they would clear it up with the capture of Robbie.

He thought about all the murders he'd been working on,

went through his notes again, reviewing the evidence, his mind churning, perusing the photographs, scouring over the injuries. He saw the escalating violence, and thought back to the connection Red had made about the link to the bars. *Sadie worked in a bar. The young kid killed on the same night Alex was mowed down worked in a bar.* Jackson understood something; something he suspected had been fueling the rage, making Robbie evermore hateful, more vicious. *You're alive, aren't you? You're somewhere out there, and you're still making him madder than hell.*

More than ever, he realized he had to find Sadie, Robbie's mother. If he did, when he did, he imagined it wouldn't take much–maybe a beer or a joint–to convince her to lead him right to her son.

Where do I start? Hodges had pointed out she couldn't still be working the bar, at least not topless; she had no further record in Sacramento, so…*maybe she's here*. With Robbie in San Francisco, it seemed logical that she might be, too. He punched in her name and ran a search through the local database. *I'll find you*, he vowed, swishing his coffee around in his mouth.

To make up for lost time, Russell Ross busied himself plowing through the list of buyers interested in the Sanders home. After Julie left, he'd taken a quick drive over to Cray Street to check out the vacant property for himself, and he had to admit, Barclay Sanders, the rich bastard, owned a spectacular pad. He'd wandered around, marveling at the luxury, the expense, and wondering what it took to become so wealthy.

Barclay's home, a large, multi-level, lavishly updated, corner home boasted large, bay windows, original oak wood floors, a grand living room, gracious dining room, magnificent entertainment and movie room, numerous bedrooms, and full bathrooms with marble baths. It came with a four-car garage and inspiring views of the Golden Gate Bridge. Russell whistled. *Wouldn't mind a piece of this for myself.*

He found it a tedious task sorting through the list of callers and scheduling appointments, motivated only by the sizable commission he'd earn when it sold, which would be considerable even if he had to share it with the temp and Julie.

Thinking of that brought his mind round to the girl lying in the hospital. He guessed he owed her something for this success and decided he ought to pay her a visit when he left the office that evening, show her his appreciation. Surely that would win him points with Julie, if he bothered to tell her, which could only make for less hassle in the office. Although he usually enjoyed the warfare, once in a while he wasn't in the mood.

By late afternoon, when Jackson had found nothing in the San Francisco database for Sadie Allure or Sadie Cox, he sat back, frustrated and annoyed. *There must be something.* He couldn't imagine she'd gone entirely straight, not with her history. *Maybe she married again.*

He wandered down to the kitchen, got himself a fresh cup of coffee, and carried it back to his desk, wondering how he could find out. *Maybe Red will get something on the plates.* He sipped his coffee, scrunching up his brow, and thinking. He'd get the list first thing Monday morning, after Red had staked out the twins apartment over the weekend. *If Robbie is stalking the apartment his plate should be among them.*

Russell glanced at his watch. Ten minutes after seven. He'd had enough for his first day back and shut down his computer. He grabbed a couple of his business cards and left the office, first stopping at a fast food restaurant for a quick bite to eat, and then heading over to the hospital to see Alex.

"Name," a surly detective asked, barring him from entry.

With a look of surprise, Russell handed over his ID and a business card. "We work in the same office," he explained, "what's this all about?"

The officer ignored the question and scrutinized the ID. He finally handed it back with a grunt and gave a brisk nod toward the door. Russell shrugged, assumed that meant he'd passed the inspection, and opened the door to her room. A tall man with a shock of grey hair greeted him when he stepped inside Alex's room. Russell didn't know him, and held out a hand. The man shook it, and introduced himself as Harry. Two brunettes by the bed looked to be the same age; late twenties. One eyed him skeptically, the other with surprise. The patient in the bed had both legs in casts and looked quite the worse for wear. One other person in the room: a blond male in a suit, sat by the window.

"Russell," he offered quickly, feeling out of place in such an intimate setting. With no card or gift to deflect their gaze, he added, uncomfortably, "We work in the same office." He smiled awkwardly at the faces staring back at him. "Actually," he confessed, "I don't know her. She's been filling in for me, so I stopped by to say thanks, and to see how she is."

"Thank you." The voice came from the blond in the suit. "That's nice of you."

"I heard it was a hit and run. That's a rotten thing to happen." Their faces softened and he felt slightly less awkward. "Do the police have any clues?"

"Yes," the brunette female said, and the other brunette, the male, stopped her with a hand on her arm before she could say anything else. Russell watched with interest. The room seemed full of secrets, but he decided not to push. He asked politely about Alex, stayed only a few more minutes, and made his excuses.

"Hospitals make me uncomfortable. I hope you don't think me rude."

"Not at all," Harry said, the only one who appeared cheerful, a smile on his friendly face. Russell bid them goodbye, stepped outside, nodded to the officer guarding the door, and left. Hospitals did make him uncomfortable; in fact, he hated them. He thought he might even be sick and needed to get outside; away from the stuffy room, the clinical odor, and the smell of death. He needed air.

"Wait."

He turned, anxious to get away, but the pretty brunette had stepped out into the hall. She thanked him for coming to visit, a shy smile on her face. She took several steps toward him, opened her mouth to say something else, but he already felt the vomit at the back of his throat. "How–"

"Sorry, I have to get going, I must get outside," he whispered. "I hate hospitals. I know you understand and I'm sorry to rush off."

"It's okay."

He pressed his hand quickly into hers. "If you'd like to talk about her, maybe help me get acquainted when she's better, seeing how we'll be working together, we could have coffee."

He flashed her a smile and strode away down the hallway, down through the lobby, and out into the cool evening air. Jessica stepped back inside Alex's room; traces of a smile clinging to her lips, Russell's business card in the palm of her hand.

Jackson decided to wrap things up for the night and got ready to go home to his wife and son. He sensed the gap closing between him and Robbie. *I'm close now.* He unlocked the door to his car. *I'm going to hunt you down until there's no place left for you to run.*

Chapter Thirty-Six

Early on Monday morning, Jackson had already begun calling local hospitals and major employers in the area, trying to locate a Sadie Cox. When Red arrived, he grinned up at him, and went to get a fresh coffee. "Got that list?"

He thought about Anderson Collins on his way back to his desk. That story had unfolded quite a bit since Red had checked on Jessica's claim. Quite a few more calls had come in over the past few days regarding sexual harassment claims, both recent and old, connected to this man. He seemed notorious for his mistreatment of women. Also, it appeared that several more of his staff had harbored similar doubts and suspicions as Jessica. They feared he might have had something to do with Alex's accident and had come forward to confirm the allegation of his inappropriate attention towards her, and her refusal to comply. A few had suffered similarly.

The case had been turned over to another division for a full investigation and, late on Saturday, he had called to share the news with Jessica. She'd been with Judd and Ben at the hospital when she'd received his call and he could tell she was elated.

Ecstatic with the news, Jessica had tried not to let Alex overhear their conversation. The nurse had warned them not to excite her; that she still needed rest. Jessica had whispered to Ben the update from Jackson.

"I'll let her know when she's stronger," he promised. "I

don't want her thinking about him yet."

Before they'd left on Saturday evening, Jessica promised to visit on Monday.

"I can't go with you," Judd had said, "and you shouldn't go alone. Jackson said Robbie might be watching."

Jessica's heart had sunk. She couldn't miss a visit. She'd hoped she might bump into Russell again, but of course, she couldn't tell Judd that, and he was right, she couldn't go alone.

"Don't worry, I'll be here late afternoon. I'll meet you in the lobby," Ben had offered. "That way, you can still visit, and you won't be alone." It had been settled, and she'd called Jackson back to tell him so he'd know where to find her if he got any news.

Over the weekend, Red had misplaced his list of vehicle registrations, and by Monday afternoon, when he still hadn't found it, Jackson finally came unraveled, launching into him with pent up rage.

"How could you be so fucking careless?" he roared. "All you had to do was sit in the fucking car, eating your fucking Twinkies and make a note of the registrations of cars that drove by, and you still managed to screw it up, you fuckwit."

Shocked, Red gaped at him open-mouthed, Jackson quickly apologized. "Sorry. I'm exhausted."

"We're all feeling the stress," Red muttered. "I'll find it and get it to you as soon as I can. We had quite a bit of traffic so I'm hoping we got something."

Jackson hoped so, too. He spent much of the afternoon calling the rest of the hospitals in and around the area, brought Red up to speed, and enlisted his help with the employers. While he waited for the results to start coming back, he went for yet another coffee, hoping somehow Sadie would have been admitted or employed, where he could find her. He'd given the hospital administrators all the name combinations for both her and Robbie.

As he headed back to his desk, Red said, "How many is that?" and nodded at his mug.

"Who's counting?" Jackson sat down with a sigh, took a slug, and glanced over at Red, eyeing him with a frown. "What? I said I was sorry."

Red just shook his head.

"So I like coffee, what's the big deal?" He took another mouthful of the hot black liquid, felt the jolt kick in again, and blinked back the headache settling at the back of his eyes.

"You need more sleep, Jackson, and less coffee," Red said, without looking up. "One day, that stuff's gonna kill you."

"Not likely." Jackson snorted, and gulped down another mouthful. "The job'll finish me off first."

"He's gotta be working somewhere close," Red said, a little while later, when none of the employers had claimed to have anyone on their staff under any of the aliases they had for Robbie. "How else does he get his money? Drugs?"

Jackson shook his head. "He'd probably have robbed his victims if it had been drugs. He drives a Mercedes, a sports coupe, so he's got plenty of money coming in. Someone knows him, someone's giving him work."

Red blew out a frustrated breath, still unable to locate the misplaced list. "I can't see how he doesn't have a rap sheet. For a kid with his lot in life, I can't believe he's clean."

"He isn't. He just hasn't been caught. And we might have a chance if you come up with that damn list."

While Red continued to search, Jackson went on to check all the local bars and restaurants. Maybe that's how he chose his victims. He asked each proprietor he called and told them all the same thing: "He'd be around one-hundred-ninety pounds; Caucasian; muscular build; probably a heavy drinker; probably just sits watching people. Likely has a long scar on his left cheek."

Most of the places he called told him the same thing in return: "Sure, we have tons of customers just like that. The city's full of weird and freaky types." He was getting nowhere. He downed more coffee. Finally, at three o'clock, he stood up and told Red he needed a break. He had forgotten to eat and thought his legs might buckle under him.

"Taking thirty minutes," he said, rubbing at his eyes, "I'll get back to it later. Find that list while I'm gone."

Jessica drove alone into the hospitals grounds, constantly checking her surroundings.

"He could be anywhere." Jackson's warning echoed in her head. She scanned the parking lot for a Mercedes, wishing this time he'd be there. He had to be here if she had any hope of luring him. He had to see her. She wanted him to see her alone, to follow her into the busy hospital, where she'd be quite safe. When she noticed she'd picked up a stranger, when she noticed a man she didn't know paying her undue attention, she'd call Jackson, from the safety of the hospital, and he'd swoop immediately. He'd check it out. She'd decided herself, without a word to anyone, that she had to do this on her own.

If Jackson thought she'd sit by and be terrorized by the idea of the sadistic bastard luring her to her death, then he'd been wrong. She'd lure him to his own demise. Robbie wouldn't suspect a thing. He didn't know they were onto him. No further visits to her mother had been reported and she and Judd hadn't gone for a while. Marianne would be none the wiser. Jessica had told Judd she felt safer close to home, and he hadn't questioned her.

Her real motive for not going was to stay local in the hopes she'd pick up her stalker where Jackson could pounce. He could act far faster if she stayed local.

She got out of her car, glanced around, stuck her chest out, straightened her shoulders, and strutted over to the hospital, swinging her purse as she went. *If he's here, if he's watching, he can't know anything's amiss.* She made it into the hospital without incident. She scanned the lobby. Nothing. Then Ben waved from reception and she hurried to join him.

"Everything all right?" he said.

"Fine."

Together, they went up to see Alex, who had opened her eyes, was tired, and pleased to see them.

From a safe distance, Robbie watched her cross the parking lot by herself. He watched her sassy strut and the way she swung her purse.

"Feeling good by the looks of it." He sneered. "Have I got something in store for you."

He followed. She didn't check behind, just strode into the building like a woman on a mission. He matched her pace, and entered the lobby a distance behind her, keeping out of sight. She stood by reception, with the well-dressed blond he'd seen before. He couldn't hear their conversation and hung back, watching from behind a group of people. They left the lobby. He checked in on his mother, made sure she didn't see him, and cursed her for recovering so well. Soon she'd be back in rehab.

He went back to the lobby and waited while they visited

Alex. *How do I separate Jessica from Blondie?* He'd already figured that Blondie must be the boyfriend. He smoothed his hands down the jacket of his navy, striped Armani suit and fiddled with his pale blue tie. He'd dressed nicely, as he always did; although it was essential today, given what he had in mind. As he tried to figure a way to get Jessica alone, she handed him a massive advantage.

Thirty minutes after they'd left the lobby, she returned alone, surprising him, and giving him the opportunity he needed. When she disappeared into the cafeteria, he got up and followed her, pushing his way through the throng of people, until he stood right behind her.

"Hello. I wondered if I might see you here. How's your friend?" He tapped her lightly on the shoulder. She turned, a scowl, a look of distrust, and then smiled. She recognized him, as he'd known she would.

"Getting better. She's improving every day."

He nodded, and let his gaze drop to the floor. "That's good. Wish I could say the same."

"Oh no," she gasped. "Your mother?" He nodded, rubbing at the wetness in the corner of his eye. "She passed away just this afternoon. I barely made it in time to say goodbye."

"I'm so sorry." He watched the sympathy climb into her face. *Encouraging.*

"It was inevitable." He kept his voice thick, choked with emotion.

"She must have been very sick."

"She'd been ill for a long time. She put up a brave fight." His finger dabbed at his eyes. "But, it doesn't make it any easier. We were so close."

He gave the performance of his life and almost killed

himself with the effort. It took serious talent to switch on the waterworks at the drop of a hat. *Shit, maybe I should have been an actor.* He watched, hoping she'd be the type of girl whose heart melted for a man in tears. She looked the type. No one knew more about loss than this little bitch. When she said nothing, he continued the charade. "I thought I'd sit here for a while and get myself a coffee before I head home. I need to steady myself before I drive. I'll have to take care of her things."

"I'm sorry."

Not as sorry as you're gonna be. "I'm her only child, and she was all that I had left in the world." He wiped his eyes again; and waited.

Chapter Thirty-Seven

Jessica's mind whirled with confusion. Upstairs with Alex, Ben expected her to be back any minute. He'd be livid if he knew what she was doing, talking to a stranger. *But he's not really a stranger. He's been kind to me, more than once.*

She thought about Ben. She'd said she be only a few minutes, had told him she needed some water and felt safe enough to go to the cafeteria by herself, smoothing over Ben's objection. "You can't watch me every second. No one can."

"He could be here, Jess. I told Jackson I'd keep you safe."

"I know, and I feel suffocated. I can't be constantly coddled."

They'd argued. Not wanting a battle in front of Alex, Ben reluctantly agreed, but insisted she use her mobile if she sensed any danger. He'd handed her his business card with his own mobile number scribbled on the back.

Jessica had headed to the cafeteria, trying to be mindful but not obvious. His Mercedes had not been in the parking lot, and if it had, if she'd missed him, if he'd stood watching from somewhere nearby, then he'd know she had someone waiting. She had Ben's number in her purse, and he was only a phone call away. *Plus, how could he drag me from a busy hospital without being seen?*

"The least I can do is return your hospitality," she said, and offered him a pack of tissues for his tears. He smiled, but refused the tissues.

"Well, maybe you could keep me company for a few minutes, while I drink my coffee."

"I really should get back." She glanced toward the lobby.

He pretended not to hear. "It'll be tough going back to an empty house. I'm dreading that."

"Your mother lived with you?" Her face registered surprise.

"Yes. I moved her in and took care of her, until she had to be admitted." He looked at her, giving his ultimate act. "Look, I'm sorry, I'm a blubbering wreck. I didn't mean to unload on you."

"No, you're not, it's fine, I–"

"I'm glad I ran into you. I knew you'd make me feel better. I know you understand."

He swallowed the bile rising in his stomach, seriously doubting he could continue the pretense for much longer. She made him feel loathsome. The sight of her made him want to tear out her heart and squash the bloody thing right in his hand. Or maybe he'd feed it to the first dog he saw; like he had with the little, drunk bitch's tongue last year, and the man's genitals back in ninety-five. The dogs had lapped those up. Great fun to watch.

"Tell your friend I said hello. I hope she feels better soon. I look forward to meeting her properly, when she comes back to work." They had reached the counter and become the next in line.

"All right." Jessica suddenly smiled. "I guess I can sit down here for a few minutes. What harm can it do?" She giggled, turned to the server and ordered two large, black coffees. "My treat," she said and walked further along the line to pay the cashier. They found a table and she set the drinks down. "I need to call someone, let him know I'm okay."

"Boyfriend?" He knew better, and watched her shy smile. *Bet she's never even had a boyfriend.*

"No." She gave a soft, shy laugh. "He's a friend. Better make the call or he'll come down here searching for me."

"We wouldn't want that." He smiled, remembering to dab at his eyes once in a while. "Before you make your call though, could you do me a small favor?"

"Of course."

"I need a little cream for my coffee."

"Oh," Jessica laughed apologetically, "I didn't think. I always drink it black."

"Well, I should have said something."

"Wait here, I'll get you a few." She got up, and went back to the counter.

"Like I'm going anywhere," he snarled under his breath. "At least, not without you." While Jessica had her back to him, fetching a few lousy little carton's of creamer, he reached over and dumped a large dose of crushed up Flunitrazepam into her coffee. He stirred it quickly with the spoon on her tray, and wiped it clean.

"Here." Jessica returned and handed him the creamers less than a minute later. She sat down and tipped two sachets of sugar into her own coffee. She gave it a good stir, blew on it, and took a huge gulp.

"Thank you." He smiled. "Don't forget to make your call."

Jessica took the business card out of her purse, and took another slurp of coffee. "For a cheap cup of coffee, it's actually decent." She laughed, and took another mouthful. He waited patiently while she pulled out her phone, opened it, and dialed a number. While the numbers connected, she drank more coffee and smiled. The call went through.

"Jess, are you okay?" He could hear the voice, and recognized it as Blondie.

"I'm fine." She smiled into the phone, and took another gulp. "I'm sharing a quick cup of coffee in the cafeteria."

"I thought–"

"I'm fine Ben." He watched her smile become apologetic. "I ran into a–" she hesitated, "a friend." She downed more of her coffee, clearly uncomfortable. "His mother just died…yes, this afternoon…he seems upset."

"Who is he?" he heard Ben question. Ben had been right to worry. Jessica should be worried, too, but time had run out for her.

"He's someone from work. Nothing to worry about." She took another slug of coffee, spoke for a few more minutes. She ended with, "I won't be long," and snapped the phone shut. He hoped there'd be no further interruptions, now that he had her all to himself.

Jessica rubbed her eyes and turned her attention to Robbie. She had never sat at a table drinking coffee with a man, other than her brother, and it almost seemed like a date. She enjoyed the sensation and wondered if he found her attractive; that would be another new sensation for her. She hadn't been entirely honest with Ben. *But, it's almost true.* She calmed herself. *He is from work, only Alex's office, not mine*. She smiled at the young man opposite. He had nice, dark brown eyes. She liked them. He seemed to like her, the grin on his face told her he did. She felt flushed, almost heady. *He seems such a nice guy.* She sipped the liquid left in her mug. *And he's just lost his mother. I can certainly relate.*

As he sat quietly, continuing to smile at her, she remembered him from four days ago at the hospital. She'd finished her first visit to Alex. He'd been so kind to her in the lobby, and offered her tissues to wipe away her tears. She thought he'd mentioned having coffee back then, although, right at the moment, she couldn't be sure. Her head felt a little fuzzy. *He seemed so nice back then, and he's so nice today, in spite of his pain.* She rubbed again at her eyes. They felt a little weird. *Why can't everyone be that nice?*

Satisfied she'd bought him enough time, Robbie engaged his game. He knew her vulnerable spot, and hit it hard. With more forced tears, he amped up the agony of losing a loved one; the fear of carrying on alone; of finding his way through his heartbreaking trauma. Before long, he had her in tears herself. She wiped her eyes, took another sip of coffee and rubbed at her temples. She blew her nose and blinked hard a few times.

Robbie decided he needed to get her out of the hospital before her blubbering drew too much attention. He hadn't banked on being quite so convincing. "Are you all right?"

She nodded, took another sip of coffee; this time she spilled a little. "I…I…don't feel…all that, ohhh," Jessica stopped, and sighed, and rubbed fiercely at her eyes. "Whhaat did–"

She couldn't finish. Her voice sounded strange, even to him, sleepy and slurred. Her movements became impaired, along with her thinking. He'd dumped so much of the stuff in her coffee it would be a wonder if it didn't kill her before he could. That would totally ruin the plan. For all his perversions, he'd never been into necrophilia.

Rape never usually factored into his plans. However, for Jessica, he'd decided to make an exception. With Jessica, that had always been his plan. He intended to taste every inch of her; after he'd nearly choked her, and before he dumped her into the river. He would make sure her brother knew every intimate detail of the ghastly things he'd done.

The drug worked fast. She tried to stand up but had become too unsteady, and sat back down with a bit of a bump. She looked at him and he could see the confusion in her eyes. He sipped politely at his own black coffee. He'd never lower his standards to use those cheap, little creamers. Besides, like her, he took it black.

"Did you put some…ughh." She couldn't orchestrate her sentence, although it looked like she'd picked up on the general idea.

"Here, let me help you up. I'll get you out of here."

He picked up her purse and hooked a hefty, strong arm, an arm as strong as his old man's, around her waist and pulled her out of her chair. He half dragged her through the busy cafeteria, out through the door, and into an even busier lobby. No one paid much attention to the well-dressed young man propping up his unsteady, probably unwell, girlfriend. They were in a hospital after all. It didn't look that unusual.

Robbie adeptly moved Jessica, almost frog-marched her, out of the lobby and all the way to his car, in the back of the grounds. He kept a watchful eye out for Ben, and apologized to everyone they passed for his unstable girlfriend. Either too dizzy, or too drowsy, Jessica didn't respond.

They reached his Mercedes and Russell propped her against the side while he opened the passenger door. He pushed her roughly inside the car, and slammed the door. He ran to the driver side and got in, and sped the vehicle out of the grounds. Quickly, he headed towards The Marina.

Jessica's head lolled about on the headrest. He thought she looked ridiculous. She made a feeble attempt to unlock the door. He wondered if she'd really have the courage to throw herself out, if she'd ever got it open. Even if she'd had her full strength, she wouldn't have been able to unlock it. The door on the passenger side didn't open from the inside. Not since he'd had it rigged.

He reached The Marina quickly, drove into his underground garage, and dragged her roughly from the car. He pulled her up the stairs and into his hallway. She tried to protest, a feeble attempt. He half carried, half dragged her down the hall, past the bathroom, past the kitchen, and into his bedroom. He threw her small body ruthlessly down onto the bed. She looked even tinier against the huge, California king. Terror flickered through her heavy lidded eyes, before she closed them.

His pleasure mounted. She had to suffer. He pulled off her boots, unzipped her jeans and yanked them roughly from her body. Surprised to see she wore lacy, black underwear, he cussed. He'd been expecting prim and proper, not sexy.

"Just a tramp, like all the others." He tore open her blouse. Her black, lacy bra matched the panties. He narrowed his eyes with distaste. He shook her roughly and she opened her eyes, long enough for him to see the horror and fear, before they closed again. *She's almost out cold.* He was thoroughly aggravated. *Shit, I should have given her less.* He wanted her to be sedated only enough to where she couldn't fully fight back, not to where she'd be passed out and miss the delights he intended. She had to know the terrible things he'd do. She had to know the humiliation when he stripped her naked, and feel the pain when he heaved his burly frame on top, and crushed her beneath his weight. She would feel him rip into her defenseless, little body, and squeeze tightly on her throat with his massive hands. He could wait. The drug would take hours, especially with the amount she'd had.

He wandered down the hall to the kitchen and got

himself a beer. He took it into the living room and flicked on the TV and watched cartoons, while she slept like a drunk on his bed.

Chapter Thirty-Eight

Jackson heard the panic in Ben's voice as soon as he answered the phone. "What do you mean, she's gone?" he thundered. "You're supposed to be watching out for her. I thought you said she'd stay with you. She should never have been left alone."

"I searched all over the lobby," Ben wailed. "She's gone."

All afternoon, Jackson had worked furiously, and he'd made enormous progress. The hospitals had all called back, and all revealed nothing. Except San Francisco General.

"We don't have a Robbie anything here, nor Sadie Allure or Cox," the administrator had said, "but we do have a Sadie Ross. That's the only name we can match."

"Admitted?"

"Several days ago. Hope that helps."

Jackson knew better than to jump to conclusions. *If it's her, she must have married again.* He had taken a drive over to the hospital, to see this Sadie Ross for himself. At four-forty-five he'd left her, recovering from her drug overdose, his mind reeling with what she'd said.

"Why are you looking for Robbie? What kind of trouble is he in?"

"He's not in any trouble ma'am," he'd lied. "We need him to help with our investigation. We think he might have valuable information."

"Oooh, valuable," Sadie's eyes had popped wide with

excitement. "That's a new one. My boy 'aint never been called that before." She hooted, a dry, hard cackle that sounded like she had a lung full of smoke. "Imagine that, him 'elping the police instead of runnin' in the opposite direction. I never woulda thought."

Jackson had let her ramble. "Always been in trouble, but never got caught. Crafty little shit, and a mean bastard of a kid." She'd looked at Jackson. He'd seen the appreciation in her eyes, the way she pushed her yellowed, shaky fingers through her bleached blonde hair, self-consciously touching the inch of black roots and trying to rearrange the blonde to cover them. His stomach had lurched.

"What do you mean by that?" He'd engaged her with a winning smile

"I never wanted 'im in the first place. Only 'ad 'im for Bodie. Ruined my figure, and he never looked at me the same after that."

He'd thought she might remember him, from Bodie's day in the courtroom, but she didn't. *Mind's probably addled by the drugs.*

"I'm sure that's not true," he'd smiled, aware of his lunch swirling threateningly. "What did you mean by him being a–"

"He used to bully kids at school, and he killed some of the neighborhood pets. He doesn't think I know about that, but I knew. Found a cats tail or two in his room."

Jackson had shuddered.

"Anyway," she'd flicked her greasy locks and given him a haughty look. She acted as if she had something to be proud of. "You really think he can 'elp you?"

"Yes, ma'am, I believe he can."

"Well, if you're tryin' to find 'im, you best know who you're lookin' for." She'd laughed the same ugly cackle and

Jackson's patience had waned.

"I'm sorry?"

"Come on, are you the detective or what?" She'd chuckled, staring at his stone-set face. "He don't go by Robbie now; not since his dad died. I 'ad to protect him, you know, from the press. I'm still 'is mother."

Her stalling had made him want to grab her and shake the information from her bony, drug-addled, greasy, rancid little body. He could almost smell Robbie, he'd gotten so close. His thoughts never drifted far from Jessica and the danger in which he'd placed her. If the yellow-haired hag didn't give him the information, so help him he might just have to beat it out of her.

Sadie wanted his attention and he wanted her information. To her, it must have seemed like a fair trade, but to him, it had been torture. With lives at stake, one in particular, he needed the name, and one way or another he'd get it. "What's his–"

"Patience," she scolded, "I'm getting to it. He uses 'is middle name." She fiddled with her hair. Jackson wanted to slap her. His fingers twitched, his heart raced, and his temper rose. "And he uses my third 'usband's last name, too." She'd added that revelation as though it was an honor, a sign of desirability, to have been married three times.

"So," Jackson had had to curb his frustration in case she refused to say any more, "who is he now?"

Finally, she gave him what he needed. "He goes by Russell Ross," she'd answered, smug and proud. "Don't that sound nice?"

"Where can I find him?" He didn't have the time.

"I don't know that. We 'aint that close."

Jackson had turned to leave.

"Detective…" she'd called feebly from her bed.

He stopped at the door. "What?"

"When you find 'im, tell the bastard to come and see me. The nurse said he's only been 'ere once, and I never even knew."

He'd left the hospital at four-forty-five and gone directly back to his office. *I was right; he's here.* Now, he had a name. Robbie, or Russell, was close. He'd been to the hospital. Jackson realized he'd been watching. He'd used Alex to draw in Jessica, like he'd feared. Which meant Robbie might know the cops were on to him, if he'd seen them posted outside her room.

Before Jackson had returned from the hospital, Red had found the list of registrations. He'd done his partner a favor and run the list through the database and the DMV, trying to make amends for his screw-up and recover lost time.

"I got a name," Jackson yelled, when he burst back into the station. He tried to get Red up to speed in just a few minutes. They had no time to waste. With Jessica meeting Ben at the hospital, he expected Robbie would be close, that he might visit his mother again. "His old lady talked, we're looking for a Russell Ross."

"Russell Ross?"

"Robbie goes by his middle name, Russell. His old lady married again, and changed his last name, too."

"I recognize that name. Wait a minute–"

"Russell Ross is the guy we want."

"He's on the list." Red smacked the list of registrations with his hand and tossed it to Jackson. "I knew I'd seen that name. He's on the list."

Jackson scanned the registrations, saw the name and the license plate, and next to it a description of a Mercedes Benz,

SL500. "Shit." He looked at Red. "This is it. This is our guy."

"How do we find him?"

"His old lady doesn't know where he is. I'll run his name through the database and see what I find. Only place I think he might go is the hospital. And Jessica's there with Ben."

"Maybe you should get back over there?"

"She'll be safe with Ben, and I don't know what the kid looks like. I need an address. Besides, he can't do much there, it's a busy hospital; they'd get noticed."

Jackson pulled out his list of employers and began working through them again with the new name; Russell Ross. "He's making plenty of money," he said to Red, "so I know he's working here somewhere."

"I'll call the dealerships, trace all sales of a Mercedes Benz SL500."

"Good, hurry," Jackson ordered.

He realized he needed to warn Jessica, to let her know they had a name. She needed to know his mother had been admitted to the same hospital. That upped the level of danger. He wondered if he should go back over there himself.

Before he could pick up his phone to call her, it rang, and he snatched it up in a hurry and hollered, "Jackson."

"Detective." Ben's alarmed voice came through.

Jackson listened in disbelief. "How could you fucking lose her?" he roared at Ben.

Red looked up, startled.

"She isn't here, detective." He listened, while Ben sounded close to tears. "I've looked all over the lobby, all over the cafeteria, and she isn't here."

"Then where the fuck is she?"

"She went to get coffee, said she'd only be gone a few minutes. I called her phone and she's not answering."

"Shit," Mac blistered, hissing to Red. "He's got her. Shit. Robbie fucking has her."

Ben's voice came back through the phone, "He couldn't have, she wasn't alone."

Jackson didn't even want to ask. "Who was she with, Ben?"

"Someone from work. That's why I didn't worry."

"Did you see him?" His voice had gone dangerously low. Right now, he wanted to kill someone himself. He wanted to strangle Ben.

"No, she went to the cafeteria by herself to get a water. She called me and said she'd run into a guy from work whose mother died this morning, she stayed to have a quick cup of coffee. When she didn't come back, I got worried, and I–"

"How long was she gone?" Jackson interrupted.

"I don't know. I'm sorry, I lost track of time. I was thinking about Alex. She left me around five-thirty."

Jackson realized he'd missed her by less than an hour. If he'd stayed longer, hadn't been in such a hurry to get away from Sadie, he might have seen them together.

"Fuck," Jackson slammed his hand on the desk. "Listen, Ben. The guy we're looking for is not Robbie Allure. He's not using that name any more. We're looking for a Russell Ross and his mother is not dead. She's–"

"Oh fuck, Russell Ross. Are you sure?" Ben shouted down the phone. "I know who that is."

"How could you know? I only found out this afternoon." Jackson thought his head might explode.

"I've met him, Detective. Jessica has, too."

"When?" Jackson demanded.

"When we visited Alex on Saturday, he came to the hospital. He told us Alex had filled in for him at work. He came by to say thank you."

Jackson could barely believe what he heard. "Did he have a scar on his face?"

"I don't know," Ben said, "I couldn't tell. He had a beard."

Jackson checked his watch. It was now six o'clock. Robbie had had Jessica for at least thirty minutes, and he prayed she wasn't already dead.

"Where does Alex work?" he barked.

"Kirkland & Associates. Wh–"

"I need a number, Ben."

Ben gave him the number for the office. "It's six o'clock. The office will still be open; ask for Kelly Kirkland. Shit, this is my fault. I shouldn't have–"

Jackson cut the call, then dialed Kirkland & Associates in a hurry. His call was immediately patched through to Kelly Kirkland. He identified himself and asked about Russell Ross.

"Yes, he works here," Kelly confirmed, "what's this about?"

"I need an address," Jackson demanded.

Kelly protested. "I'm sorry, I can't give out personal information. How do I know you're really a detective?"

"We're wasting time," Jackson snapped in frustration. "A life is at stake. Call the station right back and ask for Detective Jackson, Detective Macdonald Jackson. I'll be waiting. And have that address ready."

His phone rang within the minute, and Kelly gave him an address on Marina Boulevard.

Robbie had grown impatient. He wanted to get it over with, and get the bitch out of his house. More than that, he hungered to see her body bludgeoned by the Great American River. It would take at least two hours to drive there. He had to be at work in the morning and face another grueling day with the obnoxious bitch, Julie, and he needed to be well rested for that.

He finished another beer and made his way back into the bedroom where she lay, half naked and still comatose. A sudden urge overcame him and he left her for a moment to go down the hall and have a pee. The beers played havoc with his bladder.

Jackson raced down to his patrol car, with Red right behind, fired the engine, turned out of Vallejo Street and screeched onto Stockton.

"I just hope we're not too late," he said, racing up Columbus Avenue, his lights flashing.

"He might not be here," Red cautioned. "He could have taken her anywhere."

"I know, I know," Jackson said, turning left at Bay Street, minutes away from the Marina Boulevard address. "But this is personal. He's waited a long time for this."

"You think he took her to his place?"

"That's where he's going to do it. He can take his time and not be interrupted. He won't want to rush. He'll want her to suffer. Red, if my hunch lets me down on this one, I quit."

The patrol car sped down Laguna Street and made a swift left onto Marina Boulevard. Red looked over at Jackson.

"Don't worry. If you think he's here, he's here. You can be a real bastard at times, but you're a good detective, Jackson. Your hunches are usually right."

"I hope they are this time, otherwise it's gonna cost

Jessica her life." They screeched to a halt outside a Victorian house. The driveway was clear of vehicles. Red pointed to the garage underneath.

Robbie finished in the bathroom and began to zip up his pants. Suddenly he stopped.

Why bother? He smirked lazily, and dropped them to the floor. He stepped out of them and kicked them aside. *They're gonna be coming down anyway.* In his silk boxer shorts and white, silk shirt–the same one he'd worn to the hospital–he swaggered back down the hall to the bedroom, unbuttoning his shirt on the way.

He knelt on the bed, next to her sleeping body, and breathed heavily in her ear. "Damn shame you're gonna miss this." He dropped his full body weight down on top of her and sniffed her like a dog. He sniffed at her thick, dark hair, and thought it smelled of spring. He ran his tongue over her face, tasting the salt from her tears, and pushed it roughly between her lips. Her soft mouth didn't resist. Not the fun he'd intended. He ran his tongue over the smooth surface of her teeth, then bit down hard on her lip. He tasted the blood. *That's better*. The adrenaline rushed inside him, and he felt himself grow hard.

"What would you like first?" He sneered. When she didn't respond, he tut-tut-ted, and made her decision for her. First, he leaned in close to check on her breathing. Satisfied the drug hadn't killed her, he grabbed a fistful of her hair and yanked her head back on the pillow, exposing the entire length of her slender neck. He rubbed his nose up and down it; breathing her in, tasting her innocence, then bit her neck hard in several places. Marks immediately rose on her creamy skin. He stared at them in wonder. They colored immediately, ranging from red to purple.

He pushed himself up into a sitting position, straddled her, and placed his large hands around the base of her throat. He squeezed, lightly at first, and then harder; much harder. He laughed at the sight of his enormous hands around her ridiculously small neck. *Could do it with just one.*

The detectives got out of the car and surveyed the front of the house. Two large windows with an iron railing jutted out above the garage underneath the house. The front door was set back to the right.

"Wonder which one's the bedroom." Red came up behind Jackson. "That's where he's gonna be."

"Where're the rest of the off–?" Before he'd finished saying it, three more patrol cars screeched to a halt outside the house. Six armed officers got out.

Robbie took his hands away from Jessica's neck and looked at the range of marks. "You'll have some fantastic bruises," he crowed. He leaned over her again to check on her breathing. She gave a soft moan, which fueled his desire. He fumbled with her underwear, trying to pull it down, when he heard a knock at the door.

"Fuck." He sucked the blood from his lip and got up to look out of the window. The sight of the patrol cars, four of them, outside his house, stunned him.

"It's him, second left," Jackson shouted, spotting Robbie peering out of the left, second floor window. "He's inside the house."

"Robbie Allure. Russell Ross. SFPD. Open the door," came the order.

Staggered, Robbie stepped back. *How the–* He realized

he had no way out. The patrol car across the drive blocked any access from the garage. The cops had him cornered. He had no way to get Jessica out of the house. He threw back his head and laughed. Suddenly, it didn't matter how they'd figured it out.

"You've got no warrant," he screamed at the window, and ran back to the bed. "Can't come in without a warrant." He lost interest in devouring Jessica's cataleptic, half-naked body lying in the middle of his bed. Before the cops barged their way in, he had to take from her what her family took from him. He grabbed her by the ankles and tugged her to the foot of the bed.

Jackson heard the laugh; the chilling sound of the insane. He heard the scream. *You're right, I don't have a warrant.* He issued the order. Robbie didn't know about exigent circumstances. Jackson had to preserve Jessica's life, and that gave him the legal right to enter the house by force. *Let her be alive*. His heart pounded with the desperate hope. The battering ram hit the door. The boom reverberated throughout the house and the door caved in under the force.

Robbie heard it give, and tightened his grip on Jessica's throat. His nails dug into her smooth skin, drawing a spurt of blood. His thumbs pressed hard on her windpipe. Almost twice her size, he could choke her in seconds. She couldn't even fight back.

"Too bad you're missing the party," he hissed in her ear. Her face began to change color.

"Bedroom's to the left," Jackson boomed, certain that's where they'd find them. The officers quickly checked their way through the house, clearing each room. They made their way upstairs in pairs.

As they entered the bedroom to the left, Jackson's heart sank at the sight of a burly, two-hundred-pound man atop an unmoving, female form. He could see her face had turned purple. *We're too late.*

The detectives burst in, but Jackson hung back by the door. He couldn't look. He couldn't bear to find her dead. He'd never be able to tell Judd. He couldn't live with himself and his terrible mistake.

Robbie's insane screech pierced his ears and he flinched. As four officers wrenched the psychopath from the bed and dragged him past Jackson, kicking and fighting, the scream took Jackson back years.

"Get him out of here," he snapped.

Red made a move forward, but Jackson put out his hand. "No, let me." Suddenly, he had to do it; had to find out for himself. He stepped quickly into the room and moved to the bed, bent over her body and placed two fingers on the side of her neck. Not much of a pulse, but a pulse.

"She's barely alive," he called back to Red, unable to tear his eyes from her face. He sensed movement at his side. Red rushed past him, placing his head next to Jessica's mouth. He listened for several seconds, and turned to face Jackson.

"She's breathing, Jackson." He checked her again. "She's a fighter. She'll make it."

Chapter Thirty-Nine

Judd, Jackson, and Red gathered at Jessica's bedside in San Francisco General.

"Hell of a job, Jackson," Red said.

"No, it was just hell," he growled, "I almost fucked up." He saw Jessica move her hand, and stepped closer to her bed. She spoke slowly, her voice hoarse. "Thank...you." She reached for his hand. He saw the question in her eyes.

"No, he'll never get out."

"How did you know where to find her?" Judd said.

"Hunch." Mac and Red had answered together.

Jackson moved to the side of the room and plopped down onto a chair. Last night had taken a bigger toll than he'd imagined. He'd questioned his judgment, questioned his ethics. He didn't know if he should still be a cop. He'd taken a gamble and almost lost. If his hunch had been wrong, he would have lost; and so would Jessica. He listened to the chatter around him.

"What's going to happen to Russell, whatever he's called?" Judd said.

He heard Red answer. "He's going away for good. For all of the murders."

"Really?" The whisper came from Jessica. Jackson rose from his chair. He moved back to the bed, and took one of her hands in his.

"Yes. He kept a log. Called it his Last Breath List. It's an account of each of the murders. That, and catching him in the act of attempted murder last night, is enough to lock him up forever."

"How did you manage to hold on for so long?" Judd asked Jessica. "The cops said the man's twice your size and he dumped so much of that crap into you it's a wonder that didn't kill you."

"Allow me," Red said, a slight strut in his voice. "That's actually what saved her life. She'd been so drugged up she had no clue what was happening. She was totally out of it."

A good thing, Jackson thought.

Judd went as far as to say it.

"And," Red continued, enjoying his audience, "because she didn't know, she didn't fight. He couldn't arouse her survival syndrome, and that bought her extra precious seconds."

"You mean, that sicko tried to kill her, but actually saved her life?" Judd could scarcely believe it.

"That's right." Red beamed at Jessica. "If you hadn't been so drugged up you might have panicked and run out of air. You might not have made it. So, you see, you beat him, after all."

"Way to go, Red." Jackson slapped him on the back.

"Is…Ben here?" Jessica's whisper hushed the room.

"Not yet. He'll stop by in a few," Jackson assured her.

"I want…him to know…I don't blame him," she whispered.

"He's with Alex," Judd said.

"Is she…all right?"

"Fine." Jackson touched her cheek. "He's giving her an update from Narcotics."

"Narcotics?" Jessica sounded confused.

"Something to do with nailing a drug-dealing ex-husband she's been running away from."

Jessica lay back against the pillows and smiled. She hadn't been the only one harboring dark secrets. Everyone had them. Everyone had a past. Many had something or someone in their lives they feared, many had been running from something. Even smart, capable women, like Alex. *Alex is the bravest woman I know.* She closed her eyes.

Judd thanked the two detectives and turned to Jessica, and said softly, "Ben asked me to tell you something." She opened her eyes, gave him a tired smile, closed them again.

"What's that?" she whispered.

"He asked Alex's family about Marianne Croft, just like you asked him to."

Jackson watched her eyes flutter open, search Judd's face, saw him reward her with the gentlest of smiles, a slight nod of his head, and he saw her close them again, a tear glistening in the corner of her eye, and the most amazing look of peace on her face. He didn't know what it meant, but he knew a private moment when he saw one.

He nodded to Red, noticed the way Red was staring at Jessica, smiled to himself, and left the room. *They get us all in the end.* As the door to her room closed behind them, he just caught her whisper to Judd, "Last night…I had the best night's sleep…since Cameron died. I didn't…have a single nightmare."

Jenny Hilborne has worked in a variety of fields, including the retail music industry, residential real estate, commercial real estate, and finance. She is the second of four daughters, born and raised in Wiltshire, South West England, and relocated to Southern California in 1997. Jenny is a member of Wolfwriters, a group of professional writers who meet bi-monthly in Northern San Diego. She is also a member of Sisters in Crime. Madness and Murder is her first novel. She is working on her second suspense novel, also set in San Francisco, featuring homicide inspector, John Doucette; an experienced inspector plagued by personal betrayal.

6252399R0

Made in the USA
Charleston, SC
02 October 2010